the Luciter Stone

Airship 27 Productions

The Lucifer Stone
© 2023 Bob Madison

Published by Airship 27 Productions
www.airship27.com
www.airship27hangar.com

Interior illustrations © 2023 Kevin Paul Shaw Broden
Cover illustration © 2023 Adam Shaw

Editor: Ron Fortier
Associate Editor: Fred Adams Jr.
Marketing and Promotions Manager: Michael Vance
Production Designer: Rob Davis

All rights reserved under International and Pan-American Copyright Conventions. No part of this book may be reproduced in any manner without permission in writing from the copyright holder, except by a reviewer, who may quote brief passages in a review.

ISBN 978-1-953589-51-4

Printed in the United States of America

10 9 8 7 6 5 4 3 2 1

the Lucifer Stone

by Bob Madison

"For Mason"

EDITOR'S NOTE

I'm not a conspiracy theory kind of guy, but when city officials close down on you, when Princeton University won't provide any answers, and when the media says what you've got is all a hoax, then where am I?

So here is the true story of the Peter Armstrong Papers.

You think you know all about them. Such eminent publications as *The New York Times* and *The New Yorker* have already said they were a forgery. (*The New Yorker* went so far as to say that I created a hoax to scare an already virus-nervous public.) Experts I hired examined the papers and verified that they are authentic documents from the period, and that some elements of the stories were undeniably true. *Newsweek* examined the documents with an open mind and a battery of forensic experts and historians of the era, but would not go as far to say that they described actual events. The women on *The View* had a rare moment of agreement when they said I was "a menace." *Rolling Stone*, ever classy, said I was "full of shit."

I'm not surprised by this. I think if any of the mainstream media said the Peter Armstrong Papers were authentic, it would mean that certain fundamental beliefs and understandings about the world and our place in it would need a radical revision. And these radical revisions would not fit a narrative that the media continues to promote.

But, no matter. Here's the truth.

As the documents relate, Peter Armstrong was a professor of Astronomy at Princeton, a post he held from the Nineteen Twenties through the Forties. He was born on July 14 in 1901 in Waukegan, Illinois, the second of four sons born to William and Mary Jane Armstrong. Bill Armstrong was a haberdasher (back when people could make a living selling clothes) and Mary Jane (nee, Mary Jane Clark) was a keen amateur naturalist.

Young Peter excelled at school, especially in what are now called "earth sciences." He entered Columbia University on a science scholarship at age thirteen, graduated two years later and earned his doctorate in Astronomy two years after that. He also received his Master's Degree in Geology and another undergraduate degree in Chemistry. All this by the time he was eighteen years old.

He had his pick of academic posts, but decided instead to spend some time traveling around the world. Young Armstrong toured Europe just following the Great War, then made his way through Persia and Tibet, and finally spent several months in Southeast Asia.

It was a robust young man who returned to the States in 1921, looking for a job. Contemporary pictures show him casually handsome, well-dressed (as befits the son of a haberdasher!), with pale blue eyes and thick, wavy reddish hair swept back over a broad forehead. He had a lifelong taste for the juvenilia of his time (especially pulp novels and newspaper comic strips), Lucky Strike cigarettes and obsessive note taking. The countless notebooks he filled with his observations of the heavens (which went far in proving that the papers found later were at least "real" historical documents) fill nine bookcases at the Princeton library.

It was Princeton University that won out in the end, and Armstrong joined as full professor of Astronomy in the fall of 1921. I've looked over his employment files and they seem to be unremarkable, except for frequent absences that Princeton officials described as "government work."

He never married and lived in a small apartment in Princeton, New Jersey, not far from the college. He retired at fifty-five (which, from what I can gather, was a surprise to Princeton) and on April 21, 1956, said goodbye to his landlady before stepping into a cab to keep a lunch date.

He was never seen nor heard from again.

The disappearance of Professor Peter Armstrong caused a minor scandal. The police, and later the FBI and later still the War Department, were never able to determine what happened to him. When and where—and even if!—he died remain a mystery.

It's here, belatedly, that I come in.

My grandfather was Professor Richard Pierson, who was also a Professor of Astronomy at Princeton while Armstrong was there. I did not know him particularly well; he died when I was six. I would be lying to you if I said I sat on his knee while he told me stories of Peter Armstrong—in fact, all I can really remember about Grandpa Dick was that he once gave me a Bozo the Clown toy circus.

My grandmother survived Grandpa Dick by more than twenty years. When she died in 1992, she left the small house in Princeton that they shared for more than fifty years. My own parents had passed away, so the house was mine.

I was very busy with my own career and rented it out to a series of different tenants for nearly thirty years. It's only when I decided to move to California that I wanted to clean it up for selling.

The house was filled with all the accumulated junk found in any house where people lived for a long time, aggravated by it all being shoved down into the basement or stuck up into attic during prolonged rentals.

When I first found Armstrong's papers, I didn't know what to make of them. There were thirty volumes—gray hardcover books filled with yellowish paper, graph ruled. There were some astronomical calculations here and there, but, largely, they were dairies kept in a neat script written in fountain pen.

I paged through them, then started reading them closely, and then freaked out.

I'm sure my grandparents inherited Armstrong's journals and never bothered to read them. (I guess. Who knows? Maybe they read them and believed in them about as much as *The New York Times* would later on.) But when I read them what I found was something like a secret history of the Nineteen Thirties and Forties. A story more weird and more dangerous than the already weird and dangerous mid-Twentieth Century we already knew.

It all read like some fever dream. It couldn't be true, I thought. Since I didn't know if young Armstrong had a taste for writing fiction, I started to check up on some of the things found his accounts. I discovered that, whenever Armstrong mentioned a person or a place, they were real people and real places. As for the stories—either he was an aspiring writer or a psychotic.

But what really got me thinking was all the obstacles put in my way when I started to authenticate Armstrong's Papers. Princeton at first stalled, then stonewalled before finally shutting up completely. When some of the experts I hired to check on the paper, ink and that sort of thing started talking about what they read in them, I got a disturbing call from the State Department demanding that I turn the books over to them. It took a lot of legal wrangling (which I'm still paying for!) for me to keep them in my hands, despite a highly illegal visit from an already criminal FBI.

Then, the campaign to discredit the Professor Peter Armstrong Papers started in earnest. First in academic circles and then in the media. And so I had to think—would anyone go through all this trouble if there wasn't *some* truth in them? Is it really a conspiracy theory when there really is a conspiracy?

The papers are now with me in Southern California under lock and key. If you want to see them, you had better have a pretty damn good reason, and be prepared to have me watch you every second you page through them.

So, that's all I have to say. I have been going through Armstrong's notebooks, editing select bits for publication. There was some water damage to the original notebooks, reducing a few pages here and there to nothing more than blue-black stains. For the passages where Armstrong's writing was hopelessly smeared and unreadable, I tried to inject something that was close to his original intention (I hope!). I have also corrected his spelling. Let me say this: Professor Peter Armstrong may have been a great genius, but he couldn't hold his own in a second-grade spelling bee.

This is the first of installment of his papers to be published in something close to their entirety. Dated memoranda indicate that the following events took place in March 1934. The reception it receives is out of my hands. All I've got is what I know (and you just read it), and what I found (which follows).

Make up your own mind.

Bob Madison, Huntington Beach, CA 2023

CHAPTER ONE

I had been listening to some dance music coming live from the Hotel Meridian in New York City while I watched the sun go down. Ray Noble and His Orchestra[1] had just finished *Stardust* and I shut the radio off.

I stood by the window and looked at the stars. It would be a good night for observation. The sky was dark and cloudless and Orion's belt sparkled like a string of jewels in the sky. I could hardly wait to get to work.

I grabbed my trench coat and Trilby hat and made sure I turned the burners off. I was renting the top floor of a little house off Broadmead and nearly burned it down a couple of weeks ago when I forgot to turn off the stove. Mrs. Bradbury, my landlady, threatened to throw me out if I ever did it again.

The night outside was cool and dry. The trees were still bare and the late winter breeze blew through the branches. I considered taking the car to the observatory, but decided instead to walk.

I had only gone a few blocks when I had the oddest feeling that I was being followed. A black town car, long and sleek, kept pace with me for a few blocks. It turned off before I got to the observatory and I shrugged away my silly suspicions.

I made my way past Palmer Stadium, now deserted in the cool of the evening, and walked down FritzRandolf Road. Before too long, I saw the observatory just ahead.

The FritzRandolf was the new facility and it was fabulous. I helped with the overall design and couldn't help but feel that the observatory was somehow *mine*. It was a low brick building with an enormous domed wing. Ivy clung to the red brick and some low-cut hedges provided color. The grass surrounding the observatory was damp and the toes inside my shoes were moist by the time I got to the door.

I used my key and pulled the heavy metal door behind me. The

---

[1] At the time, it was not uncommon for hotel ballrooms to host live orchestras, or for local radio stations to broadcast live music from them. Ray Noble (1903-1978) was a famous bandleader, composer and arranger, emblematic of the 1930s sound.

laboratory corridors were dark and I cautiously walked through the building to the observatory proper.

I opened the door at the observatory and stopped—just to enjoy the view.

Few things make me happier than being at the FritzRandolf. The place I really called home was a large, semi-circular room that was dark except for the oblong split in the ceiling

The enormous telescope housed a 23" Fecker-Clark refractor. There was a new mount and dome to house the telescope. Synchro motors moved the telescope itself and there was a movable platform beneath the scope.

The telescope used the original objective lenses, focusers and eyepieces of the old scope we used at the Halstead Observatory. Old Man Cooley was miffed that the Halstead had to be moved to build dorms, but I thought the dark and seclusion provided by the new location for the FritzRandolf made it ideal.

A ticking sound filled the room as the clockwork mechanism vibrated. It was another thing that made the FritzRandolf so special—inside it was like holding a beloved pocket watch to my ear. The surrounding instruments were sleek and cobalt blue in the dim light and the entire room had a streamlined, futuristic feel, like something out of *Amazing Stories*.

I loved it.

Dick Pierson stood on the platform, peering through the lens.

"How's the view?" I called up.

Pierson kept his eye on the lens, absently making notes in the journal he was holding. "Everything's still up there."

"I'm on for tonight," I said. "Unless you're up to something and want to switch."

Pierson pulled himself away from the scope. He was a big man, tall and barrel chested and already slightly running to fat. He had broad, handsome features and sharp eyes. His jacket was draped over his chair and his tie and top shirt button were open. He had a decade on me, but treated me like an equal.

"No," he said. "Old Man Cooley has been going on about increased meteor activity, but I haven't seen anything." The large, metallic space made his baritone sound like thunder. He pressed a button and the platform lowered. "Have you?"

"I heard that, too, but I haven't seen anything."

Old Man Cooley was Dr. Mason Cooley, head of the department. He was a mentor to Pierson and like a second father to me. If he said that there was something going on, I could take it to the bank.

"What do you make of it?" He closed his top shirt button, straightened his tie and put on his jacket. It didn't matter; Pierson always looked like an unmade bed.

"I don't make anything out of it," I shrugged. "I got to see it first."

"Speaking of seeing, have you seen Cooley lately?"

I thought for a minute. "No, now that you mention it. Two weeks, at least."

"Strange," Pierson reached for his hat. "Isn't it?"

"You know Mason. He's probably working on a paper and forgot everything else. He'll turn up."

"He better," Pierson fished a pipe out of his pocket and filled it. "He signs our checks."

I started for the scope. "Go home and have a drink. I'll let you know if anything comes up."

I stepped onto the platform and slowly rose closer to the mechanism.

"Don't overdo it," he said, making for the door.

"Huuuh?" I had already screwed my eye into the lens.

"I said don't overdo it!" he called from the door.

I mumbled something I hope was polite and he closed the door behind him.

There was a smoke stand next to the chair and I pulled a pack of Luckies from my pocket and lit up. It was strange that Cooley reported meteor activity when I had seen nothing significant for several weeks. If Pierson saw nothing, too, then it must have been an isolated event and Cooley was following up on it.

I stepped away from the scope and pulled out the logs for the past few weeks. We kept logs going back for six months in the oversized graph-paper journals I'm using now. I paged through the most recent and found nothing in the notations from me and Dick, but when I went back three weeks, I saw Cooley had made a notation on February 19th. He recorded ten projectiles that burst into flame upon entering our atmosphere and made detailed calculations on the probable points of impact here on earth.

Not unusual at all by itself. Meteors often break apart or burn up completely when they travel through the atmosphere. Cooley had probably seen the fragments of a big rock that had broken into bits and tracked their descent.

Curious that he insists on a high degree of follow-up.

I paged back all the way to January and found nothing unusual. I replaced the book and stubbed out my Lucky. I went back to the scope and the echoing tick-tock sound on a note of contentment.

I had lost myself watching the farthest regions of sidereal space and only became aware of my surroundings again when I heard the doorbell ring.

The sound itself was surprising. The observatory was closed at night and anyone who should be there had a key. I checked my watch and saw that it was already ten-fifteen. I had been at it for hours.

I sighed and stepped away from the scope. I lowered the platform and walked through the dark corridors of the lab. I don't know why, but already I had a feeling of foreboding.

The door to the observatory is a large, metal plate that opens from inside by pressing the emergency bar. There is no window to check who is outside. I stood there and waited. The bell had only rung once and I hoped it was one of the undergrads being funny.

It wasn't. The bell rang again, more insistent. Bracing myself, I opened the door.

On the threshold were two men. Both wore overcoats and broad-brimmed fedoras that had seen better days. The man closest to me was my height, thin and reedy, with washed-out eyes and a dark, pencil-thin mustache. They man behind him was shorter, broad and mean looking. A scar trailed from the outside of his left eye and down to his mouth, leaving him with a permanent half-frown.

"Yes?"

The man with the mustache spoke. It was only when he opened his mouth that I realized that all of his teeth were gold. I had never seen anything like it before; the inside of his mouth looked like a threshing machine.

"I'm looking for the doctor."

I saw what it was in a heartbeat. Something must have happened on the road and they were looking for medical help.

"You mean a medical doctor," I said. "If you go to the main building, the infirmary might be open."

"Who are you?" the gold teeth flashed in the dim light.

That put me on my guard. Why would he want to know? I started to close the door. "Sorry," I said.

The gold-toothed man stuck his foot in the doorjamb. From behind him, the stocky man landed a ham-sized hand on the door and pushed back.

Gold Tooth smiled. "I said, who are you?"

I looked from one to the other. Finally I said, "Professor Peter Armstrong."

Scarface took a slip of paper from his coat pocket and checked it. "That's him."

"You need to come with us," Gold Tooth said.

"Why would I do that?"

"Cause I said."

I looked them over again. "Are you with the police?"

They both laughed at that—a nasty sound that made everything worse.

"Then," I said. "I don't think so." I started to push the door shut.

Gold Tooth pulled a gun from his coat pocket. It was a silver automatic. He moved so fast, I didn't know what he was doing until he pressed the gun right under my chin. The cold metal pushed into the soft flesh on the underside of my mouth.

"Think again, punk," he said.

Awkwardly I put my hands up.

"You coming now?" he asked.

I nodded.

"C'mon."

"Can," I stammered, "Can I get my hat and coat?"

Gold Tooth and Scarface exchanged another look. I said a silent prayer. If they let me get my coat, maybe I could leave a message of some kind for Pierson.

"Where is it?"

"By the telescope."

Gold Tooth pushed me back inside and they followed. The door slammed behind them with a hollow crash. Gold Tooth said to Scarface, "Get the man's coat. And check the pockets."

Scarface stepped into the darkness. I turned to Gold Tooth.

"What's this all about?"

"You'll find out soon enough."

In moments Scarface came back with my hat and coat.

"Anything in 'em?"

"Nothing but his keys and a book," Scarface said.

Gold Tooth reached out for the book. He read the title and said, "*Tarzan and the Lion Man?*"

"Are you kidnapping me, or assigning book reports?"

Scarface said, "He's funny."

"You keep records?" Gold Tooth asked.

"Of what?"

He rammed the gun under my jaw again. My head jerked upward.

"Of the sky, you mook."

"You mean the celestial records?"

"Sure."

"We don't keep them here," I lied. "They go to the Dean's office at the end of the day."

Gold Tooth took the gun away and stood there, digesting that. If he asked how I was able to make notes at the scope while the records were in another building, I was cooked. But he looked like he didn't have enough brains to fill a cigarette.

"All right, we'll get them later," he said. He lowered the gun.

I lowered my hands. "Well, goodnight then."

The gun was shoved into my gut. "You're still coming with us."

Scarface handed me my hat and coat and I stuffed Tarzan into my pocket. Scarface went out first and motioned for me to follow. Gold Tooth pocketed his gun. "Don't get cute, funny boy. Or you're dead."

We stepped into the late evening air and I nearly jumped out of my skin when the door banged shut behind us. The two men laughed and led me along.

We stepped over the damp lawn and at the curb was the long, black touring car I had noticed earlier. Scarface stepped around and climbed into the driver's seat while Gold Tooth opened the back door for me. I stepped in and he took the front seat. Once we were inside the car he pulled the automatic from his pocket and kept it trained on me.

We pulled away and I turned to watch as my beloved observatory grew distant.

I moved my attention to the front seat. "What is this all about?"

"You'll find out," Gold Tooth said.

I didn't like the sound of that, but I couldn't think of anything I could do about it.

We drove for nearly a half hour, mostly through New Jersey farmland. The roads were deserted and I prayed for a passing police car. But I saw no one.

I recognized Princeton Meadows and we made our way through scattered farmhouses. When we finally stopped, I could hardly believe my eyes.

I knew where I was before I got out of the car. The car stopped and Scarface got out first. He opened the door for Gold Tooth, who backed out, still holding the gun on me. Not that a gun was necessary anymore.

I pushed open the door and stepped out on my own.

The place was a small, two story farm house in the middle of four acres of uncultivated land. One wing of the house was wood, with clapboard shutters and a stone porch complete with matching rockers. There were four bedrooms upstairs, a library, a well-appointed living room and a barely used kitchen.

The right-most wing of the house was reinforced brick and windowless.

And I knew all of this because I had spent many happy hours here in the past. It was the home of my friend and colleague, Dr. Mason Cooley.

I turned to Gold Tooth. "What's going on here? Do you know Dr. Cooley?"

Scarface nodded towards the house. "Inside."

"Just one damn minute," I said. "Where is Dr. Cooley? If you've hurt him in any way…"

Gold Tooth pulled me by my coat lapel. "Move it, tough guy."

I walked up the well-known porch steps and Gold Tooth rapped on the rough-wooden door with his automatic.

I did not know what to expect, but the last thing I expected was what I saw.

It was a little man. A midget, to be precise. He had close-cropped hair, blonde, short enough to see his scalp beneath. His eyes were cold and ice-chip blue and his thin-lipped mouth was cruel and sardonic. He wore an elegantly tailored navy pinstripe suit, claret-colored tie and cream-colored shirt. His patent leather shoes glistened in the night air. At a glance, I thought he could not be more than four feet tall.

His eyes took in the scene in a glance and he stepped aside for us to enter.

"You got the records?" he asked, closing the door.

"No," Scarface said.

"They're locked up in the Dean's office," Gold Tooth said. "We'll have to get them tomorrow."

The midget looked at the two men, face colorless and blandly nasty. "You had better be right. I don't like mistakes."

"No mistakes," said Scarface. "This here is Armstrong."

The midget looked up at me. "Dr. Armstrong. Welcome." His voice was deep and cultured, but vaguely singsong in its intonation. Like he usually read Shakespeare over the radio. Whatever his story was, I had no time for him and I was getting madder and more scared by the minute.

"Who are you and where is Mason Cooley?"

"He's here," he gestured vaguely towards the inside of the house. "No worries. We had hoped to speak with you first."

"About what?"

"Romero, take the gentleman's hat and coat."

Gold Tooth stepped forward, hands out. So his name was Romero. I filed that away for future reference. I took off my hat and coat and handed them over. Scarface stepped behind me and ran his hands down the length of my body before I could make another move.

"He's clean," he said.

"Excellent," the midget said. "Come with me."

He walked through Mason's house like he owned it. We stepped through the living and dining room and into the study. I had been there many times before and just walking in conjured up happy memories. It was a cozy, book-lined room with a desk, three armchairs, a smoke stand and a large, floor-model Crosley radio. Near the desk was a low liquor cabinet and behind the desk were French doors leading out to the fields beyond.

The midget walked to the bar and took out two glasses. "May I offer you a drink, Dr. Armstrong?"

"No," I said.

He looked up. "You aren't telling me you don't drink? I thought it was a job requirement for all university people."

"I like to know who I'm drinking with first."

He smiled a bit to himself and poured bourbon for us both. He syphoned soda into each glass and held one of them up to me. "I'm Mr.—Smith."

"Smith?"

"Yes." He turned and walked behind the desk, put down his drink and climbed into the chair. "Now that introductions have been concluded, let's discuss astronomy. Shall we?"

My eyes made a tour of the room. Romero and Scarface stood on either side of the door. Through the French windows I saw nothing but darkness. There was a French phone beside a Tiffany lamp on the desk top, but I'd be lucky to barely pull the receiver off its cradle before they stopped me.

I drank the bourbon. It warmed my insides and steadied my nerves. I took a breath and settled in an armchair.

"Fine," I said. "Let's talk astronomy. Do you want to talk about absolute magnitude, or would you rather talk about occultation? Perhaps you'd like to discuss the elliptical galaxy?"

He leaned back in Mason's chair, drinking Mason's bourbon. "Why don't you do the talking?"

"Fine. Delighted to chat with a colleague." I glanced over my shoulder at Romero and Scarface. "Or colleagues, I gather. What institution did you gentlemen attend?"

If they had said they attended San Quentin, I would not have been surprised. But before either could say a word, the midget said, "They're not college boys. More the school of hard knocks."

I turned back to Smith. "And you are a colleague of Dr. Cooley?"

Smith put down his drink and slid a silver cigarette case from his jacket pocket. He opened it up offered one to me.

"I have my own," I said, and reached for a Lucky.

Smith took a slender, brown cigarette from his case and used the heavy lighter on Mason's desk. "We've done business together."

I nodded. I reached over for Mason's lighter and lit my cigarette. "So, in your expert opinion, would you say it's possible for perambulators to achieve escape velocity and transverse the ionosphere in an elliptical orbit?"

Smith puffed his cigarette and dropped ashes onto Mason's carpet. "That's a matter of opinion."

"I just asked you if baby carriages could leave the atmosphere and fly around the Earth," I said. "So why don't you just tell me who you are and where I can find Mason?"

"I told you he was funny," Scarface said behind me.

"A regular Jack Benny,[2]" Smith said. He pulled on his cigarette and ground it into the ashtray. "Now, laughing boy, you can tell me what you saw on the night of February 19th?"

There was that date again—the same night Mason recorded ten projectiles hurtling towards the Earth. And calculations of where to find them.

I let smoke dribble out of my mouth. I leaned closer to the desk to use the ashtray, cradling the desk lighter in the palm of my other hand.

"I didn't see anything."

"But Cooley did?"

"Ask him."

"I'm asking you."

---

2   Jack Benny (1894-1974) was one of the most successful comedians in the history of radio. His persona was that of a cheapskate, though the real source of his comedy was the brilliant interplay between he and his supporting cast of characters. Many of his original shows are available online.

"And I'm telling you, I saw nothing. You're Mason's friend. Go ask him."

Smith and I locked eyes over the table. I did not like where this was going. If Mason needed help, he needed it now.

I jumped to my feet—too fast, I think, as I ended up on my tiptoes. I screamed, "MASON!" I turned to see surprised looks on Romero and Scarface. "*MASON!*"

Romero reached for his gun. I hauled back and threw the desk lighter at him. It bopped him hard on the head, knocking off his hat. Scarface dived for me, but I kicked my armchair over and he stumbled into it.

Adrenaline lit up my brain. I turned and swept the Tiffany lamp off the desk and the room plunged into darkness.

I ducked and scrambled for the wall. Romero and Scarface scuffled in the black, unaware that they were pushing against one another. I had no idea where Smith was.

I felt along the wall, found the doorknob and pulled open the door. I had only run four steps down the corridor before Scarface tackled me and I fell.

I was not much of scrapper, but panic set in. I twisted round on the floor and punched at the man's head and shoulders. He just grinned in a way that made his scar show red, reached back slowly and clipped me in the jaw.

I had read about it in books and it was true—the punch was like sheets of lightning or stars exploding in my brain. I don't think I even blinked before I went down.

I wasn't out completely, but things had turned a little fuzzy. Romero and Scarface each took a leg and dragged me back into the study. There, Smith had put the lamp on the table and once more the room was lit.

"Fast little punk," Scarface said.

"This is most regrettable," Smith said. "Put him in the chair."

Romero right-sided my armchair and Scarface lifted and set me in it like I was a ragdoll. I blinked until my vision cleared.

Smith was standing in front of me. With me seated, his eyes were nearly level with my own, and I saw him shake his head in regret.

"That was not smart, Dr. Armstrong."

"Where is Mason Cooley?" I groaned.

"I'm asking the questions," he said, voice calm and dangerous. "Now, this is the last time I'm going to ask you. What did you see on the night of February 19th?"

"I told you. I didn't see anything. I wasn't even at the observatory that night."

Smith frowned. He turned to Scarface. "Get his book."

Smith stood, starting at me silently until Scarface returned. Smith took *Tarzan and the Lion Man* and paged through it. After he had seen all of it, he pulled the book apart in frustration. "It's not here," he said to Scarface.

"Hey," I said. "That was new!"

Smith came closer; his breath was stale and rank as it blew against my face. "Tell me where the records are."

"Records?"

"Records!" his voice an enraged squeak. "The observatory records!"

"I told him," I said. "They are with the Dean."

"Which Dean?"

"Dean of the Sciences Department," I lied. "Main building. All laboratory records go to the main office. Protocol."

Smith stepped back with a *what can you do?* shrug. "Dr. Armstrong, I tried to be nice. I really did. But you don't leave me any alternative."

"What are you going to do?"

"You'll see." Smith motioned to Romero and Scarface. "Take him to the laboratory."

Romero wrapped an arm around my neck and Scarface twisted my right arm behind my back. They need not have bothered—the sock to my jaw had taken any fight out of me. They pulled me from the chair and we followed Smith down the hallway.

Mason Cooley remodeled the property back when he bought it in Twenty-Eight. The farmhouse originally was no better than a cold-water shack and Mason turned it into a comfortable retreat for a scholar.

The new brick wing was designed by Mason to carry out his private researches. For some time Mason had worked with radioactivity, and wanted to keep the observatory and laboratory safe from potential alpha, beta and gamma rays. Sometimes his electromagnetic work played havoc on his instruments, but Mason continued on unafraid.

I wish I could say the same for me.

Smith flicked on the rows of overhead lights. The laboratory was much the same as I saw it last. The brick walls were lined with delicate electrical instrumentation. Several large tables were bolted to the floor, topped with black tile and equipped with Bunsen burners and running water. An oscillator hummed in the corner and Mason's high-powered telescope stood at the ready. Only two things were out of the ordinary and both had me terrified.

First, Mason's notebooks were shredded and individual pages littered the floor and tabletops. Second, the isolation room, where Mason examined space debris that might carry infectious disease, was occupied.

The isolation room was at the end of the brick wing extension; a long, narrow room lined on the inside with lead. The door was steel with a window at its center; lead lined the door interior and the glass was coated with a transparent lead film. The room was equipped with an overhead light, scientific tools (including another microscope) and a black-tiled platform in its center.

The platform was partially covered by a lead dome. Mason would keep potentially dangerous materials under the lead dome. The dome could retract into the table—like a chef opening a dinner tray—by levers both inside and out.

But what terrified me the most was the man locked inside.

The man was short and balding, fifty or so from the looks of him. He had a gray crown of hair, but was bald on top. Rimless eyeglasses covered his watery blue eyes. His jacket was missing and his top shirt button and tie were loose. He wore suspenders and spats, and when we entered, he hammered on the glass.

"Let me out!" he wailed. "I don't know anything! Let me out!"

Smith walked to the door, stood on his toes, and looked through the glass.

"Stutka," he pleaded. "Please! Please! I haven't done anything!"

Scarface pulled my arm up higher behind my back. Romero stepped back and pulled his automatic. He pressed the cold muzzle against my temple and Scarface let go.

I paid no attention. I stepped closer to the door.

The man behind the glass saw me and slapped his palms against the window. "Help! Get help!"

Smith threw a glance at Scarface and nodded.

"No!" the man screamed. "Stutka! Please, God no!"

Scarface walked around us and grabbed the lever beside the door.

The lever, I knew, which opened the protective dome in the table.

I don't know what I expected to happen, but I jumped Scarface to prevent whatever it was. He brushed me aside and I crashed into one of the lab tables, knocking a few meteor specimens to the floor. Romero grabbed me by the tie and hauled me to my feet. He pressed the gun to my temple and brought me back to the lead-lined door.

Scarface held the lever; the man inside looked at him with pleading eyes.

Smith said, "Now."

"NO!" the man screamed.

Scarface slowly pulled the lever down.

Inside the room, the dome slid into the interior of the table. Revealed beneath was baseball-sized red rock. It wasn't perfectly round, more like a rounded cylinder, and the surface was uneven with multiple facets. The stone shone a little like crystal in some places, but also flatly like a metamorphic rock.

As soon as the dome fully retracted, the rock glowed scarlet. Red light filled the room and the man inside threw his back against the door and screamed!

I tried to move to the lever, but Romero pressed the gun against my temple.

And then it happened.

The man turned, screaming, as the effects were already taking place. At first I thought the red light from the rock made his skin look red, but then I realized it now *was* red. He brought both hands to his face and screamed, "Stutka! No!"

The skin on his hands and face seemed to—soften, and then grow liquid. When he took his hands away from his face most of both cheeks came with them. I saw the upper and lower rows of teeth at what was now a screaming skull.

The eyes grew more watery still, then melted and trailed down his cheek bones like greasy tears. Hair fell from his head in clumps and his neck shriveled behind his collar.

The screaming, which had been intense and horrible, dimmed to a few choked gurgles. He put a hand against the doorway glass and slowly slid to the floor, leaving a crimson trail where his fingers had once been.

I stumbled closer and looked at him on the floor.

The figure only writhed for an instant and then grew still. The clothes compressed and shrunk until they simply heaped where a man had once been. His remaining shirt, trousers and shoes were covered with a vile, red-black ichor.

Scarface pushed the lever up and the dome slid over the stone, snuffing out the red light.

I felt the room swim around me and dropped to my knees. I was swallowing huge gulps of air when Scarface and Romero brought me back to my feet.

Supported by both men, I looked down at the midget.

"Now," he said. "Tell me about February 19th."

"I don't know anything," I said. "I wasn't even there."

The midget looked at me, and I swear I could see the wheels spinning inside his head.

"He doesn't know anything," he finally said.

I took a deep breath and recovered just enough to be stupid. I pulled my arms away from Scarface and Romero and said, "I know one thing, *Mr. Stutka*. I'm going to see you in jail for this."

Stutka, for that was his name, shook his head like a man grown old watching human folly. "That was a mistake," he said. He then reared back and punched me in the stomach. His hard little fist struck me right over the belt buckle, and after what I had just seen, I was perilously close to being sick.

Instead, Scarface pulled me up by the shirt collar and Romero once again pressed the gun against my temple.

"You want I should put him inside there?" Romero asked.

My head swam at the idea.

Stutka considered. "No. We need to be careful with this."

"What do you want we should do?"

The midget nodded at the door. "Take him for a ride. Dump him in Sandy Hook. Make it look like an accident." He straightened his tie and walked away. "But don't get too creative," he said over his shoulder.

Scarface frog marched me down the corridor, but I did not offer any resistance. He reached around me and opened the door and pushed me into the back of the touring car. I had not realized that Romero had fallen behind us, but he came through the door ten seconds later with my hat and coat. He threw these over me in the back seat and slammed the door.

Scarface drove and Romero sat beside him.

"Sandy Hook?" Romero asked.

"Screw that," Scarface started the car. "Rocky Hill. I need something to eat."

Sandy Hook was about an hour away, while Rocky Hill was only about fifteen minutes from here. Fifteen minutes. It seemed to be just about all the time I had left alive.

I wasn't afraid of dying—though I certainly was in no hurry. It's not what comes after that has me afraid—who knows what comes after?—it was dying itself that terrified me. There were good and bad ways to go, and getting shot by two gangsters in some deserted farmland was not one of the good ones.

I thought about saying something to them, maybe even pleading for my life. But I doubted it would do any good. Instead, I slid down a bit in the backseat and did what I did best. I watched the stars.

The stars looked down at me with sparkling indifference. And I wondered, what had happened to Mason? How was he connected to these people, and just what the hell fell from the sky that had everyone so panicked?

The car left the main road and sliced through the unpaved, rural back roads. I saw some silos and scattered barns, as well as a few clapboard farmhouses. In a few weeks the fields would be plowed to plant corn, and one of those machines would probably find my body.

The car made a right at the outskirts of a large private farm. The boundaries of the property were lined with elm trees and the branches just beginning to bud obliterated my view of the sky. Without the stars, I turned back to my situation.

I could let these guys murder me, or I could fight back. And if I was going to fight back, now was the time to do it.

I watched Scarface and Romero through slitted eyes. The bigger man drove silently while Romero sat nestled in his coat. Romero glanced back to check on me, saw me supine and helpless, and turned his attention to opening a pack of cigarettes.

My hat and coat were right beside me. I had no real plan, just an action. I grabbed hold of my coat and threw it over Scarface's head and pulled. Scarface roared within the folds of my trench coat. I stuck a knee against the back of his seat and pulled even harder.

Romero yelped and dropped his cigarettes and matches. I was yelling, too, some sort of primal cry of terror and attack.

The touring car went wild. Romero reached for his automatic, but things happened too fast. Trees loomed up before us in the headlights like avenging giants and the next thing I knew, the car seemed to explode in a shower of broken glass.

I was thrown to the floor of the back seat and lay there for only a second. When I climbed back to my seat, I found Scarface, still covered in my coat, slumped over the steering wheel. Romero was on the floor of the car up front, covered in glass.

Time to get the hell out of there.

I grabbed my hat and lurched from the car. The fender and headlights were wrapped around a large elm and I could hear the motor turning over in the wreckage. Then I heard movement within and turned and ran for it.

I ran alongside the trees and into the darkness. It was a moonless night, and I could barely see the ground beneath me, let alone anything up ahead.

The ground turned soft underfoot and I realized I was running through the soon-to-be planted fields, and was alive enough not to stick around to be found under a farm machine. I ran until I got a stitch and then dropped to a knee and listened.

I didn't hear anything.

Not that there was anything I *could* hear. If Romero and Scarface were behind me, the soft earth would muffle their footsteps just as much as it did mine. But hunkering down in the dark, kneeling on the cold, moist earth and unable to see anything clearly only increased my panic.

I knelt there, taking deep breaths until I felt less frantic. Then I checked the sky and found the North Star. With no other option I could think of, I rose and walked north.

I had to tread carefully, as the ground was uneven and the last thing I needed was a sprained or broken ankle. It was too dark to check my watch and I could not strike a match without them seeing me—if, indeed, they were still anywhere near me. But I must have been marching through the shadows for nearly twenty minutes before I hit another clump of elms.

I figured I finally hit the outer reaches of whatever farm I was on. I pressed a hand against the elm, felt its reassuring solidity, and paused.

I think it was just dumb luck that saved me. I stood there in the trees, trying to think of something, anything, to get me out of this fix when I heard the whispering.

It was so subtle at first that I thought I imagined it. But I held my breath and dropped down to make a poor target and listened hard.

There it was again.

It was too low for me to make out the words, but I did hear whispered voices in the darkness. It was impossible to tell where they came from, but they were close enough to hear.

I thought of running, but where? In the darkness, I could run straight into them just as easily as I could run away from them! Worse still, if I made any noise in my escape, they could just shoot at that. A lucky shot would kill me just as easily as a well-aimed bullet.

I desperately struggled for some idea when I realized I was still pressing against the tree.

Without a second thought I reached up into the branches and pulled myself up. There was a little noise as they creaked under my weight, but nothing that sounded too unnatural.

I hoped.

From above I peered down into the darkness. My eyes had become more and more accustomed to the gloom during my escape, and I could see enough of the terrain below to make out the dark earth and the even darker furrows where the corn would be laid.

I could not hear any more whispering. The wind came up a bit, but it didn't carry any sounds to me. And even though I was somewhat safer hidden up among the branches, I felt more vulnerable and easily trapped. If they somehow found out where I was, all they had to do was point and shoot.

So maybe it wasn't the best idea.

I kept still and tried to control my panic and then I saw the shadow.

At first, I couldn't tell who it was. But in the gloom I could discern the outline of a thick overcoat and wide-brimmed hat. The shadow spread over the darkened landscape as the figure itself came close.

The figure was nearly under my tree when I was just able to make it out. It was tall and slender and carried an automatic in its hand. Romero!

I realized I could have dropped down from the tree on top of him and wrestled the gun away from him. But I also realized that the idea was nearly as stupid and suicidal as climbing the tree had been.

I held my breath. If I stayed absolutely and completely silent, he would move on and I would be safe. I leaned forward to peer into the darkness.

That is when it happened. I leaned over further than I should have and the next thing I knew, I was hurtling into the night.

There was a dizzying second and then I landed with a thud on top of Romero.

I let out a yell and he howled, and for a second I expected to be perforated by a bullet. But I felt both of his hands on my lapels and next thing I knew, we were thrashing about in the dirt.

He tried to get his mitts around my biceps, but I rolled over on top of him. He brought up his knee but missed me and I swung blindly into the shadowy mass that I thought was his head. I missed and my fist pounded dirt.

He then pushed me over. In the dark he got to his knees and felt around for the gun. I shouldered into him and laid us both out for another round of nighttime groping.

I don't know how, but I found myself straddling his chest and pressing him into the dirt. He yelled, "Help!" and I feared that Scarface could track us by the sound of his voice.

I found his throat and wrapped both hands around it and squeezed. I heard a sick, gurgling sound as he struggled under my body.

I still don't know if I would have killed him there and then, but it never came to that. He rammed his forearms into mine and my left hand lost its grip on his throat. He caught hold of that wrist and pulled it to his face. He snarled and sank his golden teeth into my wrist.

It was unlike anything else that had ever bitten me before. His teeth cut through the cuff of my shirt and razored into the ball of my wrist.

I cried out in pain and pushed back off his body. My left wrist was on fire and I slid into the dirt. My right hand found something cold and metallic.

I wrapped my fist around it and swung out into the darkness.

The butt of the gun managed to clip him somewhere because I heard a metallic clang. I could not see it, but I think I clocked him right in his mouthful of gold teeth. There was a slight sigh and he went down.

I crawled on top of him and put a hand over his mouth, just in case he was still awake, and listened. I expected his teeth to snap shut over my fingers like a bear trap.

The sound of footsteps was still impossible to hear in the soft ground, but was that the shadow of a man I saw fast approaching?

Romero was out of it for now, but what if Scarface caught up with me? I could shoot him now, but if I missed, the flash of the shot would tell him where I was. One lucky shot and he could kill me.

Unless he didn't see the shot.

I felt around the ground and found my Trilby. I took it up and covered the muzzle of the automatic with it, and unsteadily got to my feet.

I had never shot anyone before. I could warn him not to move—that at least would be fair. But, then again, he could shoot at the sound of my voice.

I kept quiet. I was barely able to make out his shadow, and did not know if he was aware of me, too. Scarface walked a little to the left, then trailed a bit to the right. He stood still and I could see his head pivot, as if he were trying to smell me.

After the pause, he moved. And it looked like he was coming straight for me.

I held the gun, covered the muzzle with my hat, and fired once. Then once more.

The explosion of the shot rang out in the cold night air. I had never fired a gun before and the recoil nearly pushed me off my feet. The second shot tore the Trilby from my left hand, but any flash from the shots had been successfully shielded.

Whether I hit him or not I did not know. But if he was out there, I certainly scared him. I stuck the automatic beneath my belt and ran in the opposite direction.

I ran for nearly ten minutes, unable to see much of anything, when my foot hit something in the dirt and I did a neat somersault in the air before hitting the ground.

I closed my eyes and listened.

Nothing.

Still, I waited.

Sure that there was no one close enough to do me too much harm, I got up, again located the North Star, and set out at a moderate pace.

I walked and walked. Before too long I came upon a darkened horse barn and saw the lights of a farmhouse beyond. I almost cried with relief.

I ran towards the lighted windows. It was a small farmhouse, two story and simple, much like Mason's but without the brick addition, and clearly someone lived there. As I came closer, a hand drew closed the shades of the windows facing me.

I climbed up the stone steps and hammered on the door.

No answer.

I hammered again.

The door opened and a second later I was looking down the length of a double-barreled shotgun.

The man holding the shotgun was short and wiry, wearing a collarless shirt, dungarees and muddy boots. His eyeglasses were propped up on top his forehead and his eyes turned beady.

With quiet deliberation, he cocked both barrels of the shotgun and his mouth went grim.

"You just stay right there, mister."

I slowly raised my hands.

"Was it you doin' all that shootin' I heard?"

"No."

The shotgun trailed down from my head and rested on point right over my belt. My eyes followed and I realized he was looking at the automatic stuck behind my belt.

"I'll give you five seconds to explain. And if you don't," he said, "I'll kill yah."

CHAPTER TWO

"I can explain," I said.

"I'll bet you can," the farmer said. "But first, let me have the gun."

I reached for the automatic in my belt.

"Slow!" he barked. "Take the butt between two fingers and slowly pull it out."

I did as I was told and held it out.

He took hold of the automatic with his left hand, his right still propping the shotgun into my middle. He stuck the automatic in his belt behind his back.

"I need to call the police," I said.

"What happened?"

"I was kidnapped and a friend of mine may be in trouble."

"Kidnapped?" His eyes narrowed and he used his free hand to lower the eyeglasses over his eyes. "You mean, like the Lindbergh Baby[3]?"

"Something like that."

"Hell, why didn't you say so?" He lowered the shotgun. "C'mon in."

I stepped inside and he shut the door behind us.

The house was like Mason's but without any of the improvements. The wallpaper had grown a little thin, the living room furniture was now threadbare, but there was a Crosley floor model radio in the corner and a stack of *Detective Story* magazines beside it.

I turned and asked, "Do you have a phone?"

"Do you have a nickel?"

"Yes."

He held out a hand. "Let's see it first."

I fished a nickel out of my pocket and pressed it into his palm.

He looked at it and for a mad moment I thought he was going to bite it to ensure it was genuine. Instead he stuck it in a pocket and said, "Phone's in the kitchen."

"Thanks. You can put that shotgun away. Someone is liable to get hurt."

"This?" He brandished the shotgun again and stuck both barrels in my face.

---

3 Charles Augustus Lindbergh was the 20-month old son of famed aviator Charles Lindbergh (1902-1974), the first man to fly nonstop from New York to Paris. The kidnapping, and eventual murder, of the Lindbergh Baby caused a national furor.

"Let's see it first."

"Wait!" I screamed.

He pressed the trigger. I heard one, sharp, metallic click, and then another. I nearly wet myself. It was a moment before I could breathe again.

"Hell," he said, "I ain't had money for no bullets in over a year."

I collapsed onto the arm of his couch and put a hand to my forehead.

"Hey there, big feller," he said. "You ain't doin' too good." He walked into the kitchen and came back a moment later with a jelly jar filled with clear liquid. "Here, I made it myself."

I took the glass and sipped. It smacked my head and lit up my brain harder than Scarface's fist.

"Thanks," I choked. I handed the jar back to him. "Now, you were saying about a phone?"

I followed him into the kitchen. It was neatly kept, sink clear and clean and the drain board empty. There was a hand pump in the center of the sink for water and an old model ice box in a corner. The shelves were stocked with jars of dried corn.

There was a wall phone beside the back door. The man lifted the receiver, turned the crank furiously and waited for an operator.

"Is that Phyllis? Howdy! It's Fred. Let me have the police—What? No, everything's fine."

He shot me a glance while waiting and in moments spoke into the receiver once more. "Fred Clarke here. Who's this? Tom? Hold on, I got somebody here who needs you."

He stepped aside and held the earpiece out to me.

I stepped up to the phone. "Hello, police?"

"Yes."

"This is Peter Armstrong. Dr. Peter Armstrong from over in Princeton."

"How can I help you, Dr. Armstrong?"

I considered—what best to tell him to do the best good. "I was just abducted from Princeton Observatory by two men. They took me to the home of Dr. Mason Cooley. I think they may be holding him hostage."

"Calm down, Dr. Armstrong." Pause. "How did you get away from them?"

"They were going to kill me—take me for a ride, they said."

Pause.

"And?"

"And, I got away from them. I—well …, I made them wreck their car. I'm calling from a farmhouse nearby."

"I know where you're calling from." The officer on the other end let loose a long and hard sigh. "Where did you leave them?"

"Near a clump of elms not far from here."

An even longer pause.

"Dr. Armstrong, could you please put Fred Clarke back on the line?"

I stepped aside and Clarke got back on the phone.

"No, I don't know anything about it," he said. "Just came pounding on the door. Oh—and he's got an automatic." Clarke listened to the officer talk and then said, "No, I took it from him." A longer wait. "Sure, we'll be waiting for you. Take your time."

"Don't take your time!" I shouted at the phone. "They could get away!"

"Just calm down, young feller," Clarke said, hanging up. He eased over to the sink, took another clear jar and poured more moonshine from a jug. "Here. Have another. It'll steady your nerves."

"My nerves are fine!"

"Then I'll steady mine," he said, and took a sip.

He put the jar down and pointed with the empty shotgun to the living room. "Might as well sit a spell till they get here."

We went into the living room and I sank into an armchair that had seen better days. Clarke went to the radio and switched it on while I rubbed my eyes. The music of Paul Whiteman[4] filled the room and I found myself wishing for some more of the man's home-made liquor. I held back, though. It would be hard enough to make the police to believe me even if I was stone cold sober.

Which made me wonder—just what would I tell the police when they *did* get here?

Farmer Clarke sat on the couch opposite. He winced when he sank into the cushions, pulled the gun from the back of his belt and rested it on his lap with a sigh.

"This is rather awkward," I smiled at him.

He nodded at me.

"Did they say how long it'll take for them to get here?"

"However long it takes."

"Thanks."

If I told the police about the man who was murdered in the laboratory, I doubted they would believe me. I wasn't sure I believed it myself! Also, if I start talking about Mason's astronomical journals, they may be confiscated before I could examine them myself. In fact, it might make more sense for me to get back to the observatory even before I spoke to the police.

---

4   Paul Whiteman (1890-1967), also known as The King of Jazz, was a celebrated bandleader who championed the mix of jazz sound with symphonic flourishes. Much of his music is available online.

I smiled at the farmer again. "I don't suppose you have a car or a truck I could borrow?"

"Sure do."

"How much?"

"Just wait until the police get here and we'll settle it all out."

Great. I got to my feet. "If you don't mind, I'll just go to the end of the road and meet them there."

He took the automatic and pointed it at me. It seemed to be the recurring theme of the evening. "Just sit tight."

I sat.

It was nearly thirty minutes before the police arrived. Clarke got up when he heard the car pull up and the front door was open by the time the officer approached.

"Here he is."

A uniformed policeman walked in. His uniform was dark navy blue with yellow piping, with a thick leather belt around his middle to hold his gun and nightstick. He was a long drink of water, maybe thirty pounds underweight with a prominent Adam's apple and pockmarked cheeks.

I got to my feet.

"Hello. I'm Dr. Armstrong. I called earlier."

The officer turned to Clarke.

"Tom, he pounded on the door," the farmer said. "Damn near scared me to death. Had this in his belt." He handed the officer the automatic. "Said he needed the phone. Thought it best to call you."

"Correction," I said. "I asked for the phone to call the police."

The officer stuck the gun in his belt and stepped closer. "And you are?"

"Dr. Peter Armstrong of Princeton University."

The officer nodded, showing as much trust as if I said I was Ming the Merciless.[5]

"And what happened?"

In as few words as possible, I told him about the two gunmen who took me from the observatory, the trip to Mason Cooley's house, and then my escape. I did not say a word about the dead man or about Mason's notebook.

The officer took no notes, he just nodded absently while I spoke. When I was done he asked, "You got any identification?"

I reached for my pocket and he reached for his gun. I put up my hands.

"I'm just going for my wallet."

---

5   Ming the Merciless was the antagonist in the groundbreaking Science Fiction comic strip Flash Gordon, created by artist Alex Raymond (1909-1956). He was undisputed dictator of the planet Mongo, and often set his sights on the conquest of Earth.

"Do it slow."

My hand snaked up to my breast pocket and patted. Then I checked my pants.

"Hell," I said. "I guess my wallet was in my coat."

He nodded again.

"Officer, if you don't believe me, I'm sure we can find their wrecked car. It can't be far from here."

The officer turned to Clarke. "What do you think, Fred?"

The farmer shrugged. "Can't hurt none to check."

The officer turned. "Come on."

I followed the officer outside. The policeman and farmer traded a little local gossip while I sweated by the patrol car and then I got into the back seat.

"Elm trees, you said," he turned the ignition.

"Elm trees."

The patrol car eased off into the night air. We took a winding road leading from Fred Clarke's home and reached the outer boundaries of the farm. We were circling it for nearly fifteen minutes when I shouted, "Stop!"

The officer hit the brake. "There's no car here."

"But look!" I tried to open the back door, but it wouldn't budge.

The officer got out and opened the door for me. "They only open from the outside."

I was angry he didn't tell me that first, but let it go. Instead, I pointed to a grouping of trees illuminated by the eerie light of his headlamps.

There was a deep gouge in the tree nearest the roadside. "That's where we hit."

"Then where's the car?"

I walked to the tree and touched the damaged part. "Look! This break is fresh. It didn't happen too long ago."

"So where's the car?"

"Houdini[6] made it disappear! How the hell should I know?"

The officer folded his arms and looked at me, a smug half-smile on his face.

We might have stood there for days, glaring at one another if his car radio did not come to life. He ignored me and opened the front door. I turned my attention to the tree and paid no attention to the muffled voices

---

6   Harry Houdini (1874-1926), born Erik Weisz, was the foremost escape artist, magician, ghost-buster and vaudeville entertainer of his age. His other accomplishments include aviation, motion picture production, writing several books, and magic historian. Someday, when you have a year to spare, spend it in the study of Houdini.

behind me.

I saw the tracks of the car. Bits of black paint were in the freshly exposed wood where the tree had broken. I even thought I caught the smell of motor oil, but that might have been my imagination.

"Where did they say they took you?" The officer stood beside the car, leaning on the open door.

"The home of Dr. Mason Cooley."

"Well, that house is on fire."

"*What?*"

"Let's go take a look."

I raced around and reached for the passenger side of the patrol car.

"You sit in the back."

"But I—"

"In the back!"

I slammed the door and climbed into the back seat.

The officer turned on the siren and we sped down the road.

I didn't say anything other than give the occasional direction. I saw the house fire from the distance and my sense of foreboding grew as we drew closer. Tongues of flame reached into the night sky and the air was full of smoke. Even from a distance the smell of fire and carnage filled my lungs. There was a fire truck in front of the house and they were hosing it down, but I could already see that there was nothing to salvage.

If Mason Cooley was in there, he was never getting out. I never had the chance to find out if those men were holding him there, or if they had simply taken over his home.

The crowd parted as we pulled up and the officer got out and opened the door for me. I ran as close to the front steps as I could, but the inferno was so hot I could not get any closer than a few feet.

There were maybe five firemen and a dozen police. The police watched as the firemen worked, as was usual. One plainclothes officer stood there, drinking from a flask and watching the drama. He was a short, fat man in need of a shave wearing a shabby duster. His gray porkpie hat looked like he had used it to shoo away bumblebees.

The officer who brought me over walked to the plainclothesman and the two talked in hushed tones. At length they both came over to me.

"So you're a professor," the plainclothesman said.

"Yes." I couldn't take my eyes away from the fire. I barely looked at the firemen as they worked. I only saw the flames and thought of Mason.

"So what do you know about this?"

That brought me out of my reverie. I turned and told the detective exactly what I told the officer.

He took another drink from the flask and it vanished in the folds of his duster. "Anything else?"

"Yeah," I said, turning back to the flames. They glowed red and hotly upon all of us. "When your men go through the wreckage, they might find traces of a dead man."

"A dead man? Cooley?"

"No. No one I know. The men who brought me here killed him."

"Killed him?" His voice was deep, like it crawled up from behind of several layers of fat. "Why'd they do that?"

"I don't know."

"How'd they do it?"

I turned and looked at him closely. "They exposed him to some kind of rock."

"A rock?"

"Yes. Something I had never seen before. It had properties of terrifying potency. Rays, perhaps cosmic rays. I don't know."

The fat man and the policeman exchanged glances. Then the plain-clothesman held out his hand and the officer handed him the automatic.

"Is this yours?"

"No."

"Was it taken from you?"

"Yes."

"If it wasn't yours, then how did you come to be carrying it?"

"I took it from one of the men who kidnapped me."

"I see." He handed the gun back to the officer. "Dr. Armstrong, if that's your real name, you're under arrest."

I don't think my eyes could have popped any wider.

"I'm what?"

"You're under arrest."

"On what charge?"

"Suspected arson, for starters."

"But I told you my story!"

"You told us a story all right," he said. He motioned to the officer, "Lock 'im up. I'll make some calls and get back to you in a few hours."

"But I—"

The officer pulled his nightstick. "You're not going to give me any trouble, are you, *Professor*?"

"Jeez!" I said, holding my hands out.

The officer cuffed my hands behind my back and I felt my cheeks grow hot, and not because of the fire. If Mason needed my help, I wasn't going able to do anything for him now.

~~~

I spent the night in jail.

I had never been arrested before and nothing can really prepare you for the experience. I've read about innocent people getting arrested since I was a kid, but I never reckoned on how devastating it can be. The helplessness and isolation were just about the worst moments of my life.

The officer drove me to a small police station—hardly larger than a Princeton student locker—and walked me through the offices to a cell out back. I demanded a phone call and he just chuckled and unlocked my cuffs before shoving me inside.

He closed the cell and I watched him walk out, closing the door behind him.

I sat on the musty cot, head in my hands, finished.

Who knows what was happening with Mason, and who would be able to help him now? And what would happen to my place in the faculty if they actually prosecuted me? And what would my folks think?

I loved both my mom and dad, but I couldn't say that it was easy being "the brain of the family." My father was very successful in his field, and thanks to him I always look like a million dollars. He was very proud of me, gave me every opportunity and was always there for me. But when he called me "Tom Swift,"[7] I always had the feeling that he sometimes wondered—where did this strange kid come from? He never loved me any less, but whenever he looked at me, that question was always floating just behind his eyes.

My mom had been an amateur scientist, and in a way, she understood me better. But not completely. As I started to outpace all of my classmates, she got oddly possessive, as if I was living the life she had imagined for herself. She got to be very interfering, so much so that she would go through my notebooks and letters—looking for what, who knows? But it always infuriated me. Things got much better with her after I left home,

---

[7]   Tom Swift was the hero of more than one hundred (and counting!) Science-Fiction/adventure novels for boys from 1910 through 2022. Swift was a boy inventor with limitless know-how and enthusiasm. Tom Swift novels have, to date, sold more than 30 million copies worldwide.

but still, when she calls I instantly start to think about my "cover story."

And what would these two people, who love me even when they make me nuts, say when I tell them I was arrested? How could I explain what happened tonight? Hell, could I even explain it to myself?

Of course, Mason would understand. In many ways, Mason Cooley was a second father to me. It happened like this.

Several universities were interested in me when I returned from my travels abroad. Columbia was a real possibility for me, as was Yale. But when I met with Mason something about us just "clicked" and he actively campaigned for my recruitment.

When I joined the faculty, he made it a point to mentor me in every way. He gave me unprecedented access to the telescope, put me on an equal footing with Dick Pierson; even had me chair the occasional staff meeting.

And it was fun to work with Mason. He didn't teach me things as much as lead me to conclusions, all the while asking me the questions that guided me to thinking with greater clarity. Often he would just sit there, usually holding a drink and clinking the ice in his glass.

We also had some of the same challenges. I'm the world's worst speller, and Mason would sometimes transpose numbers. His notebooks would sometimes read 1913 when he meant 1931, and that played the very devil with his math. But nothing seemed to stop him. When he started making preliminary experiments with radium, I even helped him design and build the fortified wing of his farmhouse.

He would often host parties in the farmhouse, and especially famous were his New Year's celebrations. They would start at the observatory proper, with our colleagues and their wives taking turns at the scope, looking at the stars as the galactic clock counted down the last few moments of the old year, and then we would all drive over to his farmhouse and spend the day eating and drinking ourselves into hangovers and stomachaches.

And Mason knew *everybody*. His parties wouldn't just be Princeton faculty, but he also knew artists and poets and intellectuals from Greenwich Village, screenwriters from Hollywood, dissidents from overseas—everybody.

The one point where we would clash is in what we read. Mason would push Theodore Dreiser and Frank Norris on me, and I would give him books by Edgar Rice Burroughs and Jules Verne.[8] But he would sniff at my

---

[8] It would be difficult to consider four more different writers than Theodore Dreiser (1871-1945) and Frank Norris (1870-1902) and Edgar Rice Burroughs (1875-1950) and Jules Verne (1828-1905). Dreiser was a novelist of the realist school, while Orwell was a gifted essayist and political polemicist. Burroughs and Verne, on the other hand, were entertainers, creating between them many classic novels of Science Fiction and adventure.

books and I would doze over his. It was our sole point of misalignment.

Of course, the observatory was more than home to both of us. I can't even count (and he certainly couldn't!) the many nights we spent in the lab, taking turns at the telescope and making meticulous records of the celestial movement. It was a quiet domesticity of like-minded academics.

And I realized that, with him missing and his home burned to the ground, those days were over for good.

I sat there brooding for several hours. It was nearly two in the morning when the fat plainclothesman came back to see me. He smelled of booze and the burnt-out building as he stood on the other side of the bars.

"You ready to talk?"

I got up. "I already talked."

He nodded to the officer, who unlocked the cell. "Come on. Let's get a statement."

In minutes I was in his office, a small room barely large enough for his desk and two chairs opposite. A stenographer, her hair a tidy bun atop her head, took it down in shorthand as I spoke.

I told him everything, except any details about the observatory journals.

He asked me for people to call to verify that I was who I said I was, and then I was escorted back to my cell while calls were made and my statement typed up.

I kept hoping to doze off, but a feeling of dread would not let me go. The faint, dull white light of dawn was just beginning to light up the cell window when the policeman returned and brought me back to the office.

The detective sat at his desk, a sheath of typescript in front of him, and sitting in the chair I had occupied earlier was Dick Pierson.

"Dick!" I pushed past the policeman to Dick and nearly shook his hand off.

"Peter!" he grinned at me. "What trouble have you gotten yourself into now?"

"You know this man?" the detective asked.

"Definitely," Pierson turned to him. "This is Dr. Peter Armstrong, one of the most important professors at Princeton Observatory."

"Has he been in trouble before?"

"What does that mean?"

"You just asked," the fat man leaned back in his chair, "what kind of trouble he's gotten into *this time*."

Dick turned from the cop to me and then back to the cop. His neck got read—I watched it turn like the mercury of a thermometer going up.

"I don't know what game you're playing," Dick said, "but you'll find that I'm not as nice a man as Dr. Armstrong. Either charge him with something concrete, or let him go. At any rate, I'm going to advise him to institute legal proceedings against you."

I hadn't even thought of that, but Dick is faster on his feet than I am.

"Now, don't get bent out of shape," the detective said. "Your friend shows up talking about getting kidnapped and a dead man and the next thing we know, some house is on fire. What would you think?"

"Pal, leave the thinking to the guys who are paid to do it. It's out of your line."

Now the detective turned red. For a minute I thought Dick and I would be sharing a cell, but instead he just pushed the typescript and a fountain pen over to me. "Sign your statement and get out."

I reached for the pen but Dick grabbed my wrist. "Read it first."

"I'm sure it's all right."

"Read it, you dope."

So, I sat down and read it. As I finished each page, I handed it over to Dick, who read it again. After I signed the bottom page and initialed the others, we were let go.

A change had come over Dick as we made our way to the car. The sun was now up and pale sunshine made for a sad morning. We walked to his silver Chrysler Airflow and I got into the passenger side. He keyed the ignition and drove silently until we were well past the police station.

"Peter."

"Yes."

"What happened?"

"You read the statement."

"That's it?" he asked. "You're not holding anything back?"

"No. Yes. Well …, maybe yes. One thing."

"What?"

"Those guys wanted the observatory journal for February 19th."

"Who was on that night?"

"Mason."

He chanced a look at me. "Why?"

"I don't know."

We drove in silence.

"What was in that rock?"

"I have no idea," I said.

"And it was red? With smooth, almost crystalline angles?"

"It was red and it glowed."

"It can't be a contagion or a virus," he said. "At least, I never heard of one that worked so fast."

"Unlikely."

"And if it's radioactivity—Well, I've never heard of radioactivity doing *that*. It would take almost unimaginable concentrations of it."

"And who was that man?" I asked. "It was horrible. I can still hear his screaming. And what were they doing in Mason's house?"

"And what happened to Mason?" he asked.

"Don't know," I said. "It doesn't look good."

Before too long we were out of the Jersey farmland and approaching Princeton.

"Would you mind dropping me off home? I need a shower and a change of clothes."

The town had started coming awake when Dick pulled in front of my place on Broadmead. I took his hand again and thanked him. I clutched the door handle and said, "You know, maybe you should grab that journal and stick it somewhere safe."

"Where?"

"Anywhere."

"All right. I'll put it—"

"Don't tell me!"

His face fell. "Why not?"

"In case I run into those guys again," I said. "I don't want to be able to tell them anything. And listen. Don't even tell the Dean you've taken it. Just hole it up somewhere until we decide what to do next."

"Deal," he said. I stepped away from the Chrysler and he drove off.

It was cold on the curb and I missed my trench coat. But I don't think I had ever been so happy to be back home. My place is a simple, two story frame house. Mrs. Bradbury, a widow, is my landlord. She had the lower floor and I had the upper. Right past the front door was a stairway. At the base of the stairs was a door leading into Mrs. Bradbury's home, while the door to my apartment was at the top of the stairs. Now and then she would knock on my door and ask me down for breakfast. And though I was starving, I was hoping to avoid everybody until I had a shower and some sleep.

No such luck. When I keyed the front door Mrs. Bradbury was on the landing in a flash. She's a stout, older woman in her fifties with a thatch of bright white hair and thick, round, black-rimmed spectacles that gave her an owlish look.

"Dr. Armstrong," she inquired. "Are you okay?"

"Yes, thank you," I lied. "Sorry if I was making noise."

"No. I was awake anyway. Your friends were here earlier and I let them in to wait for you."

"Friends?" I instantly went cold. "What friends?"

"From the college. They said they worked with you."

Oh no. "Where they a guy with gold teeth and another with a scar?"

"Good heavens, no!" She actually brushed the question away, like I was having her on. "You know. Just those college types."

I looked up the stairs with apprehension. "Are they still there?"

"I think so."

"Thank you, Mrs. Bradbury." I turned to go.

"Oh, Dr. Armstrong?"

"Yes?"

"Was she pretty?" She asked the question and then blushed behind a palm.

"Was who pretty?"

"Well—you were out all night and I just figured…"

"No," I said. "I was in jail."

"Jail!"

"It's a long story. I'll tell you tomorrow."

"But—"

"Tomorrow," I took the stairs two at a time.

My door was open just a crack. I placed a sweaty hand on the panel and gently pushed it open. Suddenly, I wished I still had the automatic I had taken away from Romero.

Inside, nothing but quiet. Pale morning sun streamed through the windows and in a moment I saw that my morning visitors had not been neat.

My pillows on my living room couch had been thrown about and the couch itself upended. My armchairs had spilled over and my reading table and smoke stand knocked to the floor. The two large windows facing the street had their shades pulled down and out.

I stood there, sniffing, as if I could smell an intruder. But I sensed nothing. On the floor near my reading table was the fossilized tibia of a mastodon the geology department gave me as a gag last Christmas. I hefted it in my right hand, appreciating the weight.

Holding the bone ready, I stepped into the kitchen. Cabinets were opened, dishes haphazardly tossed onto counters and the floor. Pots had been opened or turned upside-down; a quick check told me the icebox had also been searched.

I tiptoed into the spare bedroom, where I setup a small telescope along with a simple deal table laden with a few experiments. Everything had been upended and pawed over. In my own bedroom, the bed had been pulled apart, my night table drawers were opened and my clothes strewn all over the closet floor. I also stored some artifacts from my travels here—trinkets from all over Europe and Asia, along with a few Central American native masks—all kicked around like so much trash.

I went back to the living room and that was where my heart grew heaviest. My bookcases had all been emptied, their contents strewn all over the floor. Books on astronomy, celestial mechanics, geology and physics had been paged through and tossed aside onto the carpet. All of my magazines had been pulled from the shelves and thrown to the winds: *Amazing Stories*, *The Shadow*, *Argosy* and *Doc Savage* lay helter-skelter at my feet.

Worse still, some books that I had really treasured were treated very shabbily. Things by Jules Verne and H.G. Wells and John Taine and H. Rider Haggard.[9] I started to gather them up and put them back in the shelves and stopped when I came across my copy of *At the Earth's Core* by Edgar Rice Burroughs. My father gave it to me for my twenty-first birthday but first sent it to Burroughs to autograph.

I opened it to the two inscriptions on the cover page:

<blockquote>
To My Son On His Birthday,
Love Dad
Your Pop Says You're FANTASTIC
And That's Good Enough For Me!
Happy Birthday From Your Pal,
Edgar Rice Burroughs
</blockquote>

The book's cover had come partially detached from the pages, hanging by a few bookbinding threads. It was ruined.

Well, I like to think I have a high boiling point, but this on top of

---

9   H.G. Wells (1866-1946) was, of course, along with Jules Verne, the Father of Science Fiction as we know it today. Most of his political and social thinking does not bear close examination. John Taine (1883-1960) was a popular Science Fiction writer of the time, and, H. Rider Haggard (1856-1925) wrote some of the greatest adventure novels in the genre, including *King Solomon's Mines* and *She*, which are still considered classics.

everything else was just too much. I sat down on the upended couch and bawled like a kid.

After I calmed down a bit, I dropped the mastodon bone and stood at the door and called for Mrs. Bradbury.

Something in my voice must have alarmed her because she was up in a flash. I didn't say anything, I just stepped aside and let her come in and see for herself.

"Oh, my goodness," she said, stunned. She put a hand to her mouth and asked, "What happened here?"

"Those people you let in—"

"But I never dreamed—"

"I'm not blaming you; I'm just asking you."

She turned, eyes even wider behind her spectacles. "But they said they were friends from the school."

"Fine, fine, fine. How would you describe them?"

"Oh—just ordinary men."

"Was one of them about my height, thin and all his teeth were gold?"

She shook her head *no*.

"Was one of them a big man with a scar? Or—a midget?"

"NO!" She surveyed the wreckage of my apartment once again. "They were just ordinary—men."

"What did they look like?"

"Well, one was tall—"

"How tall?"

"Taller than you. He wore a gray hat and topcoat."

"What color was his hair?"

"I don't know. He wore a hat."

"And the other man?"

"About your height. My age, maybe, white mustache. He was average build, I think. Oh, and yes, he wore very shiny patent leather shoes!"

"Can you think of anything else?"

She stood there and I could almost hear the gears turning in her head. "No," she said finally. "Nothing. I'm sorry."

I turned from her to my apartment. "That's all right. It can't be helped."

"Do you want me to call the police?"

"No. I've had enough of the police for one day."

"You mean—you weren't joking? You really were arrested?"

"Yes."

"For heaven's sakes why?"

"Because Dr. Cooley was kidnapped and his house burned down."

"What's that got to do with you?"

"I wish I knew." I slipped out of my shoes. "If you'll excuse me, Mrs. Bradbury, I need a shower and something to eat."

She took one more glance at my apartment and her face brightened. "Why not clean up and I'll make you something to eat. You must be all in."

I could have hugged her. "That would be great. Thanks."

She left and I opened my tie. But as I stepped into the bathroom, I realized that I had better update Dick. I right-sided my candlestick phone and clicked for the operator. In seconds I had Dick on the line.

"Everything all right?"

"Yeah," I said. "But someone broke in last night and gave my place a good going over."

"Cripes!"

"If I was a guessing man, I'd say someone was looking for Old Man Cooley's notes. Did you put them in a safe place?"

"Don't worry. I'll always have my eye on 'em."

I sighed. "I'm going to wash up and have breakfast and maybe catch an hour or two of sleep. Let's meet at the observatory at one. That work for you?"

"See you then!" and the line went dead.

I showered, the hot spray loosening the tortured muscles in my neck and back. A quick razor and then a brush through my teeth and already I was feeling better. Then I took up a clean, button-down white shirt from the closet, along with a purple tie and my gray tweed suit with the elbow patches that Mrs. Bradbury likes so much, and dressed.

When I came out, Mrs. Bradbury had already started setting the living room to rights. She cleared the coffee table and set up the couch and had ready a pot of tea, a side of toast and a heaping plate of ham and eggs.

"Oh. Wow."

"It's the least I could do," she said, unfolding a napkin. "Now, you get that inside you and tell me all about it."

So, I did—everything except the murdered man. I didn't want to scare her more than necessary. She listened as I crunched toast and drank tea, hardly asking any questions at all. Once I was done she said, "Well—it seems to me the key to all of this is Dr. Cooley."

"No kidding."

"I mean, once you find him, I'm sure he'll be able to explain everything."

"Well, maybe, maybe not. At any rate, his house is gone, and he hasn't been at the observatory for days. So, where do I look for him?"

"Well, you used to go to his parties and things."

"Yes?"

"Well, try his friends."

I put down my teacup. "You know, that's brilliant."

She shrugged as if to say, *of course*.

"But do it later," she said, gathering the breakfast things onto the tray. "First, get a little rest."

I didn't need a lot of persuading. I ushered her to the door and locked it. I carried the mastodon bone to the couch—it gave me an increased sense of security. It was nearly ten. I figured I would sleep for a couple of hours and then meet Dick.

If I could sleep. I was so keyed up, I thought it was impossible.

I was out the moment I put my head down.

~~~

It was the phone that woke me.

I'm sure it rang several times before I opened my eyes. A quick look at the window told me it was late afternoon.

I got off the couch, the mastodon bone tumbling to the carpet beside me. I took up the receiver and made a sleepy, "Hello?"

"Dr. Armstrong?"

"Speaking."

"It's Dean Elson."

That woke me up. Thurgood Elson was Dean of Sciences at Princeton. "Yes sir?"

"I would like to see you in my office." His voice was cold and flat. "Could you be here in thirty minutes?"

I looked at my watch. It was a little after three. I was surprised that Dick didn't call when I stood him up. Maybe he already briefed Elson and they wanted to compare notes. I could get there in twenty minutes, but wanted the extra time to brush my teeth and hair.

"Thirty minutes," I confirmed.

"Be there," Dean Elson said and hung up.

Just on a hunch I called Dick at the observatory. I let it ring ten times before I hung up. Then I called his number at home, but again no luck.

That didn't mean anything. I hoped.

I cleaned up a bit, grabbed a fedora and checked in with Mrs. Bradbury before stepping outside. I debated walking, but suddenly felt vulnerable in the open. I would take the car.

I have a sleek, black 1931 Lasalle 345 and it's a honey. With white-and-yellow tires, trippe lights and a silver goddess radiator mascot, it's probably the thing I prize most right after my books. I parked at the corner two days before, so trotted over. I was just paranoid enough to check the rumble seat (empty!) before I hopped in.

I made it to the University in less than ten minutes. I stopped off first at the observatory. Dick wasn't there, and my colleagues had not seen him all day. Probably with Dean Elson, I figured.

I hiked over to the Sciences Administration Building and took the elevator to Elson's office. His secretary had me wait outside for just a moment before I was ushered into his office.

Dean Elson was not alone, but Dick wasn't with him. Instead, a tall man in a gray hat and overcoat stood by the door, and seated in one of the two armchairs facing the desk was a trim man with an iron gray mustache. He turned and rose when I entered and extended a hand.

"Mr. Benet," Elson said, "this is Dr. Peter Armstrong. Peter, this is William Benet, from the War Office."

I reached out to take his hand and my eyes fell on his shoes. He wore highly-polished patent leather pumps.

Elson nodded towards the man in the gray overcoat. "This is Mr. Watterson, also from the War Department."

Watterson didn't offer a hand, so neither did I.

Elson stood behind his desk, watching our faces. Elson was only a fair scientist, but he was a *brilliant* administrator. He was a small, plumpish man with wispy white hair and impish eyes. He had a soft, almost lilting voice, except when he was angry. Then it got weirdly metallic. Right now, it was still soft and lilting.

"Dr. Armstrong, would you like to take a seat?" he asked.

I must have looked pretty suspicious, because when I didn't move Elson said, "Don't worry. Everything's all right."

I sat.

"Mr. Benet and Mr. Watterson told me about the trouble you had last night," Elson started. "They just wanted to ask you a few questions."

"I already gave a statement to the police," I said.

"Yes, we know," Benet said, using the plural as lots of government types do.

"Then what else can I tell you?"

"You can start by telling us where we can find Mason Cooley," Watterson

"...this is William Benet from the War Office."

stepped away from the wall and came closer to my chair. "And you can finish by telling us what the two of you were up to."

CHAPTER THREE

The question hung in the air.
"What are you talking about?"
"Come off it, Armstrong!" Watterson snapped.
Benet raised a placating hand. "Please forgive my colleague." Here he threw Watterson a look that would do credit to a disappointed aunt. "He's a little high strung."
I turned my attention to Benet.
"What can I do for you?"
"We could start with your being so kind as to repeat your statement to the police."
"Why?"
"Sometimes things come back when you just think of them again." He smiled benignly. "Humor me, Dr. Armstrong. I wouldn't presume to understand your business. Please, don't presume to understand mine."
"Fair enough," I took a breath and settled back into my chair. I looked at Elson and he nodded me on. So, I started from the beginning and told them everything I told the police, but I still kept back any of the stuff about Mason's observatory journal. When I had the chance, I would tell Elson all about it, but not anyone else.
"I see," Benet said, when I had finished. He smoothed the points of his mustache and his eyes got cagey. "Are you sure there's nothing else?"
"Nothing."
"Well," I said. "One thing. Someone broke into my apartment last night."
Benet and Watterson exchanged looks.
"How do you know?"
"They wrecked it, along with several valuable books and personal papers. If you could find out who did that, I'd be very grateful."
"Dr. Armstrong, now I have something to tell you."
I expected what came next, but it didn't make me any the less angry.
"We were in your apartment early this morning to conduct a search," Benet said.
"You went through my stuff? Who the hell said you could do that?"

Benet waved a placating hand.

"Don't give me that!" I snapped. "How dare you! My stuff is private!"

Watterson, standing near Elson's desk, made a baby face and whined *my stuff is private*. "What are you? Twelve?"

That did it. Without a thought I got to my feet, balled a fist and clocked Watterson on the jaw. The big man staggered back a few steps, tumbled over a lamp and slid down the wall, taking a portrait of George Washington with him.

Elson was on his feet. "Dr. Armstrong!"

Watterson lumbered to his feet and there was murder in his eyes.

"He ruined my Edgar Rice Burroughs!" I barked.

"Watterson!" Benet snapped.

The big man stopped.

"Dr. Armstrong, we did search your apartment, but that was all. At least, that's all he was instructed to do." His eyes grew flinty. "Watterson, did you damage any of Dr. Armstrong's property?"

"I was just searching."

Benet nestled primly into his seat. "I take it that means you did." He turned to me. "Dr. Armstrong, when I left Agent Watterson there, it was simply to review the materials in your home, not damage them. If your—Burroughs or anything else needs to be replaced, let me know and I will do my best."

"What the hell were you doing in my place?"

Benet did not answer. Instead, he said to Watterson, "Apologize to Dr. Armstrong."

"The hell I will," he said.

Benet's voice was now flat and dangerous. "Apologize."

Watterson looked at me and gritted his teeth. "I'm sorry," he choked out.

"The hell with that," I said. "You still haven't told me what you were doing in my house."

Elson trotted from behind his desk and rehung the portrait of Washington. Watterson just stood and glowered at us both.

"Dr. Armstrong, I'm sure you realize from your description of the murder that something very dangerous is at hand. Whatever that stone is or was, it could be used as a very powerful weapon."

I sat down.

"You yourself said that the man died within minutes, and in a great deal of pain. Imagine, if you would, if that should fall into the wrong hands?"

"It's already in the wrong hands."

"That's why we need to get hold of it."

"Why would your hands be any better?"

"What is that rock?" Watterson asked.

"Why should I know?"

"Certainly as a geologist," Benet said, "you must have some idea?"

"I'm not a geologist. It's just one of my undergraduate degrees."

"Well excuse me," Watterson sneered.

"Indulge me," Benet said.

I thought back to my talk with Dick Pierson. "Well, I don't think it's bacteria."

"Why not?"

"It worked so fast. Or, let me say that if it is a virus or bacteria, I never saw anything like it."

"What else?"

"Well," I racked my brains. "I can't imagine it being part of the natural world."

"Why not?"

"It's safe to say that if anything like that had been uncovered before, we would've known about the effects."

"What if it had never been uncovered before?" Elson asked.

"There's that," I admitted.

"Do you think it could be manufactured?" Benet asked.

"I guess it would have to be. But I couldn't begin to imagine how."

"Nothing that your colleagues would be working on?"

For some reason, I had a moment's worry for Dick. But I pushed it back and answered, "That's not the kind of work we do here."

"Certainly not!" Elson said.

"But if it was something manufactured," I said, "you're talking about a weapon of terrifying potency. I saw it at work and I hope it's something I never have to see again."

Benet sat back, lips pursed. He deliberated for a moment, then he took a leather satchel from the floor. He opened this and removed a file of file folders.

"Dr. Armstrong, how well do you know Mason Cooley?"

"Very well."

"Did you often discuss politics?"

"I don't discuss politics with anybody," I said. "I'm just an American."

"Dr. Cooley has been known to us for some time as a Communist sympathizer," Benet went on. He took a sheet from the folder and handed it to me. "Do you recognize any of these names?"

I read it through and knew most of them. "Yes."

"From where?"

"From Mason's parties. What is this all about?"

He took the paper back and slipped it into the folder. "Many of Dr. Cooley's associates in New York are Communist or fascist sympathizers. The prevalence of Communist thinking in certain New York artistic and intellectual circles is so vast that we have taken to calling the city Moscow on the Hudson."

"Not here in Princeton," Elson said.

Benet pivoted in his chair with the grace of a dancer. "Of course, Dr. Elson. Of course."

"What's this got to do with the rock?" I asked.

"Dr. Cooley's political interests were not limited to some cocktail party sedition," Benet said. He pulled a handful of cablegrams from his satchel and handed them over. Some were in Italian, many others in Russian and a few in German. "Dr. Cooley was mentioned prominently in multiple European cablegrams. It's how he first came to our attention."

I looked up from the telegrams to Elson and back to Benet. "Has he broken any laws?"

Now Watterson spoke up. "Not yet. But we have learned that he also has built up a considerable amount of gambling debt."

"Gambling! That's nuts. I've never seen Mason bet on anything in his life!"

I looked at Elson. He shrugged with a *me neither* look.

"It's true," Benet continued on. "We haven't been able to calculate the exact amount of money he owes, but it's in excess of forty thousand dollars."

I whistled. "Forty thousand! But—who does it owe it to?"

Benet opened another file. He pulled out a small, three by four snapshot and passed it over. It showed two men ducking into a taxi parked in front of a nightclub. "Do you recognize those men?"

"Yes! The guy with the mustache is named Romero. The guy with the scar is the other man I told you about. They took me to Mason's house last night."

"That is Antonio Romero. He's a big-time mob enforcer, largely in New York, but he was also active in Chicago in the Twenties. Suspected of multiple homicides, previously convicted of racketeering and money-laundering. He was released after three years in Joliet on a technicality."

"All his teeth are gold," I said.

Benet nodded. "Yes. He got in Dutch with a Chicago mob and they punished him by pulling all his teeth. Romeo then went to a leading

Chicago dentist to have them replaced with solid gold, and then murdered the man once he was done."

"But that's crazy."

"So is he."

Elson folded his hands on his desk. "Why isn't this Romero in jail?"

"It's easier to know these things than it is to prove them," Benet said. "The other man is Raymond O'Brien. He emerged from the Lower East Side gutters and moved west to become a gunman with the Spangled Mob in Las Vegas. He got involved with the wife of a mob boss and had to lay low. He spent his time in hiding strike busting and committing a few murders for hire, some of them very important men. He is not as crazy as Romero, but a very dangerous man."

"I would bet the guy who gave him that scar was more dangerous still."

Benet laughed. "It was a woman—that moll of the mob boss we told you about. She tried to leave him and they got into a fight. She broke a bottle and carved the side of his face."

"Score one for her."

"Not really. She was found dead a few days later, her face terribly disfigured by vitriol."

"Well, if you know who these people are, get after them."

"One more," and here Benet took an eight by ten photo from the pile. "Recognize him?"

"It's the midget!" I said. "Stutka."

"Leon Stutka," Benet nodded. "The most dangerous gangster in North America today."

"I've never heard of him."

"I'm not surprised. Stutka was born in rural Pennsylvania, near Lord's Valley. He had a remarkable facility for numbers. He was the product of an incestuous relationship between Verner and Mathilde Stutka, brother and sister German nationals who arrived in the country in late Nineteen Hundred. Despite his genius, it quickly became clear that young Leon was emotionally unstable. His parent's farm burned under mysterious circumstances and their bodies burned beyond recognition. No matter, because soon after the fire Leon started touring the country as a sideshow attraction at the Gollmer Brothers Circus.[10] For several years authorities

---

10 Although lesser known than the famous Ringling brothers, the Gollmars made lasting contributions to American circus history. The Gollmar Bros. Greatest of American Shows operated out of winter quarters on Baraboo's Second Avenue from 1891 until 1916, with brothers Walter, Fred, Charles, Ben, and Jake Gollmar as proprietors. For the following decade, the Gollmar name was leased to other circuses, last being used in 1926.

were interested in the circus, as there were often high-profile homicides wherever the show appeared."

"Stutka?"

"Yes. Though little more than a young boy, he was implicated in several murders-for-hire, usually for middle-aged women looking to get rid of their husbands. Despite his size, Stutka holds a peculiar fascination over women, particularly the middle aged and motherless. When police started connecting the dots, he disappeared from the circus. Little is known of his early adulthood, but by the time he was thirty he was big, if you'll pardon the pun, in Los Angeles rum-running. He quickly rose to head the largest illegal liquor enterprise in the country. When Repeal came along, he maintained his distribution line and used his established criminal organization to branch out into racketeering, numbers games, book makers, protection scams and dope."

"But I don't get it," I said. "What's Stutka got to do with the War Department?"

"When he switched his base of operations to New York City, he also became interested in radical politics. Stutka's organization soon became the largest criminal enterprise in the United States."

Watterson chimed in, "Bigger than the mafia, bigger than the Chicago rackets, bigger than the tongs."

"But the big difference was that Stutka was too slick to ever be implicated in any of his illegal enterprises. He has run a legitimate import-export business for years. Oh, his underlings might be caught, but Stutka himself was untouchable."

"But where do you fit in?" I asked.

"And Professor Cooley?" Elson added.

"Stutka's import-export business has brought him to the attention of several European agents who are interested in …" and here Benet gave an eloquent shrug. "Shall we say, state secrets?"

"He's a spy?"

"Of a sort."

"And Dr. Cooley?" Elson pressed.

"Needless to say, we keep track of everyone who becomes involved in Stutka's affairs, legal and illegal. Some months ago, Stutka bought up Dr. Cooley's gambling debts and now holds his marker."

"Jeez," I said.

"This would still be no concern of ours, except Dr. Cooley's name is mentioned is several international cables between Stutka and certain

European powers. If they wanted something from Dr. Cooley, and Stutka had control of him, well …" And here he once again shrugged his shoulders.

I got up and walked a bit. "Let me get this straight. You're saying that Mason might have something to do with that rock, and that Stutka might control Mason and that European fascists might control Stutka?"

"Something like that," Watterson said.

"That's fantastic, if true," Elson said.

"There's more," Benet said.

"You're kidding."

"No. There is still yet another player."

"Who?"

"You tell us," Watterson said.

"Me?"

Benet shushed Watterson and went on. "Our research has told us that there is another player in the game."

"You haven't even figured out what this game is!"

"True. But it's probable that Stutka has one more pay master, more powerful and more dangerous than any European fascist."

"Who's more powerful than that?" Elson asked.

"We have indications that there is an international criminal organization, bigger, more dangerous, more terrible than anything that Stutka has put together. So big, in fact, that it might have the power to topple nations."

"Who runs it?"

"As my colleague said, we were hoping you could tell us."

I laughed. "How the hell would I know?"

"Surely you're not suggesting that Dr. Armstrong…" Elson started.

"I'm not suggesting anything. But it is possible that this person, this Mr. X, was also known, however unwittingly, to Dr. Cooley. If that's the case, you, Dr. Armstrong, and you, too, Dr. Elson, may be acquainted with one of the most dangerous men in the world without knowing it."

"Of course," Elson said at length, "Dr. Armstrong and my office will do anything we can to assist you. Won't we, Dr. Armstrong?"

"Well, sure," I agreed.

"I hoped so," Benet said. "I'll be sending one of my agents to see you later today."

"But I already told you and the police everything I know."

"Yes, but we are also pursuing other possibilities. If we want to ask a few scientific questions—just to get your professional opinion—I'm sure you won't object."

"Not at all," Elson answered for me.

"I'll arrange a meeting later today," Benet got up and shoved the files into his satchel.

"And if you hear from that commie Mason Cooley, you're to get in touch with us," Watterson was now on his hind legs.

"Here's how to get in touch with us." Benet had removed two business cards from his pocket and placed them gingerly on Elson's desk. "As Agent Watterson advised, you will get in touch with us if you hear from Dr. Cooley. *Right?*"

"Yes," Elson and I said in unison.

Benet took a black hat from under the armchair and placed it on his head *just-so*. "Gentlemen," he said with a nod, and Watterson followed him out the door.

I turned to Elson. "Well!"

"Well, indeed," he sat and once more folded his hands on his desk.

"I'll go back to the Observatory," I said. "If anything comes up, I'll let you know."

"Peter, sit down."

I didn't like his tone of voice.

"Yes, sir." I sat.

"What are you not telling me?"

"Me?"

"Don't give me that *who, me?* look. I've known you long enough to know when you're holding something back."

I sat there, thinking. It only at that moment occurred to me that Benet and Watterson never told us what they were looking for in my apartment. It could only be Mason's laboratory journal. Whatever was in it was hot, as hot as that rock used to kill that man in Mason's home. I needed to look at it for myself before I could put anyone at risk.

"No, I'm not."

Elson took a deep breath and looked at me critically. "Peter, we're going to have to assume that Mason, when and if he ever resurfaces, is a lost cause. He's a valued member of this faculty, but we cannot allow his personal behavior to compromise the integrity of this institution. If it means saving Princeton, I'll cut him out like a tumor." He leaned forward. "I would cut anyone out like a tumor, regardless of how I feel about them personally. Do I make myself understood?"

"Yes, sir."

"Now, get out of here and stay out of trouble. And for heaven's sakes, cooperate with these people in any way they want."

I thanked him and opened the door.

"Oh, and Dr. Armstrong?"

"Yes?"

"What the devil is a—Burroughs?"

"It's a long story," I said and left.

A glance at my watch told me it was going on four-thirty. I hustled over to the administrative offices and checked on Dick Pierson, but he wasn't there. His assistant told me he had not been in the office all day. With mounting dread, I dashed back to the observatory and looked for him there. But still no sign of him.

I checked observatory journals—they had all been pawed over, and recently. It was a safe bet that Benet and Watterson had been here before their visit to Elson.

I picked up the phone and called Dick's number. After ten rings I gave up.

The next step would be Dick's apartment. I was missing the automatic I had earlier this morning now more than ever. If Dick was in trouble, I didn't want to keep him waiting. But I didn't want to go looking for him unarmed.

I left the observatory and hopped into my Lasalle. In a few minutes I was home and taking the stairs two at a time.

Mrs. Bradbury had already started putting my place back together. The couch and armchairs were upright, the coffee table reset and she had piled my books and magazines neatly on the floor so I could put them in their proper places in the bookcases. And leaning against the couch, where I had left it earlier, was my fossilized mastodon tibia.

Better than a baseball bat, I thought.

I grabbed this and made for the door. Just as I reached for the handle, there was a knock.

I stood on my side of the closed door.

"Who is it?"

"Dr. Armstrong?"

A woman's voice.

"Yes?"

"I'd like to speak with you a moment."

Holding the tibia in my right hand, I slowly opened the door with my left.

"Yes?"

"Dr. Armstrong?"

She was beautiful, easily the most beautiful woman I had ever seen in my life. She had a sweet, heart-shaped face with lips that were full and half-smiling. She had auburn hair, mostly hidden by a yellow cloche hat, and the eyes that regarded me were clear and blue and deep.

She was dressed in a smart suit of Lincoln green that lovingly highlighted every contour of her figure, carried an unusually large handbag of yellow that matched her hat, and her feet nestled in black heels.

"Yes?"

"You already said that."

"Oh, yes." I cleared my throat. "Can I help you?"

"My name is Penelope Welles."

"Wells? Like H.G.?"

"No, like Orson.[11]" She looked me over and then stood on her toes to peer into the apartment beyond. "You met with my boss, Mr. Benet. He told you to expect me."

"A girl?"

"You don't miss a thing, do you?"

I stood there, silent. I didn't know what to say.

"Well, are you going to invite me in, or am I supposed to just stand here and admire your bone?"

"Huuuh?" I looked down at the tibia. "Excuse me, Miss Welles. You see, I was just stepping out."

"Really?" she pushed past me and entered my living room like she owned the place. She pivoted from side-to-side, taking in the furnishing and the Charles R. Knight[12] reproductions that hung on my walls. That little half smile never seemed to leave her mouth.

"Do you think you could come back at a later time?"

As I asked, she had drifted over to the piles of books where she made mental note of the titles. Finally, she turned and said, "Well, I'm busy, too, Dr. Armstrong. Perhaps I could come with you and we can talk on the way?"

"Oh, that's, um, that's to say that isn't going to be convenient. You see, I'm going to visit a friend."

---

11   Orson Welles (1915-1985) was one of the most significant thespic talents of his century, making significant contributions to film, theater, radio and television. His first film, *Citizen Kane* (1941), which he wrote, directed and starred in when he was only 26, remains a cinematic classic.

12   Charles R. Knight (1874-1953) was an artist famous for painting dinosaurs. His work is showcased in the American Museum of Natural History in New York City.

"Who?"

"No one you know."

"How do you know?"

"Do you know Professor Richard Pierson?"

"No," she said, "but I will once you introduce me. Come on. We'll take my car."

"Um …,"

"Don't be bashful, it's no problem."

She strode across the living room like Hannibal took the Alps. I held the door for her.

"You're bringing the bone with you?" she asked.

"Oh. I was just returning it to Dr. Pierson. I, um, borrowed it from him."

"You *do* have interesting friends."

We stepped outside and she led me to a car parked behind mine.

I gaped for a moment.

I had read about them, of course, but had never seen a Duesenberg Model J in real life before. It was long and low and sleek, more Rocketship than car, and painted a bright, metallic blue. The top was down, despite the cool late afternoon air.

"Climb in," she said.

She stepped around to the driver's side and I climbed in beside her. I let the mastodon tibia rest against my calf.

"Where to?" she keyed the ignition.

I gave her directions to Dick's place and we pulled away from the curb. The Duesenberg hummed like an airship.

"This is quite a car."

"It's a Nineteen Thirty."

"I bet it goes fast."

"I could do one hundred and sixty, if I had to."

"Good thing you don't have to."

"Not recently."

Dick Pierson lived in a bungalow outside of Princeton proper, mostly to get away from the night-time lights of the city. Light made telescopic observation much more difficult, and living out of town also provided him with additional privacy.

She steered us out of town and towards the boonies.

"Do you mind if I ask a personal question?"

"Not if you don't mind one in return."

"Fair enough," I said. "How much does a car like this cost?"

"How much do you make a year?"

"About three thousand."

"You can buy one of your own in a little over six years, provided you don't eat."

"Wow. And how can you afford this on a government salary?"

"I don't work for the government. I'm more of a consultant."

"Consultant?"

"It's a word. I'm sure a smart guy like you has heard it before."

"What kind of consultant?"

"Usually when they are up a tree, they come to me for help. I have a knack."

I let that sink in. "You mean, you're some kind of secret agent?"

"Some kind. Now I ask personal questions."

"I thought you already had." She was taking the country roads so fast, I had to shout into the slipstream.

"Does Pierson have Cooley's notebook?"

"I don't know what you're talking about."

"Don't play dumb, Dr. Armstrong. It's not convincing."

"But..."

"Doctor, there's a notebook of Cooley's missing from the observatory." Here she took a country-road turn at the speed of light, nearly blowing my fedora into the distance. "It's not in your apartment. We checked. You spend the afternoon looking for your friend Pierson, and when I come to your door, you're on your way to his place armed like Alley Oop.[13] Who are you kidding?"

I looked ahead and folded my arms.

"Don't sulk, Doctor. It's not a good look for you."

"I can explain."

"I don't want an explanation. I want that notebook. When did Pierson get it?"

"After he picked me up last night. I told him to get it from the observatory and hide it somewhere."

"Why?"

"Because Stutka wanted it. I don't know what's in it, but I know I didn't want him to have it."

"You didn't tell Benet."

"I'm not sure I wanted him to have it, either."

---

13 *Alley Oop* was a popular comic strip featuring the titular caveman. It first started in 1932, written and drawn by V.T. Hamlin (1900-1993). The strip continues to this day.

"Why not?"

"Because I don't know what's in it. Haven't you been listening?"

"What could be in it?"

I turned to her and said, "It probably tells us where Mason got that rock."

"And where's there one, there might be more?"

"That's what I'm afraid of."

Dick lived in a small community of like-sized bungalows off a patch of unused farmland. I had been to his place many times. It was a one-story home, with a smallish kitchen and a large living room and dining room. There are two bedrooms; I don't think Dick ever made his bed in his life, so I had seldom been inside there. The spare bedroom faced north, and there was a large-size table telescope at the window. As we approached in the dwindling sun, the windows were unlit.

We pulled in front and I got out, holding the tibia. I went to the driver's side to get the door for Miss Welles, but she was out and grabbing her handbag before I could get there.

"Dick didn't really do anything wrong," I explained as I led her to the door. "I asked him to hide it."

"We'll worry about that after we get the journal." We walked up the stairs and I froze as I reached for the buzzer.

The wood around the lock and door handle was crushed. I pressed the door gently with a finger and it opened a hair.

I hefted the tibia and said "Stay here."

Miss Welles opened her purse and pulled an Old West-style six shooter. She cocked the hammer and pushed past me. "Back off, sonny, and let the adults handle it."

With her free hand she pushed open the door. It creaked in the cool night air.

The living room beyond looked normal. She stepped inside, gun at the ready, and looked through the living room. Then she turned and motioned me inside.

I stood behind her, brandishing the tibia. I didn't see anything out of place; the books were in the bookcases and Dick's astronomical maps were still hanging on the wall. His table-size telescope was on the dining room table and his suit coat was draped over one of the chairs. She led us through the swinging door into the kitchen, where we found nothing but an unfinished glass of Coke, then went to the bathroom, also empty, before hitting the bedrooms. His bedroom was the mess that it usually was, and his observatory room was neat as always; the window shades where he usually used the telescope were drawn. Nothing seemed out of place at first glance, except for the fact that my friend was gone.

She un-cocked her gun and stuck it in her handbag.

"We're too late."

"Oh, no," I said. "Do you think he's—dead?"

"Probably." She gave the place another glance. "And they probably have the book, too. Let's go."

"Wait."

"What?"

I tossed the tibia on the couch and put my hands on my hips, thinking. "If they were going to kill Dick, why move the body? They'd just leave him here."

She came closer. "Good point."

"So maybe they kidnapped him, the same way they kidnapped me."

"Why?"

"Because …" and it only hit me as I was thinking aloud, "Because they need someone to explain to them what's in the notebook!"

"That doesn't get us anywhere. If they have your friend, that means they have the notebook."

"Not necessarily. It doesn't follow that just because they have Dick, they have the notebook. The door was broken open. If Dick had any warning of their arrival at all, he may have hidden it."

"But they would've searched."

"The place, yes," I said. "But not his mind. If it's still here, we have to search Prof. Pierson's mind."

"What do you mean?"

"Dick knew all about the dead man, and he knew what we were up against. If it was at all possible, he would've kept the notes away from our enemies. Do you mind if I smoke?"

"Go right ahead."

I always think better when I'm smoking. My mom says I can't think at all without a cigarette, but that's an exaggeration. I took a Lucky from my pocket and lit up. The smoke calmed my nerves and focused my attention.

"Any scientist will tell you that every component of the physical world tells a story." I surveyed the room. "It just is a matter of interpreting what the data really means."

Whatever happened must have happened early morning, since he never made it back to the university. I put myself in Dick's shoes. I'm home. I've just returned with the journal. I haven't yet had breakfast…

I went to the kitchen. There, on the counter, was the half-consumed glass of Coke. I threw my Lucky into the sink and held the glass.

"Well, Einstein?"

I sipped it.

"It's warm. But watered down. Dick came back home and poured himself a Coke with ice. He started to drink it, but something caught his attention. He put it down to investigate and didn't touch it again."

I surveyed the kitchen, looking for anything else out of place. I absently opened some of the cabinets and found nothing but assorted cups and dishes, boxes of Wheaties and coffee tins. I kept opening doors until I hit the back door, leading from the kitchen to the rolling fields outside. I absently opened it and looked around.

"Look at this!" I said.

Miss Welles came over. "Tire tracks."

"Yes. Dick heard a car approaching. He wasn't necessarily worried, but he was cautious enough to take Mason's journal and hide it somewhere."

"But where?"

I closed the door. "Wherever he put it, he knew I would have to find it." I stepped past her and went back to the living room. It was possible that he would hide the book in plain sight. I browsed the bookcases and she did the same.

"It's not in the bookcases," she said.

"How do you know?"

She ran a finger along the shelves. "Dust. Nothing's been moved anywhere near here for a few weeks."

Dick, I thought, *how would you tell me where it was?*

Miss Welles was looking behind the photos and prints on the walls. My eyes trailed her as she went to the dining room.

"That's it!"

"What?"

I rushed past her. "Put yourself in Dick's place. You're an astronomer and you must hide something. Something that another astronomer needs to find. Dangerous men are here to take you away. What do you do?"

"Is this a quiz, or are you going to tell me?" She folded her arms and regarded me from under her yellow hat. I have to admit that she was absolutely adorable.

"You race into the room with the telescope and bring it here." I pointed at the table-top scope on the dining room table.

"It's too small to hold a journal."

"But not," I said, turning the scope on its axis, "too small to hold a few pages." I grabbed the large, objective lens and twisted. The glass unscrewed and I reached inside.

It was two sheets of graph paper, torn from Mason's notebook. "And here they are."

Her face lit up.

I unfolded the pages. "That's it. Observations for February 19th. Safe at last!" I refolded them.

She leaned forward and took the folded sheets from my hands. Pulling forward her Lincoln green jacket, she stuffed the papers beneath the elastic band of her brassiere.

"Now they're safe."

Thump-thump. It was a muffled sound.

"Let's go."

"No," I said. "I need to check to see if I can find any clue on where they've taken Dick."

Thump-thump.

"Do you hear something?" I asked.

She listened. All was quiet.

"Just the house settling," she said. "These country houses aren't built to last."

"Shush," I said. There it was again.

"I think it's coming from the bedroom," she said.

Holding the tibia, I rushed through the house and into Dick's bedroom. Miss Welles was right behind me.

"I don't see anything," she said.

We listened. Dust motes floated in a shaft of light; it was almost as if I could hear them.

Thump-thump.

"There it is again!"

"Not here," I said. "Next door."

She led the way to the spare bedroom. Before another *thump* could sound, she went to the only possible place and threw open the closet door.

An old man lay huddled on the floor. He was balding with a grizzled mustache and beard. He had a wide nose and mouth, large ears and ill-fitting dentures. He was dressed in a blue button-down shirt, causal trousers with suspenders and he wore brown carpet slippers.

There was an angry bruise on the side of his head running down his temple to his left eye. His eyes were at half-mast and he was bound and gagged.

"Mason!" I cried.

I dropped to a knee and undid the gag. Mason took a deep breath and made a low, mewling sound. I reached around to undo the ropes that held him.

"Don't!" Miss Welles barked. "The knots might tell us something. Get a kitchen knife. And bring some water while you're at it." She ran a soothing hand over Mason's forehead and I dashed for the kitchen.

I got a carving knife from the kitchen draw and a bottle of Coke from the icebox. I opened it with my teeth and spat the lid into the sink.

"Here," I said, handing her the knife when I got back.

Miss Welles sliced through the bonds at his hands and feet and dropped the knife. She stuffed the ropes into her handbag and guided his hands from behind his back. She vigorously rubbed his wrists.

"You identify this man as Mason Cooley?" she said, her eyes still on him.

"Yes." I got to my knees again. "Mason? Are you all right?" I brought the Coke to his lips. "Here. Drink this."

I held the bottle while Mason took a tentative sip. He sputtered at first and took a breath, then drank some more. Now was the first chance I had to really look at him. Not only was there a nasty bruise on his forehead, but there were fingermarks at his throat and wrists and I was sure his nose was broken.

"Mason, who did this to you?"

He mumbled something, dentures churning in his mouth. I couldn't make it out.

"What?"

He looked from Miss Welles to me and mumbled again.

I gave him another sip. He pushed the bottle away and motioned me closer. I put my ear against his lips and felt his breath as he whispered, "They're still here."

"What did he say?"

"He said, *they're still here*."

Miss Welles got to her feet. "Help me lift him. We need to make tracks."

"What's wrong?"

"Shut up and help me, will you?"

I put the Coke down and squeezed behind Mason and got my hands under his arms. He is a big man and heavy. Miss Welles got him by the hands and pulled. With a lot of pulling and tugging, we got him unsteadily to his feet.

I draped one of Mason's arms around my shoulders, keeping hold of the tibia. Miss Welles draped the other arm around her shoulders.

"This is going to be hard, Dr. Cooley," she said, "But try to walk."

Mason took a loose and unsteady step. But she did not wait for him to gather strength or regain his balance. She pushed-and-pulled us all out of the bedroom and into the living room.

We were approaching the couch when it happened.

The window shattered and suddenly the front of the house was on fire. The fire was so fast and so fluid—it was like a *splash* of flame. The fire spread across the floor, suddenly throwing up a wall of flame. Instantly the door caught fire, the window curtains went up and floated away like burning clouds and fire licked the furthest walls.

"Molotov cocktail!" Miss Welles shouted over the roar of the fire.

She pivoted us around and we pressed on into the kitchen. We pushed through the swinging door just as *that* window shattered. Instantly the sink and floor around it were engulfed in flames. The fire roared heavenward and started to consume the roof.

It was the second fire I had seen in twenty-four hours. I realized that this was probably the way they burned down Mason's home, and now they were using the same method to kill us.

Miss Welles pushed us back into the living room.

Already the house was a smoke-filled inferno. During the scant few moments we were in the kitchen, the living room became a rapidly-burning death trap. A solid wall of fire blocked the door and windows as the flames crept closer to the center of the room. The heat, the smoke and the roar of the fire nearly overwhelmed me. Mason slouched more heavily on my shoulders.

"Leave him!" Miss Welles said on the other side of him. "We have to get out of here."

"NO!" I shouted. "You go. I'll find a way to get him out!"

She did not answer. Instead, she steered us to the spare bedroom.

Mason, helped up by us both, sputtered in the smoke-filled room. The three of us made it to the window. We all averted our eyes while I swung the tibia and shattered the window. The open air pulled the smoke outward, making things worse—like standing in the center of a chimney.

Then the gunfire started.

Miss Welles pushed the two of us aside and reached into her purse.

She pulled the six-shooter and cocked it. Too much smoke was funneling out of the window for her to take aim, but she fired blindly into the field behind the house.

She took six shots, then gave orders while she reloaded. "Drag that chair closer with your foot. I'm going out. Once I'm out, dump him over the window and jump out as quickly as you can yourself."

"That's crazy."

She looked at me, her clear blue eyes visible through the smoke. "You want to stay here?"

"Good luck," I said.

She pulled off her heels and hitched up the skirt of her suit. She kept her gun in her right hand and climbed onto the chair. "Ready?"

"Yes!"

She fired once, then once more into the distance and then flung a leg over the side. She was out.

I shook Mason. He looked at me blearily.

"Mason!' I yelled. "Pay attention. Step up!"

I don't know how I did it, but I propped one leg up onto the chair and helped him haul his weight up. And then—it's all a blur now—I slouched him over the sill, grabbed him by the ankles, and dumped him outside.

Two more shots. Close; I was sure it was Miss Welles. At least, I hoped it was her.

I grabbed my tibia, took one last look at poor Dick's ruined home, and plopped over the sill.

CHAPTER FOUR

I fell on my tibia.

The burning farmhouse filled the air with ashen smoke and I could barely see a thing. I was just able to make out Mason lying on the ground beside me and Miss Welles crouched next to him, shooting into the distance. The wood overhead splintered as bullets hit the wall. My fossilized mastodon tibia bit into my backside where I landed on it.

"This is hardly an improvement," I said.

"Can you drive?" she aimed and fired once again.

"Yes!"

She reached into her handbag and passed over the keys. "Take your

...Miss Welles crouched next to him...

friend and let's make tracks."

She got up and spat two more bullets into the smoke. I saw flashes of light as they returned fire, but could not get a bead on them through the haze.

For an instant I lost sight of Miss Welles. I stuck my tibia in my belt and got Mason to his knees and then draped him over my shoulder and got up. He was dead weight and I groaned under the pressure.

Crouching and trotting while carrying an unconscious man is something I hope to never do again. I ran my hand along the overly hot exterior wall to guide me as my eyes watered in the hot soot. I turned the corner and quickly made it to the front of the house.

Miss Welles crouched behind the open passenger door of the Duesenberg, gun at the ready. "Dump him in the back!"

I did and raced around to the driver's side and got behind the wheel.

The window exploded as I keyed the ignition when a bullet hit it. "JEEZ!"

"Just drive!" She got in beside me, kneeling on the seat and facing back.

I wasn't used to the car and it took a second to get the gears down pat. I heard another bullet whiz by just as I had it figured out and the Duesenberg lurched to life so abruptly that she almost spilled over the side.

I was so frantic with haste I had no clear idea of where to go. I hit the gas and we sped through open farm country. The cool evening air swept over me and I felt my hat fly away from my head, this time for good.

I took the dirt road at sixty miles an hour. Miss Welles sank down beside me and cracked her six shooter to reload.

"Where to?"

"Head for Princeton. The more people, the better." She stopped and twisted the rearview mirror. "More trouble."

I looked. There was a black Packard gaining on us. The top was down and a man stood on the passenger side. His motions were difficult to read, but when we saw a flash of red flame, we knew what was coming.

Miss Welles turned round and shot in their direction. The bullet went wild and I saw an arc of flame sail overhead.

There was an explosive *whoosh* and for an instant the earth beside us was enveloped in fire. They were lobbing Molotov cocktails at us. If the throw had been any better, the center of the Duesenberg would be a fireball and we three dead.

I jerked sideways without meaning to and fought to regain the road as we slid through the soft earth. Loose earth flew on either side of our tires and the car lurched from side to side.

"Steady!" she screamed.

The skid cost us precious seconds. As I scrambled to get back on the road, the Packard got dangerously close. I heard the engine rev as it gained on us. I snuck a look at the rearview mirror and they were now scant feet behind us.

"Hit the gas!"

I looked for the proper gear and, nervous, mistakenly slipped us into first gear. I hit the gas anyway and the Duesenberg made unhappy noises as I burned through the gears and clutch. I depressed the clutch in a heartbeat and shifted gears again. I felt something connect in the undercarriage of the car. Nothing happened.

Miss Welles fired again and swore under her breath.

I didn't need the rearview mirror to tell me that they were closer—the Packard rear-ended us and our fenders locked. I was thrown against the steering wheel by the impact and saw stars for an instant. I shook my head and hoped the breeze tearing through me would keep me awake.

The gun Miss Welles used grew silent. "Damn!" She cocked and then re-cocked the six shooter, but nothing happened. She slid back down on the seat and cracked the barrel. "It's jammed."

I saw in the rearview mirror the man standing in the Packard. He shouted something to the driver beside him. Then he started to flick his lighter. Two tries and the rag atop his Molotov cocktail came alight.

Miss Welles jerked the gear and slammed her foot over mine. The Duesenberg jumped like it was hit by lightning. There was a terrible *crunch* as our fenders unlocked and we were free.

The cars unlocked just as he threw the firebomb and he was knocked back onto his seat. We saw the burning missile fly overhead and explode a few feet in front of us. We sped through the flames, and I think the screaming I heard as we pushed through was all done by me.

Miss Welles got the six-shooter righted. "Keep her steady!" she said and knelt on the seat again.

"I'm doing my best!"

But I hadn't handled a car like the Duesenberg before. Panic and the newness of the car got the better of me. In seconds we were now going too fast. The speedometer hit sixty, then seventy, then eighty and then one hundred. Our surroundings were nothing more than a blur as we cut through the backroads of New Jersey.

And then things got worse.

The road curved right and I took it hard. The Duesenberg reared up on its two left wheels and we drove at a slant for a good count of ten. I expected the Duesenberg to flip over and then the car right-sided itself with a *bang*.

It was then that the other car came into view.

I saw it in the rearview mirror. It had been waiting, hidden at the curve in case of trouble, and now our number of pursuers had doubled.

The new car was a silver roadster. A hand reached out of the passenger side window and bullets started flying once more. Because of the turn, the silver roadster was now directly behind us and the Packard was behind them. The Duesenberg jolted as bullets pelted it.

The speedometer was creeping up to one hundred and twenty. At that rate, we would outpace them, but the unpaved road was harder to hold and the car was getting away from me. I lifted my foot off the gas for a couple of breaths and we slowed to something more manageable.

"What the hell are you doing?" Miss Welles yelled over the sound of the engine.

"Keeping you from getting killed!"

"And who's going to keep *you* from getting killed!"

We hit a patch of road where elm trees now lined both sides of the path, protecting the farmlands beyond. The gunfire behind us continued and I saw the Packard swerve dangerously right and disappear behind the trees.

Miss Welles kept her eyes right. Through the trees speeding by she could see the shadow of the Packard. They had increased their speed and were almost parallel to us.

The roadster also hit the gas and the shooter in the passenger side let loose another barrage of bullets.

"I'm open to suggestions," I yelled.

"Faster!" was all she offered.

I shifted gears and hit the gas again. The engine roared louder than any plane. Somehow, the roadster was keeping pace. The occasional gunshot hit the rear end of the car.

The spacing between the trees as we sped through then grew wider and we were able to see the Packard better. The driver must have had his foot to the floor because they were nearly ahead of us.

Then, the line of trees stopped. Both cars were now in open view.

The Packard revived with a fury and the driver swerved left. They were now a scant few feet off to the side. Miss Welles turned to shoot at them, but the gunfire from behind increased and she took cover by dropping low onto the front seat.

The passenger in the Packard got back to his feet and grabbed another

Molotov cocktail. We saw him try and work his lighter.

Miss Welles jumped up on the seat to take a shot, but the roadster opened fire and she again ducked for cover.

The lighter came to life and the cocktail was lit. At this distance, a child could just toss the burning bottle into our car.

I yelped in terror and swerved hard right. We mostly left the road and the side of the Duesenberg crunched against the side of the Packard. The Molotov cocktail flew from the man's grip and fell over the side. Brilliant streams of fire spread over the open field.

Miss Welles took advantage of the confusion to rise up once again. She swung backwards and threw two bullets at the roadster and then pivoted right to fire an additional two at the Packard. The man in the passenger seat ducked.

I swerved left to get back on the road and hit a muddy patch. The Duesenberg seemed to glide over the mud for a mad instant and then the world around us spun.

We were going so fast and things were so insane that all that registered for an instant was a terrifying blur. My body jolted left and right and I hit the brake. When the Duesenberg came to a stop, the roadster was not only bearing down on us, it was *facing* us.

We had turned completely around.

"Go!" Miss Welles screamed.

I didn't need to be told twice. I hit the gas and I drove past the roadster so fast that Miss Welles and the driver didn't even have time to exchange bullets.

I switched gears and went even faster. In the rearview mirror I saw the roadster stop, pull off to the side, turn, and take after us once more.

The Packard was now somewhere to our left, but we were also driving through the trees again and I was damned if I could see them.

"What now?" I asked.

"Can you get to Princeton this way?"

"A little longer, but sure."

"Then don't waste time talking," she said. "Just drive."

And I did. The roadster sped up and was once more in firing range. I saw the flashes of light in the rearview mirror as they fired and the faint *pop-pop-pop* was almost lost in the sound of the wind.

Now the trees subsided once more and I could see the Packard on the left. Miss Welles hadn't killed the man in the passenger seat because he was on his feet again and reaching for a Molotov cocktail.

"Do they buy those things by the gross?" Miss Welles yelled.

I hit the gas, but so did the Packard. For a moment we were nearly neck-and-neck. All they had to do was approach a near parallel position and the man could light another bomb. With luck, I could hit the gas and outdistance them, saving us all. I hoped.

But, no such luck. Up ahead was the turn that had nearly up-ended us. I didn't brake, but I took my foot off the gas and we slowed perceptively.

This gave the man all the chance he needed. Out of the corner of my eye I saw him light the cocktail as the Packard bore down on us.

I was nearly blinded by the flash, but it wasn't the Molotov cocktail. With a fluid motion that would do Annie Oakley[14] credit, Miss Welles slung her gun nearly in front of my face and fired.

The flash and powder not only startled me, but it hurt like a fiery slap. But her shot did exactly what it had to do. The man with the Molotov cocktail fell within the car. The driver went wild and the car turned, heading straight for our path.

We were lucky by inches. The Package jumped the side of the road just as we were about to turn. We sped past it and just at that moment, the entire thing exploded behind us.

The car simply became an enormous fireball. Flames engulfed the center of the car and spilled out onto the road.

Miss Welles whooped like a baseball fan. I turned the rearview mirror and watched in horror as the roadster behind it, moving too fast to maneuver, rear-ended the burning Packard. It hit the burning car with a tremendous *crack*, jack-knifing upside down on top of the flaming car. The driver and passenger doors opened and I saw two figures start to climb out when it got even worse.

A white flash, brighter than any lightning I had ever seen, lit up the early-evening landscape. Both cars exploded as the heat hit their gas tanks. I felt the shockwaves catch up to the Duesenberg and then vibrate beyond us despite our terrific speed.

We were now nearly back where we started. Night had fallen and a bright red beacon shined in the distance: the burning ruin of poor Richard Pierson's house. The night breeze had brought columns of smoke from the burning house low to the road and I squinted to see the path ahead.

We dived into a thick patch of smoke. The only thing visible was the

---

14 Annie Oakley (1860-1926) was born Phoebe Ann Moses in Ohio. She would rise to great fame as a sharp-shooter, touring the world with celebrated cowboy and showman Buffalo Bill Cody (1846-1917). Oakley is the subject of the Irving Berlin musical *Annie Get Your Gun*.

glow of the burning house barely cutting through the haze. I prayed that I would be able to keep on the road.

Miss Welles was on her knees on the front seat, bracing herself on the dashboard. "Watch it!"

In the dark and smoke, I nearly missed it. Two metallic forms emerged from within the smoke and were blocking the road. We were heading for a crash.

I spun the wheel rightward and we flew off the road and onto the soft farmland beside it. The Duesenberg hit every dip or rock on the road and Miss Welles bounced on the seat beside me. I spun leftward at dizzying speed, hoping I wouldn't over throw the road and emerge on the left side of it.

Somehow, I got back on the road. Though unpaved, it was lined with gravel to maintain it and the sound under our tires was like controlled thunder. I took a second to glance at the rearview mirror.

Behind us was nothing but a low-lying pillar of smoke. From that smoke, like pits shooting out of a squeezed grape, were two more roadsters.

The first car to emerge was another silver model, identical to the one just destroyed. Behind that was a bright red roadster, also with the top down. How they were able to breathe back there in the smoke was a mystery to me.

"What now?" I said.

"Drive!"

I hit the gas and the landscape around me became a blur.

The pursuing cars, though, must have had super-charged engines as well. The silver car quickly shortened the gap between us, and the red roadster was not far behind.

Miss Welles cracked her six shooter yet again to reload. "Are you all right?" she panted into the breeze.

"I've been better."

"Let's hope it doesn't get worse." She snapped the gun barrel in place.

Miss Welles turned and took a knee, firing behind us. She only let out two shots before she ducked down beside me.

"It got worse," she said.

I took a look in the rearview mirror.

A man was sitting on the windowsill of the passenger door and he was aiming a rifle at us. There was a shot and the side view mirror on my right shattered.

"Superior firepower," she said. "If he hits a tire we're dead."

I don't know why, but I instantly swerved left. It threw her against the passenger door. At that instant another shot rang out. The Duesenberg was not hit.

Miss Welles dropped to the floor of the car. She pulled a lever between the seat and the door and her side of the front seat opened up. I couldn't see what she was fiddling with inside the hold, but in seconds she emerged with an item no bigger than a violin. It was short, black and had a round magazine hanging at its underside.

It was a Thompson submachine gun. She calmly lowered the seat back in place.

She stuck the stock under her left armpit and clutched the front handle.

"Jesus!" I yelled. "Did you always have that there?"

"Yes!"

"What the hell were you waiting for?"

"I was waiting until we got into a jam," she turned and hefted the Tommy gun rearward. "Cover your ears!"

What followed next was the loudest noise I ever heard in all my life. Her side of the car seemed to light up with the flare of her gunfire, and the thudding sound of her clip of bullets was like all the thunder in the world exploding in my head at once.

The sound startled me so much that I lost the road again as we swerved right. I was driving on the loose soil again and Miss Welles continued to pelt our pursuers with gunfire.

"Keep it steady for God's sakes!" she yelled during a break.

I over-reacted and took the road too fast. This time I actually did drive over the road and then onto the left-hand farmland on the other side.

That might have saved our lives. The rifleman had been knocked out of the window by her machine gun and the driver was probably dead behind the shattered glass of the windscreen. The roadster drove blindly behind us, made a sharp right turn and then spun madly, somersaulting three times before it landed upside down in the center of the road.

I was so busy watching the ruined car in the rearview mirror that we almost got killed ourselves. Miss Welles bopped me on the top of the head just in time for me to see that we were about to hurtle into a sea of cows. I turned hard left, but we were close enough to the animals for me to hear a startled *moo!* as we swept past them.

I had just turned the car around, now going back towards Pierson's burning farmhouse, when we saw the red roadster screech to a halt, skid from its own momentum, and then slam into the up-ended car.

"Make tracks!" she yelled.

I stayed on the loose earth, running parallel to the road. As we approached the two cars, I saw a large husky man in a top coat and fedora get out of the red car and try to push it free of the other.

In seconds it seemed we dived back into the black cloud of smoke of Pierson's burning home. I choked and struggled to see but kept the warm glow of Pierson's home-fire to my right. It was nearly a minute before we were clear of it and we were about to take the turn again. I checked the speedometer and we were clocking in at one hundred and twenty miles an hour.

"Take it hard and stop behind the burning cars!"

"What?"

She yelled in my ear. "Take it hard and stop behind the burning cars!"

"That's what I thought you said."

We careened through the turn and were almost instantly upon the two burning cars. I sped around them too fast for comfort and then hit the brake. We threw up a spray of gravel and earth. Miss Welles, brandishing the Tommy gun, climbed barefoot over the passenger door and onto the road.

"Keep going. And when you get to the trees up ahead, turn around and get me."

"Are you crazy?"

"GO!"

I went.

In the rearview mirror I saw her step around the fiery wrecks and brace herself and the machine gun. I turned my eyes toward the road, suddenly unable to breathe.

Over the roar of the car I heard the retort of the machine gun followed by a terrific crash and then another explosion. I chanced another glance in the rearview mirror and saw a blinding fireball engulf the road and then reach heavenward in a flaming cloud.

I wasn't going to wait for the elms. I hit the brake, turned hard and raced back.

When I arrived, the two burning cars were now *three* burning cars. The bullet-riddled red roaster had slammed into both cars and was now covered in flames. I thought of the men who had been inside and shivered.

And then I thought of Miss Welles. I stopped the Duesenberg and hopped over the door. Through the fire and smoke I saw no sign of her. I don't know if it was the gasoline in the tanks, the bullets in their guns or the Molotov cocktails they had as readily as candy, but the fire was monstrous in its intensity. I ran towards the heat and wreckage. "Miss

Welles! Miss Welles! Can you hear me?"

She stepped from behind the inferno, holding the Tommy gun, with all the calm aplomb of a debutante stepping out of the cotillion.

I ran to her.

"Are you okay?"

"Yes."

I looked at the burning cars. "Should we try to help them?"

She pulled me along by the elbow. "Too risky. Let's get out of here." We sprinted to the Duesenberg. When we were close to it, she said, "Take this," and tossed me the Thompson. "I'll drive. You look a little green."

I carried the Tommy gun to the car while she hurried into the driver's seat. I put the Tommy gun next to my tibia and opened the back door.

"What are you doing?"

"Checking on Mason," I said, as I knelt in the back. I could barely see him by the flicking firelight. His eyes were closed and his glasses askew and his face was twisted in pain. I put a hand on his shirt and it came away bloody.

"He's been hit!" I said.

"Is he alive?" She turned over on the seat and looked down at us.

I looked at my bloody hand, wondering absently where to wipe it before I examined Mason more closely. I just smeared the gore on the sleeve of my forearm and then stuck two fingers on his throat.

"He has a pulse," I said.

"We're not doing him any good here," she said. "Get in. We'll head for a hospital."

Instead of sitting upfront I climbed into the back seat and hovered over Mason. The car pulled away, throwing me against the seat backing.

I ran my hand across Mason's face. "Mason. It's Peter. Peter Armstrong. Can you hear me?"

Miss Welles shouted something over her shoulder, but the sound of the wind speeding past us and the roar of the motor made it impossible to hear. No matter. I focused solely on my friend.

His eyes fluttered and focused on me. I reached down and righted his glasses and he smiled weakly once he was able to see me better.

I didn't know what to say. Mason reached up and took my hand and held it tightly. I stayed scrunched down in the back seat, holding the old man's hand as we raced for help.

In just the last twenty-four hours I heard many things said about my dearest friend. He was branded a Communist, a possible traitor and a mob tool. I did not know if any of that or all of it was true. All I knew was that Mason Cooley was a friend and mentor to me when I needed one. And now that he was in trouble, I'd be damned if I wouldn't be loyal to him in return.

We sat there, not speaking, for the rest of the trip. Miss Welles went through the farmlands like a rocket and only slowed when we arrived at the outer reaches of Princeton. She navigated the city faster than code and I did not look up at my surroundings until I saw we were at Princeton Hospital right off Witherspoon Street.

The car stopped on a dime and Miss Welles climbed over the driver's seat and opened the back door.

"How is he?"

I looked up; my bloodstained hand still locked in Mason's.

"He's dead," I said.

~~~

One of the benefits of being young is that I have never had to face death.

Both of my parents are still alive. My three brothers have never been sick a day in their lives, and my one dead grandparent died before I was born.

I've been lucky. All I knew of death was when people died in books. And that was no preparation for the real thing.

As I huddled in the backseat of the car, I cradled Mason in my arms. He was looking directly at me and I could feel the beating of his heart beneath my hands. And then, with little more than a blink, I felt his heart flutter and stop.

The eyes, which had looked at me with his usual keen intelligence, fluttered and grew blank. And he was gone, never to be seen again.

Where do they go, I wonder, the people who mean so much to you and then are dead? If there is some place, then it's beyond the detection of any telescope.

I heard Miss Welles get out of the car and run into the hospital. In moments attendants came out with a stretcher. She helped pull me away from his body and I watched as the men took Mason from the car and placed him on the stretcher. It was all very cold and business-like. Mason, never a sentimentalist at the best of times, would have approved.

They picked up the body and took it into the hospital. Miss Welles reached into my empty hand and closed her fingers around it. She gave it a squeeze and said, "Wait here."

She went back into the hospital and I climbed into the passenger seat of the Duesenberg. She was gone for nearly a quarter of an hour, and just as she stepped from the doors a black touring car pulled into the hospital lot.

She walked to the oncoming car. Two tall men in dark suits left the back seat and they loomed over her during a brief conference. After a moment, she left them and returned to me and opened the car door. She grabbed her yellow purse and turned to me.

"Come with me," she said, reaching out her hand.

I took her hand and followed her to the black touring car. She climbed in the back seat and I followed, closing the door behind me.

I watched the two men go to the Duesenberg. One got behind the wheel while the other ran a shocked hand over the damaged chassis.

It was only when Miss Welles leaned forward to speak with the driver that I realized there were two people up front.

As she gave the driver my address, Benet turned from the passenger side and assessed me coldly. The brim of his gray Homburg left his eyes in shadow, but I could still detect the star-like coldness at their center.

"Is he all right?" he asked Miss Welles.

"Just a little shaken," she said. "He'll be fine tomorrow."

"Did you get the notebook?"

Odd. I could not see her face, but I quickly realized that she was still holding my hand. She gave it another squeeze. "No."

Benet turned and watched the scenery change through the windshield as the car started. "A disappointment."

"I'm not finished yet."

"I wouldn't expect you to be," he said, absently. "I'll have a full report by morning?"

"At the latest."

"Mason is dead," I said. It was all I could to say.

"Yes, Dr. Armstrong," Benet said without turning. "I know."

"Whatever it is, he's out of it."

"He may be the lucky one."

We drove the rest of the way in silence. We turned down Broadmead and pulled in front of Mrs. Bradbury's house. I opened the door and stepped into the street. It was damp and the pavement glistened underfoot. I made a point of slamming the car door.

The touring car eased away before I had completely turned around. To my surprise, Miss Welles stood on the curb. She reached out a hand.

Unthinking, I took it and we walked up the front steps. I unlocked the door and we climbed the stairs to my apartment.

I turned on the lights. Mrs. Bradbury had done a good job of putting my apartment back together, but a quick glance at the bookcases told me it would be ages before I put the books back where they belonged.

I sank onto the couch.

Miss Welles went into the kitchen and in a moment returned with two glasses of bourbon. She handed me one and sat down beside me. I absently twiddled my glass so the ice tinkled, like I had seen Mason do countless times at staff meetings.

I took a sip. "Why did you lie?"

She took a sip. "About the notebook?"

"Have you lied about anything else?"

"Probably," she shrugged. She bent at the knees and tucked her feet under her. I saw that she was still barefoot and several tears stretched up the length of her stockings.

"Well?"

"I wanted you to examine it first," she said. "I thought we owed that to you."

"Is that all?"

"And I wanted you to tell me what it meant."

"Wouldn't Benet?"

"I wanted the truth."

"You don't trust Benet?"

"Trust everyone," she said. "But before they deal, cut the cards."

I took another drink. "Just how did you get into this line of work?"

"There aren't many opportunities for women with my unique capabilities."

"Unique is one word for it."

She finished her drink and nodded at mine. "Bottoms up."

I finished and she took my glass. She padded into the kitchen and returned with another round. I took the glass; it was cool and damp in my grip.

She sat. I reached out and took her glass and gave her mine.

"What gives?"

"I'm cutting the cards."

She laughed. It was a light laugh despite the throaty quality it had. "You learn fast."

I wiped away a lipstick smear at the rim with my palm and drank. "So what's next?"

"First, you climb into bed."

"Alone?"

She laughed again. "Alone. You're not quite at the point of life where you need a mercy screw."

"Thanks," I drank.

"Then, you tell me all about this." She reached under the strap of her brassiere and pulled the pages from Mason's notebook. "If I could do math, I wouldn't be doing the work I do."

I put my glass on the coffee table and unfolded the pages. I yawned and looked at the numbers. They swam before my eyes.

"I'm really sleepy," I said.

"I'm not surprised," she said, finishing her drink.

I took up my glass and looked at it, then put it down. "Hey. Is there something in this?"

"Nothing," she said. "Oh. Just a light sedative."

"What?" I wanted to jump to my feet, but I yawned instead.

"Relax," she said. "You just lost a friend. It will help you sleep."

I yawned and edged forward to get up.

She put her hands on my shoulders and bore me down on the couch. I felt the crush of her breast against my chest and blinked.

She pulled off and lifted my feet one at a time to slip off my shoes. She then put my feet up on the couch and, once horizontal, I felt consciousness slipping away.

"But I took your drink," I said.

She came so close I could feel her breath on my face. "Never trust a woman."

CHAPTER FIVE

I almost never remember my dreams.

And when I do, there is a "sameness" to them that is easily predictable. For the past couple of years I've been dreaming about Fred Astaire. Just usual dreams—he's visiting the observatory while I'm working, I pass him in a restaurant or he's Mrs. Bradbury's guest for dinner. For a while I was almost disappointed if my dream *didn't* have Fred Astaire.

I spoke to Dr. Joyce in the Psychology Department about that once, and he said I was really dreaming about my father. It's answers like that which kept me away from soft sciences like psychology and into more measurable realms, like astronomy.

The second most usual dream also followed a usual pattern: I am in a big house (it's never the same house) and I discover hidden rooms or basements. In my dreamscape homes I've found unused wings, secret staircases, subbasements, hidden towers and rooms beyond closets.

Dr. Joyce has also said I was an interesting case. I've since told Dr. Joyce to go suck an egg. ("How very *interesting*," he said to that one.)

But the dream I had the night Mason died was unlike anything I had before.

It started with a field of stars. There were two north stars—an impossibility, I know—and my attention focused on them. Most people use Polaris as a means of navigation (even Berbers in North Africa use it to navigate the deserts), and I wondered how I would get my bearing with two stars. Then the stars seemed to—coalesce into eyes, and then these were covered by eyeglasses and the next thing I knew, Mason was looking down at me from the sky.

The face then came closer and, next thing I knew, it was still nighttime and I was standing atop a grassy mountain and Mason was beside me with his arm over my shoulders. I pointed north (right between the two stars) and he smiled indulgently and pointed in the opposite direction.

I pointed north again and he shrugged before turning and walking south. I watched as his figure receded into the darkness. He was just a barely visible dot when I called out to him.

I guess I did that in real life, because next thing I knew, Miss Welles was shaking me awake.

The living room was flooded with sunlight. I sat up in surprise as Miss Welles gently pulled away from me.

"You were dreaming."

"Yes. I know." I looked around the room.

One of the armchairs held a bedroom pillow and was swaddled in blankets. Her yellow purse was on the floor and her six-shooter sat on top of that.

"You've been here all night?"

"Relax," she said. "You were a perfect gentleman."

I ran a hand through my hair. "What time is it?"

"Ten."

"Ten!" I got to my feet. "I'm late for school."

She shooed me back onto the couch. "Don't worry. I spoke to Elson. He said stay home."

"Did you tell him about Mason?"

"No."

"Why not?"

She went to the chair and folded blankets. "Benet wants it quiet for now."

"But… but what about a funeral?"

"Does he have any family?"

"No."

She shrugged. "Time enough for that later. Go wash up. Breakfast will be here in a moment."

I lurched to the bathroom and washed my face and hands. The face that looked back at me from the mirror was more like a Skid Row hop head than the face I was used to seeing. I rinsed my mouth out, straightened my tie and went back to the living room.

Mrs. Bradbury was at the door just as I entered. She handed Miss Welles a tray; once that was out of her hands, she took up a bundle from the stairs. "That package you ordered arrived."

"Thank you, Mrs. Bradbury," she said.

Mrs. Bradbury caught sight of me. "Good morning, Dr. Armstrong."

I mumbled something.

Mrs. Bradbury looked at me knowingly. "Jail. Sure." She closed the door and I heard her climb downstairs.

Miss Welles took the tray to the coffee table and poured coffee. "Here, have a slug of the mug."

I took the cup and drank gratefully.

"Well, my reputation is shot," I said.

"Or made," she said. There were two plates of scrambled eggs and bacon and a stack of toast. She buttered two slices and put one on each plate. "I don't know about you, but I'm starved."

She spooned scrambled eggs on top of her toast and ate.

I stood there.

After a moment, she looked up. "It's getting cold. I promise I won't bite."

I sat beside her and took up my plate. "Did you drug me last night?"

"I helped you get over a trauma," she said. "Sometimes, sleep is the best doctor. Feeling any better?"

"I don't know."

"Eat something."

I chewed on a piece of bacon. "What's in the package?"

"Clothes."

"Oh, I got plenty of clothes."

She laughed again, that light but oddly throaty sound. "For me, whiz kid."

"Why did you need clothes?"

"Girls *do* change their clothes, you know. Every day."

"Sorry. I wasn't thinking." I forked some eggs. "Why didn't you go home?"

"Triggermen have already tried to put the bag on you twice," she said.

I nodded sagely.

Then I asked, "What's *put the bag on you* mean?"

"Kidnap you, Tom Swift."

"Oh."

I had emptied my cup and she poured me another. "Food helping?"

I nodded.

"You were really close to Cooley, weren't you?"

"He was a second father to me."

"You didn't know any of the dicey stuff, did you?" She was looking at me from behind her toast.

"No. I'm not even sure it's true."

"It's true."

I took another bit of toast. "So you say."

"Look, Dr. Armstrong, I'll level with you."

"Please do."

"A long time ago, I learned something about my father that did not make me happy. After it my parents divorced."

I had never met anyone whose parents had divorced before. "That's a shame."

"Yeah," she said. "But here's the point. People are complicated. No matter how smart you are, and trust me, you're plenty smart, no one can know fully what goes on in the human heart. Learn that and it'll save you lots of grief."

I thought about that as we finished breakfast. Then she took up her bundle, said, "Excuse me," and trotted off to the bathroom.

I waited until I heard the water running.

I got up and quickly searched the room. When I didn't find Mason's papers, I gently put her six shooter aside and checked her handbag.

Bingo! Both pages were inside it. I took them out and popped over to my desk. I pulled my Box Brownie camera from the bottom drawer and photographed both sides of each sheet. Then I put the camera back in the drawer and slipped the papers back into her purse. As I gently put the gun back on top I thought, *well—she said never trust a woman.*

I rushed back to the couch and was working on my third cup of coffee and a Lucky when the bathroom door opened.

Miss Welles was now dressed in a cream-colored dress spotted with subtle, maroon dots. She wore a thick, bright yellow belt around her slender waist, and matching yellow high heel shoes. Her hair, still damp from the shower, was brushed and fell on either side of her face in delicious folds. She smiled at me and I felt my heart do funny things in my chest.

"The bathroom is yours," she said.

"Of course it's mine," I said. "It's my apartment."

"Gee, I wish I had an advanced college degree," she said. "What I meant was that you can go shower and change now."

"Oh." I got up and stretched. "I'd say make yourself at home, but you already have."

She returned to the armchair she slept in and threw yesterday's outfit over the back of it. "Good thing for you. You're still alive."

"I wish I could say the same for Mason."

She turned and faced me. "It's not like I didn't try."

I saw that I had hurt her feelings, and that was the last thing I wanted to do. "I'm sorry. I didn't realize how that sounded."

"No worries," she said.

"No," I stepped forward a bit. "It's not fair. Gosh, the only thing standing between me and those goons was you. And a Tommy gun."

For some reason that touched her funny bone in just the right spot and she giggled before she full-on guffawed. I laughed too, but mostly because she was.

"No hard feelings, Einstein," she said. "Get dressed. You got work to do."

"Just what exactly do you want me to do?"

"Two things—tell me where that rock landed, and, maybe even more important, where it came from. Is that something you can do?"

"It'll take some time to do the math, but I should manage."

"Do you need anything special?"

"A slide rule and some paper. I got those."

"And that great brain. Now, hop to it."

I was reluctant to leave her alone in my place. I certainly wasn't afraid for her safety, and by this time I was used to having no privacy at all. But, despite all she had done for me, I did not entirely trust her.

Not to mention that last night, she told me not to.

I nodded and went to my bedroom. I peeled off my soiled suit, shirt and underthings and got into my dove-gray silk robe. I took a fresh towel from my dresser and then hit the bathroom. My brief glimpse of Miss Welles as I passed by showed her sitting in the armchair, deep in one of my nonscientific books.

A hot shower, a shave, and fresh clothes can do tremendous things for even the most shattered spirits. I had changed into mahogany-colored tweed suit with a green knit tie and put on fresh shoes. Thus braced for the outside world, I went back to the living room.

I went directly to my desk and sat. I took out my slide rule and put a bunch of pencils on my desk. "All right," I said. "Let's have it."

She took the papers from her bag and put them in front of me. I lit a Lucky and read them through again.

"You've looked at them yourself?"

"Yes," she said.

"Then you see—it's ten projectiles, right?"

"Oh, yes."

"I only saw one that night at Mason's place—if what I saw really was one of them."

"The point is?"

"The point is that there may still be nine others just lying there."

"If they weren't taken away already," she said. "Oh, for God's sake just get on with it."

I started doing calculations while I smoked. She stood over my shoulder, as if she was afraid I was going to run off with the pages.

The great thing about focused brain activity is that everything around me just—goes away. I forgot about Mason, I forgot about this strange and fascinating woman with more guns than the average racketeer, I forgot about the man who died horribly in Mason's laboratory. The numbers were all that mattered, and I lost myself in the problem.

Thirty minutes later I absently rose and went for the charts and maps I kept in the bedroom. She didn't follow me, but she never took her eyes off of me.

She pushed the coffee cups and pencils aside as I spread the maps over the desk. I took a protractor and did a few more calculations. I stuck the protractor into the map and swung the arc on its axis.

"There," I said.

She leaned over.

"Where?"

"East Amwell Township," I said. "About fifteen miles from here."

I reached into my desk and grabbed my almanac. I licked a finger and paged through it. "East Amwell," I said. "Mostly farmland, lightly populated."

"How close can you figure to the point of… where this stuff hit?"

I shrugged. "Within a few dozen feet at best, but only just a little more at worst."

"And where did it come from?"

I took up a Lucky. "That's a more difficult question. For that, I had to make a few assumptions on the arc of descent based on the orbit and trajectory."

"And…?"

"Europe," I said. "Near, or, rather, not far from, Berlin."

She whistled.

"How likely is it that the other nine pieces are still there?"

"How do you know Stutka doesn't already have all of them?"

"Why would he want these pages if he had all of them?" She chewed on her bottom lip. "No. Whoever wants this, wants the whole ball of wax. Mason told them that there were ten. They got the one from him and now want the other nine. So, I repeat: how likely is it that the other nine pieces are still there?"

I stubbed out my cigarette. "Math isn't going to tell me *that*," I said. "You're going to have to find out for yourself."

She wagged a finger at me and went to the telephone. "First rule in this game: know when you're outclassed. If you don't know what these things are, then it's too dangerous to play guessing games." She said into the receiver: "Hello, Operator? Get me the Hotel Metropole in New York City."

I reviewed my calculations while the call went through. Once she was connected she said, "Benet? It's Penelope Welles. We know where the other nine pieces are." Pause. "No, we've found the pages. Long story. But I got the brain-trust to dope it out for us." Another pause; longer this time. "Look, do you want the dope, or not? Swell. Listen."

She gave him the estimates and then fell silent as she listened. Then she leaned forward, took a pencil and scribbled notes on my map. After a few moments of this, she looked up at me while speaking to Benet. "No, there's no time to get him security clearance, but I think we can trust him. At any rate, I trust him." She winked at me. After more listening she said, "Right. Two hours."

She hung up.

"What's going on?"

"In two hours, Benet and a special science force will be knocking on your door. We'll hop into a series of jeeps and from there, it's off to East Amwell."

"Nope."

"Nope?"

"Nope. Not doing it. I told you what you wanted to know. I've figured this out, and now I am done. Finished. Not happening. I resign and leave you to your own little secret agent games."

"Says the man who reads Tarzan."

"No one ever tried to kill me while I was reading Tarzan."

"We may need your expertise in the field," she said. "And I just vouched for you."

"Un-vouch. I'm not going."

~~~

Two hours later I was in a jeep heading for East Amwell.

It happened like this. Miss Welles alternately hectored and cajoled me, but no dice. I wasn't going. Then she tried to appeal to my sense of adventure, but I told her guys who spend their lives looking through telescopes have no sense of adventure. And if adventure meant speeding over farmland while lunatics threw Molotov cocktails at me, I would pass.

Then she went low and said I owed it to Mason.

"How's that?"

"Well," she said, "Benet got a file this thick saying your second father was a Bolshevik and probably a traitor. If you don't get involved in all this, that's going to be the official version, the end, *ad infinitum*. How does that taste?"

"Lousy."

"Good. Help us get to the bottom of this, and maybe Cooley comes out smelling a little rosier."

I looked at her for a moment. Her eyes, clear and lovely, regarded me from beneath her luxuriant lashes. There was a sardonic hint to her full lips, and her chin struck a defiant note. "You know, no matter what you did for me, I'm not sure I like you."

"I get a lot of that."

I sighed. "Okay. I'm in."

She actually walked up and shook my hand, like we had just become joint partners in a business. Or a suicide pact. "I should let you know something about Benet," she said.

"What's that?"

"I don't think he trusts you."

"Me? Why wouldn't he trust me?"

"Because you're Mason's friend. I think he's looking for a reason to clap you into jail."

"You tell me now, after we shook hands?"

"I'm not stupid."

"I must be. Why do you keep dragging me into this?"

"You're cute when you're scared."

"Thanks."

"Seriously, I know how Benet works. I think you've gotten a raw deal on all of this, and the way Benet operates is to shit on the people who've already gotten it the worst. It's almost like a game to him—it often is, with those government-for-life types. And I don't want him to shit on you."

"Gosh. That might be the nicest thing anyone has ever said to me."

"Well, you can take a knee and propose later. Right now you need some training."

"What kind of training?"

"First," she tugged on her index finger, "only talk when you're asked a question. And answer *only* the question. Don't ever offer other advice or insight. More people get caught up by talking too much than anything else."

"Okay."

"Second," she pulled on her middle finger, "if you have any ideas, let me know about them when we're alone. I'll let you know if they're any good or not."

"Fine by me."

"And, finally," she said, "keep your chin up and don't let them push you around."

When we were standing outside two hours later, a convoy of four converted Willys Jeeps rolled down Broadmead Street and stopped in front of my home.

Benet sat in the passenger seat of the first car. He was an incongruous figure in a dove-gray suit, gloves and homburg with a military topcoat thrown over his shoulders. He pulled up at the curb and the three remaining cars just idled in the road, blocking any traffic that might be coming up.

Miss Welles approached the car and saluted, which he returned with a blasé formality. She then opened the map we had used upstairs and showed him the notations and estimates.

"Dr. Armstrong, you're certain of this?"

"Okay, I'm in."

"Reasonably certain, yes."

He looked up from the map.

"Well, all science is just speculation until field or laboratory work shows that you're right."

He turned and motioned to second jeep in the convoy. Watterson sat in the driver's seat, and the man occupying the passenger seat was dressed like an Army Lieutenant. He jumped over and saluted smartly.

Benet gave him the lay of the land.

"We've deployed men in a mile-wide perimeter we estimate would lockdown the center of the circle, sir," he said. "And I wouldn't approach it without protective gear."

"Understood," Benet said. "Let's head out."

Miss Welles climbed into the back seat and I followed suit. Without further word from Benet the front jeep sped away with the remaining three close behind.

As we left Princeton, I had the oddest feeling that my life had gotten completely away from me. Just two days ago, I was an astronomer with nothing more to worry about than whether I would have enough room in my apartment for more books. Now I was driving off with the War Department to look at a European Secret Weapon. It was almost as if I was a stranger, watching these events unfold in someone else's life.

Oddly, it was Miss Welles who kept me in the here-and-now. When I felt myself becoming unmoored from reality, I had only to look at her and realize that this was indeed happening to me. Her beauty and her staggering capabilities brought the whole thing into a focus I would not otherwise have.

The day was sunny and I squinted into the distance. People on the streets of Princeton turned and watched as we drove through the town, but soon we were once again in farmland and the people grew scarce.

East Amwell was about forty minutes from my home. The open-air driving of the jeep made conversation difficult, and I had next-to-nothing to say to Benet anyway. I remembered how Miss Welles held my hand in a reassuring way last night and wished she would do it again.

After nearly thirty minutes we approached a corn field. The jeep left the road and drove through the stalks, cutting a path by flattening them into the earth. I turned and saw the three jeeps follow in the groove we cut.

We stopped at a line of military men. Benet got out, followed by Miss Welles and myself, while the driver stayed put.

The soldiers were spaced about twenty feet apart. The corn had been cut in a five-foot-wide path and that path went on for as far as the eye could see.

The soldier closest—a short man with close-cropped red hair—saluted as Benet approached.

"Report."

"We cut a mile-wide perimeter, sir," he said, pointing along the path. "Men posted every three yards, sir."

"Who owns the farm?"

"Hickey's Sunset Farm, sir. We moved Mr. Hickey and his family out about ninety minutes ago. We told them that a possible enemy plane had landed and they were cleared for their own safety."

"Very good." Benet turned and motioned to the people who came in our jeeps. Twelve men—including Watterson—approached. Four men carried two large packing crates; two men for each crate.

"Set up over there," he pointed.

The men put the crates down and Benet turned to me.

"Dr. Armstrong. We will need you to guide us and identify the rocks."

I shook my head. "You haven't seen what those things can do," I said. "I have no idea at what range they can be deadly and I would just as likely lead your people into a death trap as anything else."

"We've taken precautions with that," he said.

The first crate was opened and a tall, lanky man with eyeglasses pulled out a pendulous tunic and a pair of trousers. "How do you do, Dr. Armstrong?" he started. "I'm Doctor—"

"Never mind that," Benet said. He turned to me. "Dr. Armstrong, I'm sure you'll appreciate that members of our staff must remain confidential." He turned again to the man with glasses. "Proceed, Doctor."

"Yes, of course," the man sniffed. I could see that my colleague here liked Benet just about as much I did. "Dr. Armstrong, these experimental suits are designed to protect the wearers from the effects of radium or radioactivity. You should be perfectly safe."

"That's reassuring," I said. "How do I see through them?"

He held up a pair of goggles and some boots. "The goggles are coated with a layer of clear lead. They fit directly into the cowl or hood and then seal up tightly. You'll find the boots a little heavy, but they will also completely protect you from any harmful contamination."

Two other men from the team went back to the jeeps as the lanky doctor spoke and returned with a shoulder bag that looked like it was covered with sequins and sparkled in the sunlight.

"This is a specimen bag," he said. He took the bag and opened it. "It has an airtight lock that you activate by depressing the button *here*." He demonstrated. "It will keep whatever you bring from the field in isolation and protect whomever is near it." He took out a pair of gloves that looked like oven mitts. "You should be able to pick them up with these."

He held them out to me.

I pushed them back. "I *should* be able?"

Watterson said, "What are you afraid of?"

I took the glove and handed them to Watterson. "If you're not afraid, you do it."

That wiped his smile away, and quick. "I'm not the college boy. I'm not the expert."

"Good. That makes you doubly expendable."

"Now, now, gentlemen," Benet said. "Let's not start talking about who is and who is not expendable." He smiled at me, a rather cold smile. "Dr. Armstrong will be the first to say that all human life has value."

"You bet. Starting with mine. You didn't see what that stuff can do. I did. I signed on to help find it. Not commit suicide. Get yourself another pigeon."

"The gloves," the lanky doctor said, voice plaintive now, "should work."

"I should be able to spit ice cubes when it's cold outside, but that doesn't work either. Nope."

I don't know how this stalemate would've broken if it wasn't for Miss Welles. "Men," she said and took the gloves. "I'll get the specimens. Just be sure to point them out to me."

Watterson leered at me, all but saying, *sissy*.

I mumbled some of my filthiest language under my breath and pulled the gloves from her grip. "Permit me."

The lanky doctor then took out a metal box about four times the size of my Box Brownie Camera. "This is a Geiger Counter. It—"

"Yeah, I know. What makes you think that it's radioactive?"

"The reports I read—"

"The reports you read should've said I had no idea what caused the reaction. This might be as worthwhile as taking a pea shooter on a bear hunt."

"It's our best guess," the man said.

"Let's get into these togs," I said. There were four of us going: me, Miss Welles, the lanky doctor and Watterson. It would be a fun little party. The men from the jeep helped me get into the gear. It was heavy—like putting on a wet overcoat. The hood rested thickly on my head and shoulders, and then one of the anonymous gentlemen fitted a pair of goggles that looked more like binoculars into the slot at my eyes. Someone else pulled a cord and the hood fastened tightly around my neck. I gasped once in panic but found I was able to breathe easily.

I held onto Benet and another man as the boots were fitted over my shoes. As I leaned back I saw Miss Welles behind a jeep, changing into her protective gear all by herself. She tossed her yellow, high heel shoes over her shoulder and into the back of the jeep.

"Gosh, help her, not me," I said, but no one seemed to pay any attention.

The lanky doctor with glasses and Watterson were suited-up next. Then the three of them huddled with me; they walked like lumps of mashed potatoes that had somehow come alive.

"Can you hear me?" I shouted under the hood. Watterson and Miss Welles nodded; the doctor shouted, "Yes!"

I picked up the specimen bag and draped it over my shoulder. "If I'm doing this, I'm in charge." I pointed a thick-fingered glove at Watterson. "Got it?'

I couldn't see his face, but he nodded.

I turned to Benet. "Once we get them, get the specimen bag away from these people as quickly as possible. And do not examine it in anything other than a lead-lined room."

Benet provided me with a curt nod of the head, eyes closed.

"Listen," I said to the others. "There is not too much ground to cover, and I want us to stick together. I don't know how far our voices will carry through this junk, and I don't want anyone doing anything that I don't oversee personally."

I held out a glove. "Give me the map."

Now, in a lifetime of saying stupid things, that may have taken the cake. According to my estimates, the rocks landed in an open field. Unless I was going to compare piles of dirt on the map illustrations with piles of dirt on the ground, it wasn't going to do me a darn bit of good. But I felt that if this was my show, I wanted to hold the damn piece of paper.

Benet handed it over.

I picked up the Geiger Counter and turned it on. The lanky doctor went to the jeep and pulled out a large flash camera.

"Follow me," I said and the soldiers standing at the circular perimeter of the corn field parted like the Red Sea.

I pressed through the corn and we were off. The Geiger Counter was on, but there were no readings at all. Every now and then the lanky doctor would snap a photograph, but since there was nothing to see, if was simply a matter of form.

If the perimeter was a great circle, I thought the first move would be to move straight ahead and bisect the circle at its center. A quick look at the sun gave me my bearings and we headed off.

The going was slow and painful. The boots were heavy and every step had to be navigated through the high stalks of corn. Worse still, the strange material of the suits made an annoying sound while we walked—like engines wearing corduroy trousers. I kept my eyes to the ground while regularly checking the Geiger Counter.

After nearly a half-hour of slow walking, we hit the opposite line of soldiers guarding the outer rim of the circle. They had their backs to us, and despite the noise we made, looked resolutely forward.

"Okay," I shouted into the hood. "It's not in the middle. That makes it to either our left or right." I looked at the one I thought was Miss Welles (it was almost impossible to tell who was who) and said, "Pick a side. Ladies' choice."

Miss Welles twisted from side-to-side within her contamination suit and shrugged. She pointed to the left.

"Okay," I said, making my voice as loud as possible. I could hear my own words echoing under my hood. "I want us to spread out a bit now side-by-side in a straight line. No more than two arm's length away. Got it?"

Nods.

Miss Welles moved beside me and off about six feet, then Watterson and then doctor. The doctor took a few photos documenting our position, and then we marched forward in lockstep, each of us watching the ground under us.

It was slow going, but we made it back to Benet without finding anything. We turned around and moved back, going back and forth repeatedly until we had checked the ground for half the mile-wide circle. The Geiger Counter never registered, there were no breaks in the corn consistent with extraterrestrial impact, and the ground was unblemished.

We were moving on the curve of the outer rim of the circle before too long and rather than regroup, we followed the outer perimeter to the other side of the circle first. But by the time we have made our first full foray into a straight line on the opposite side of the circle, I suspected that we were going to come up empty.

And we did. Benet was still rooted where he was, arms folded, when we returned hours later.

I was first to take off my hood. I put the Geiger Counter down on the ground, chucked the specimen bag and said, "They're not here."

Benet did not say anything. He waited until Watterson and the other took off their hoods and looked an unspoken question at Miss Welles.

"We checked everywhere," she said. Sweat had plastered her hair to her forehead and she was heavy with fatigue. "We went over everything inch by inch and there was nothing to find."

The man with glasses shook his head in agreement and Watterson wiped his damp forehead with his arms.

Benet finally addressed me. "Well, Dr. Armstrong?"

"Well, what?"

"Where are they?"

"Not here."

"I can see that," he snapped. "Now I need you to tell me where they really are."

I shrugged. Or, I shrugged as well as I could in that get up. "Hell, you have Dr. Cooley's notes. If my math is wrong, you find them."

"That is, if you're telling the truth," Watterson said.

"Wait a moment—" Miss Welles began.

"What do you mean, telling the truth?" I asked.

"We all know Cooley was a Red," he said. "You're probably one of them, too. I'm sure if we locked you up you'd remember where the rocks were pretty fast."

"A Red?" I bellowed. "Listen, idiot. I'd like to remind you that they have kidnapped my friend Dick Pierson!"

He sneered. "He's probably a Red, too. Or he's hiding. Maybe—hey, maybe Pierson's not Red. Maybe he's yellow!"

I threw my hood and jumped at him but Miss Wells grabbed the folds of my tunic and I didn't get very far.

"Wait!" Benet said, voice commanding. "Let's not fall out now. Dr. Armstrong is quite correct. We'll have our experts confirm his calculations. And if this where they were supposed to fall, and they are not here, then there's another piece of this puzzle we're missing." He turned to me. "Dr. Armstrong. Is there anything else—anything—that you could tell us that might lead us in the right direction?"

"No." I jerked a thumb at the cornfield behind me. "They're not here, and I don't think they ever were. If they had landed here, there would be breaks or scorching on the earth or the corn. But we found no sign of that. And if they are radioactive, the Geiger Counter would've picked up trace signs of radiation. I'm stumped."

Disappointment and distrust struggled for dominance on Benet's face. At length he said, "So we will have to explore other avenues."

"You want me to take him in?" Watterson asked.

"On what grounds!" I howled. I had enough. I marched to one of the jeeps and threw the hood into the back and then started pulling off the tunic. "If you want to discuss anything with me at all, please consult my lawyer first. I will have no further discussions with you without legal representation." I sat on the fender and pulled off one of the boots.

Benet waved a placating hand. "No need for that. Dr. Armstrong, we'll take you home and you have the thanks of an anxious nation. I formally request that you think deeply about any avenues we can go in this investigation."

I immediately thought of several places they could go, but I kept my mouth shut. I managed to get the gear off by myself and then, without waiting to be asked, helped Miss Welles out of her outfit.

Benet and the lanky doctor spoke in hushed tones, Watterson standing over them like an over-protective basset hound. Benet then gave orders to the military men and then they all marched to the jeeps. Benet thanked me again and made a point of asking for the pages from Mason's notebook. I handed them over without regret.

Two military men took the front seat of a jeep and Miss Welles and I took the back. We drove away from the spot and I noticed that the other three cars went in an opposite direction.

Fortunately, we were heading home. I thought of maybe a dozen things I could say to Miss Welles, but I waited for her to speak first.

I didn't have to wait long. "They don't really suspect you of anything," she said.

"Do you?'

"No. But they are afraid."

"Me, too."

"What do you think happened?"

"Who knows?" I said. "Mason's calculations could be wrong. Or, maybe the rocks have nothing to do with anything, and you and Stutka are on a wild goose chase."

"And Mr. X."

"And Mr. X," I said. "If there is such a person. I mean, think about it.

Mason says he has something for Stutka, a powerful weapon that he'll deliver in exchange for cancelling his gambling debts."

"And?"

"Everyone is just assuming that it's something he caught sight of through the telescope," I said. "What if it's something he discovered elsewhere? Or invented himself?"

She smiled at me. It was a beautiful smile, but it was the indulgent smile of a parent who caught a talented child telling whoppers. "Cute, but I wouldn't try a line like that on Benet. He'll take Watterson's advice and lock you up until your grandchildren can vote."

"I'm not saying it's so. I'm saying it's possible."

"And I'm saying go peddle your papers. If you want to get serious, think of where the mess up is and let's get that poison before Stutka does."

"Or Mr. X."

"Or Mr. X. If there is such a person."

Twenty minutes later the jeep pulled up in front of my apartment on Broadmead. I climbed out, tired down to my very bones. I thanked the driver and smiled at Miss Welles.

"When will I see you next?" I asked.

"Did you want to?"

"Yes, but without the machine gun."

She reached into the back of the jeep and handed me the tunic, pants and hood. As I held them out, she piled the googles, and boots on top.

"What's that for?" I asked.

"A souvenir," she said. "It looks like you keep a lot of them in your place."

"I have a better idea," I said. I leaned forward. "How about a kiss?"

Instead she patted my head. "I'd love to kiss you," she said, "but I've just washed my hair."

She plopped down into the seat and pinged the driver on his helmet. He shifted gears and the jeep drove away.

CHAPTER SIX

It was now late afternoon and, despite my drugged sleep last night, I felt tired enough to climb into bed for the next four years.

I tossed the protective gear into the corner of my living room and made myself a grilled cheese sandwich in the kitchen. I polished two glasses of milk before returning to the couch and lighting a cigarette.

I was thinking it would be nice to have something to read and cast my eye over my bookcases. I then remembered that my copy of *Tarzan and the Lion Man* was ruined, and that I would have to get another if I was ever going to ever learn how it comes out.

I finished my Lucky Strike, tossed the burning ember into my smoke stand, rose and stretched. If I was going to the drug store for a book, I could also take the film from my camera over to be developed. I didn't think I had made any mistakes when reviewing Mason's numbers, but I couldn't be sure unless I had them in front of me to double check. I was very happy to have photographs of all the relevant data. I popped open the back of my camera and stuck the reel of film into my jacket pocket.

Outside I felt odd. Now that I was out of the protective gear, my step seemed lighter and the day seemed brighter. It was almost as if the last two days were some horrible nightmare and I had just come out of it. I walked down Broadmead and felt the cool air do good things to my aching head.

Princeton is a very special place. In addition to loving my observatory, I am happy with the town of Princeton itself. It is very much a small town and I just would not be happy in a big city. The thought of New York is enough to make me cringe (I'm still amazed that I actually considered joining the faculty at Columbia University for longer than a minute), and I find I still miss Waukegan, where I grew up. Both Waukegan and Princeton are small towns, which is what I like most about them, but they are very different.

Waukegan has a small-town, middle-America feel to it—it wasn't surprising to see Penrod[15] types when I was growing up. But Princeton…, well that has a more genteel small-town air to it; as if any minute a spinster detective was going to find the vicar's body near the astrolabe. It has a lot to recommend it, but it can be awfully stuck up at times and never feels as homey as Waukegan. No matter how comfortable I am here, I often have the feeling that I don't quite fit in.

Part of that is that my work takes up a great deal of my time. But also, lots of my colleagues want to spend time talking about politics or grand theories of history or about the eternal struggle between the proletariat and the bourgeois. (I've been hearing this stuff for going on ten years and just who is the proletariat and who is the bourgeois has never been clearly

---

15   *Penrod* is a collection of comic vignettes by Booth Tarkington (1869-1946) published in 1914. The book follows the misadventures of Penrod Schofield, an eleven-year-old boy growing up in the Midwest prior to the Great War.

defined for me.) And when the talk gets too silly, as it too often does, I pack up my Tarzan books and go home.

It's easy to know lots of people in Princeton, and we all feel some kind of connection through the University itself; it's like a company town but the product is college students. I waved at a few of the kids as they walked through town, most carrying books and more than a few holding hands.

Nick and Andy's was my drugstore of choice in Princeton. It was a small place with black-and-white tiled floors, an overhead ceiling fan, and a stainless-steel soda fountain in the rear. There were three book racks and usually Mabel was at the counter. They were also fast at developing photographs.

Luckily Mabel was there today. She gave me a warm hello as I sidled up to the cash register.

"Hello," I said.

"What can I do for you, doc?" Mabel is a big girl with her black hair pulled back in a severe bun and a gap between her front teeth that made her unconventionally sweet-looking.

I held up my film. "Pictures. When can they be ready?"

She took the roll of film and placed it in an envelope and wrote my name on it. "Day after tomorrow. Two of each shot?"

"Yes, please," I said absently. I turned toward the back of the shop. "Are the new books in yet?"

"Yes," she said. "Got a new issue of *Amazing Stories*, too." She took it from behind the counter. "I put one aside for you."

"Thanks!" I said. I ambled over to the rear of the store. No one was at the soda fountain, though the red headed kid behind the counter smiled at me as if desperate for business. I smiled at him and made a beeline for the books.

In moments I had a new copy of *Tarzan and the Lion Man*. I was looking for some other books by Burroughs when I saw that some dope had accidently placed some of the books by authors with B-starting last names over in the M-starting last name section. I didn't know how anybody was supposed to find anything when all the books were twisted round.

I bent to refile the B-books when it hit me. I stood up like I got a jolt of electricity.

Twisted round.

I ran back to the register.

"Mabel, is there a way to get those pictures any faster?"

She looked at me, surprised by my alarm. "No. Otis comes in the day after tomorrow and after…"

"Can he come in today?"

"Today?"

"Today. Now. This minute. Can we call him?"

"Are you all right, Doc?"

"I'm fine, but I must have those photographs. Can we call him?"

She shrugged. "I can call. I can't guarantee he'll come."

"Tell him it's an emergency. Tell him I'll give him two bucks if he comes right away."

"Two bucks!" Mabel stepped from behind the counter and went to the phone out back "For two bucks, I'll learn how to develop 'em myself."

I realized I was nearly standing on my toes when she came back a moment later.

"He says he can't come over," she said.

"But it's an emergency."

"But he said go over to his place and he'll develop them there."

"Great!"

She went behind the counter and pulled out the envelope with my film. "What's this all about?"

"I lost some notes and just realized that I had photographed them," I lied. I was surprised at how easily it came to me. "I need them for class tomorrow."

"He'll help you out," she tore open the flap and gave me the roll of film. "That's thirty-five cents."

"Thirty-five cents? What for?"

"The copy of *Amazing Stories* and *Tarzan* that you got in your other hand."

"Oh," I reached into my pocket and took out the money. "Thanks!" I said, running for the door.

Once I was outside, my mind raced. *Twisted round.* Of course. Mason always had trouble transposing his numbers. How often had he written "1963" when he meant "1936," or said turn right when he meant turn left…? And then I remembered my dream.

So that's what it meant! I was following the stars due North—but there were two of them. One of them True North, and the other, "Mason's North." No wonder he motioned me in the opposite direction. If I went the *right way* I would be going in the *wrong way.*

I ran all the way to Otis Dickerson's house.

Otis lived thirteen blocks away on Murray Street. He opened Nick and

Andy's years ago, improved it with the soda fountain, and only recently started developing film for his customers. He had a full photographer's studio in the basement of his house where he did all the developing two days a week.

Otis was in his mid-fifties, round and with a wide mouth that was usually smiling. He was addicted to the dime store jokes he sold, and it was rare that I could get out of his shop without touching a joy buzzer, looking through fake X-ray glasses, or admiring the new shipment of fake poop.

Even the name of the drug store was a private joke. Once, when I asked him who was Nick and who was Andy, he said he was.

He lived in an old two-story Victorian on the corner. He was actively expecting me because when I got to his house, he was standing at the open door in his undershirt and a pair of tan slacks. His feet were bare.

I pushed through the door by way of hello.

"Hey, Pete, what's the rush?"

There was a table that held his keys next to the front door and I put Tarzan and my pulp magazine there. "I need this for school tomorrow," I said, passing the film.

"C'mon down," he said, leading the way to his basement.

Otis was a bachelor and his house was a mess. I had been over several times for a Coke and to listen to the radio with him on summer nights, but if any of his other customers ever saw his place, they'd call the Health Department.

The wooden stairs groaned under his weight. We walked past his work bench into a small room built of cinderblocks. We went inside and he put on an apron and lit a dim, red light. The room smelled of chemicals.

The whole thing only took twenty minutes. I stood by the door, gnawing on my bottom lip as he worked. Finally, he placed 5-by-7-inch photographic sheets into the developing solution and watched as the images appeared.

"Wow," he said. "That's fascinating. I never knew about that…" he said.

I was so involved in my thoughts about Mason's calculations, that I thought he was talking about that.

"In what way?"

Otis held up a wet photograph. "A Buck Rogers bicycle. I didn't know you had one."

I had forgotten that there were a bunch of other photos on the roll of film.

"That's not mine," I lied. Actually, it was and I kept it in Mrs. Bradbury's basement. It was brand new and there was a tin carapace over the chassis that made it look like a Rocketship with *Buck Rogers* printed in red on both sides. I only rode it at night so guys like Otis wouldn't rag me.

"It's not?"

"It's for my nephews."

"You never told me about any nephews," he said, clipping the wet photos to a clothesline stretched from wall to wall. "You never told me about no sisters-in-law. Sure it ain't yours?"

"Are you developing film or cracking wise?"

"Both, if I put my mind to it," he said, soaking more sheets. "Oh, here it is."

"My notes?"

"No, those pictures you took of the new moon last month." He held it up to an appreciative eye. "You get good shots with that dinky camera."

"My patience is wearing thin."

The next four photos were what I wanted. Though Otis delighted in giving me a hard time, he was also a good guy and I saw he took extra care when the pages of notes finally started to appear on the photographic paper. He marinated them for a few minutes, shaking them with a special pair of tongs. At length he took them out and held them up to the red light.

"Clear as a whistle, Pete," he said. "You can read these easy." He then clipped the four of them to the drying line and wiped his hands on his apron. "These should take about ten minutes to dry."

I walked past him and gazed at the photos in the dim light. He was right—reading Mason's notes would be no problem. I could do it with a naked eye, and with a magnifying glass, it would be even easier.

"Would you do me another favor?" I asked.

"For the same two bucks, or is this a different commission?"

"Just hold onto the negatives for me, will you? In case I need them again."

"Sure." There must've been something in my voice, because Otis asked, "Pete, you sure everything is okay?"

"Just overworked," I said. I unclipped the four photos I needed.

"Those need more time to dry."

"No worries," I said, walking out of the developing room and making for the stairs. "They'll dry on the way home."

I took the stairs two at a time. At the door, I separately put each photo between the pages of *Tarzan and the Lion Man*. The developing solution instantly warped the pages, but it could not be helped. Otis had made it up the stairs by the time I was done.

I opened the door and with a nod stepped out.

"Hey, Pete, you forgot something!"

I turned and saw Otis standing at the doorway with an expectant look. I smacked my head and reached into my pocket. I peeled off two dollar-bills and handed them over.

"Not that," he said, pushing them away, mouth wider than ever as he grinned. "You forgot this."

He handed me a limp photo of my Buck Rogers bike.

~~~

Home, I put down my book and magazine and made a pot of coffee. Once it was hot, I carried everything over to my desk and got to work.

When I pried open *Tarzan and the Lion Man*, I saw that the developing solution seeped into the surrounding pages. The text had run a little bit, but it was still readable—I hoped. I put the book aside with a silent prayer that I would be able to get to it later.

Now, I wondered... how best to do this? The problem was not going to be easy. My guess was that Mason had transposed his numbers, as he often did. But which numbers? And how many of them? And how would I know that I had the right calculation once I was done?

To keep from going completely crazy, I was going to work on the assumption that Mason transposed numbers, rather than recorded completely inaccurate numbers. Otherwise, I could be at my desk for the rest of my natural life while I imagined completely different figures, and every minute that Dick Pierson was missing meant the longer his life was in danger.

But, lighting a cigarette, I also figured it was not as bad as all that. Working on the supposition that Mason found those rocks, they still had to be relatively close by. It was improbable—if not impossible—to think he went cross country to examine meteors that he had no way of knowing were in any way exceptional.

And what *that* meant was—it was unlikely that widely divergent numbers were the ones transposed. For example, if Mason wrote "19" rather than "91," that would create too wide a variable—eight separate data points from where I actually should be looking. No. It had to be numbers that probably had no more than one-or-two variables away, such as "23" for "32."

Working on that principle, I copied the data from the photographs onto some scratch paper and started to work. I would frequently take-out maps and charts of the surrounding area, but when I was led too far afield, dropped those solutions as untenable.

I only broke for another cheese sandwich at nine that evening, and, three hours and another pot of coffee later, hit what I thought was the correct solution. I reached for the map and traced where my calculations led me.

There. Where East Amwell Township was northwest of Princeton, Grover's Mill, New Jersey, was southeast. And both were nearly equidistant from where I sat.

I checked my almanac. Grover's Mill, like East Amwell, was mostly farmland. Meteors or other foreign bodies could land there for some time before they were ever noticed. In fact, it was a good bet that whatever the State Department, Stutka and Mr. X were all searching for was just a brief car ride away.

I reached for the phone. My first instinct was to call Miss Welles. But I took my hand away before I could lift the receiver. *Never trust a woman*, she said. I decided to take her at her word. Dick Pierson had vanished—probably taken by Stutka and his men. I couldn't call my folks. Who else did I trust?

So, I called Thurgood Elson.

"Hello?" His voice was thick with sleep.

"Dr. Elson," I said. "Sorry to awaken you. It's Peter Armstrong."

"I know who it is," he said. Over the wire, I could hear him throwing back the covers. "It's midnight. Is everything all right?"

"I think so. It's about Mason."

"What about him?"

"I think I figured out where those rocks actually landed. I'm on my way to get them."

"Where?"

"Let me check it out first," I said.

"Son, that's dangerous."

"I'll be careful. If I do find them, I want to deliver them to the University first. Maybe have our people examine them before we hand them over to the War Department. Can you set up a lab where we can keep them safe?"

"That's not the deal that we made," he said. "Just stay put until I can get there. We'll go together."

"No—too dangerous. Stay put and I'll call you when I get back."

"Peter–"

I hung up before he could say anything else. I went to the corner and picked up the contamination suit I used earlier. Then I remembered that I would need a specimen holder that would provide sufficient protection. I was stumped, and for a moment considered cancelling the whole project until I remembered Mrs. Bradbury's lead-lined planters in the backyard.

I grabbed a hat and tramped down the stairs and went around back. Mrs. Bradbury had a small shed at the end of a brick-lined walkway with flowers on either side. Around the shed were elaborate planters filled with wisteria.

These planters were elaborately sculpted, mostly the size of soup tureens, squarish, but with slotted bottoms to allow water to seep through. Each planter was fitted with had a lead-lined plate underneath to catch the water.

I turned one over, feeling guilty, and scooped out the dirt and wisteria. Then I lifted another, took the plate from its bottom, and fitted it on top of the now empty-flower pot. Not airtight, but with a plate on top and on the bottom, I should be able to secure it with a couple of belts and it would be safe enough for me to get it to the lab.

I hauled the empty planter to the backseat of my Lasalle, grunting under its weight. I then went back for the plate and stuck that in the car before returning upstairs for the contamination suit, a flashlight, my car keys and a couple of belts. I also stuck *Tarzan and the Lion Man* into my jacket pocket. If I ended up back at the University, I might get some reading in before Dean Elson arrived.

Behind the wheel, I checked the map once again and set out for Grover's Mill, a tiny place that no one had ever heard of, but which just might be the most important place in the world right now.

The streets were empty at this hour and the drive an easy one. I was soon out of Princeton and back in the farmlands of New Jersey.

I had used my protractor to cordon off a circular, mile-wide perimeter where I thought the stones must have fallen. Before long I found myself in a cornfield that looked eerily similar to the one in East Amwell.

I cut the ignition and stepped out of the car. It was difficult getting into the containment suit on my own in the dark, but I managed. I left two leather belts near the planter and picked up the flashlight. I had no Geiger Counter, so this was going to have to be rough and dirty. And fast.

I put on my gloves, moving the flashlight from one hand to the other, and set out.

Doing this at night made it doubly worse. Stalking through a cornfield on a dark, moonless night is not work for the faint-hearted, even when not looking for a weapon that can turn you into a molten pool of blood and bone in a matter of minutes. I was uncomfortably aware of the sound of my own breathing under the hood, and each corn stalk pushed aside sounded like a thunderclap. The goggles, which seemed to work so well that afternoon, seemed desperately limited in the dark of night.

I swerved the flashlight back and forth on a wide arc, covering as much ground as I could with each step. I also let the light trail up the length of the cornstalks, looking for any breaks or singeing to indicate impact.

An owl hooted in the distance and I nearly jumped out of my suit. I could feel the sweat run down under my hood, despite the cool of the evening. Each step in the heavy boots felt like a trek through damp cement.

I had been deep into it for nearly three quarters of an hour when I had my first intimation of success. I let the beam of my flashlight trail up a length of corn; insects danced in its ray. As it crept to the top of the stalk, I saw the top of it had been sliced off, leaving a burnt cut at the point of impact.

After that, it was fairly easy. The burning and cutting followed a slight incline downward. I had only to follow the stalks as they grew shorter and more burnt.

Finally, there it was—a series of deep holes in the cornfield, each puckered with hot, tumultuous earth. They looked like little wounds, the kind you get when an infected pimple is squeezed and the surrounding skin is red and tender. The heat generated by the projectiles must have been terrific—there was still a burnt smell in the area, despite the passage of many days and exposure to the open air.

The holes were all somewhat bigger than a baseball, and none were so deep that the rocks plowed deeply under the soil until they were hidden. I could swear my heart stopped as I slowly counted each declivity.

I quickly found the first five. They were spaced close together, though none had impacted against the other over the course of their trajectory. I found the sixth about ten feet away, then the seventh and eighth nearly fifteen feet from there.

I hunted for almost twenty minutes before I found the ninth, and final, rock. A let out a sigh of relief and dropped to my knees to rest.

Now that they were located, I had the problem of picking them up and securing them in the lead-lined planters in my car. I went back to the first group of five and brushed away the loose earth. In the beam of my flashlight, the rocks looked smooth and oval-shaped; nothing at all like the many-faceted, hard-edged stone I saw at Mason's house. I wondered, for a mad instant, if these were the same rocks.

Trembling, I ran a gloved hand over one of them.

You should be able to pick them up with these, the lanky doctor said.

Over the course of my career, I have examined hundreds of rocks that have fallen from the heavens. A host of atmospheric conditions—the origin of the rock itself, the terrific rate of heat at re-entry into the earth's atmosphere—leave meteors uneven, pitted or full-of-holes.

These rocks, however, were perfectly smooth. They looked more like over-sized, black eggs than anything else. The closer I got to them, the more certain I was that what I had here was man-made, and not the natural flotsam of outer space. Using Mason's incorrect numbers, I had deduced that the rocks had come from Europe; once I got home, I would have to re-examine the correct numbers and make a better estimate of their origin.

I dug away at the loose earth surrounding the first rock and, finally, I was able to pull it from the earth like a diseased tooth.

I was surprised at how heavy it was. Given its size, it should not have weighed in excess of two-or-three pounds, but I guessed this specimen weighed at least fifteen. I did not want to carry more than one at a time; they were deadly and I had already pushed my luck to the breaking point.

I carried the first stone to the car and opened the back seat. I pushed aside the makeshift lid of the planter, and gently placed it inside. I closed the cover and went to front seat and took a comb out of my glovebox.

Returning, I used my comb to gently dig up the second stone. I stuck my comb into the earth and carefully carried the rock back to my car. As I lifted this one into the planter, I thought I felt something *shift* inside the rock itself.

I froze, holding my breath.

No! the man at Mason's house screamed. *Stutka! Please, God no!*

Once my heart started beating again, I raised the rock once more to the lip of the planter.

There it was again—a shifting sound, like there was something *inside* the stone. Was it possible the smooth, black exterior was merely a casing for the red, crystalline rock I had seen earlier?

I wasn't going to perform an experiment in the dead of night in the middle of a deserted cornfield in equipment that *should* protect me. Best to wait until I returned to the lab and Dr. Elson threw the resources of Princeton at them. I quickly put the stone inside the planter and went for another.

And so it went, carefully digging up each rock, taking it to the car with the utmost caution, and then sealing up safely (I hoped!) inside the lead-lined planter.

I was grateful when it was over. With the last stone I left my comb in the field and pushed my way through the corn. I walked deliberately around my car and placed it in the planter. Then I took the two belts and cinched them cross-wise over the planter. I gave the lid a push and it held tight.

Thank God that was over. I pulled the goggles from my hood and threw them into the backseat of the car. Then I took off the hood and gulped the cool air.

Then the lights hit me.

I blinked. It was dark and, after looking through the googles, I wasn't ready for light of any intensity.

It was three lights; large, round points of light pointing directly at me. Shadowy figures hid in the darkness beyond. I squinted into the distance.

"Put your hands up, Dr. Armstrong."

I dropped my flashlight on the ground and raised my hands. My movements were slow and heavy in the containment suit.

"Please move the light," I said, still squinting. "It hurts."

The lights were lowered and, once my eyes readjusted, I gaped at the sight.

There were two black touring cars just beyond me. Five men huddled together, almost forming a perfect V, with a tiny figure at the apex.

"Stutka!" I said.

Stutka stood there, elaborately dressed and immaculate. He wore a finely tailored blue suit offset by a canary yellow vest. He sported a white pocket square and, even in the damp farmland, his spats were immaculate.

His chief goons were on either side of him. Romero grinned on his right, his gold teeth catching the glare of the flashlight, and O'Brien glowering on his left. Both held silver automatics that pointed right at me.

"Good evening, Dr. Armstrong," Stutka said.

"What are you doing here?"

"No doubt, the same as you."

"How did you know where to find them?"

He smiled and preened, looking like an over-dressed child chomping at the bit to win a spelling bee. "I didn't. We just followed you."

"Where's Dr. Pierson?" I said.

Stutka did not answer. Instead, he turned to his bevy of goons. "Take the box and put it in my car." He paused for effect. "And, gentlemen, be

...and placed it in the planter...

very careful."

One of the men broke ranks and opened the rear door of the first car while two others approached my car. Their faces were not happy.

"What you're doing is very dangerous," I said, to everyone in general.

"I'm touched by your concern."

The two goons eased me backward and reached into my car. Each took an end of the planter and eased it out of my car.

"If you drop that," I said, "we could all end up dead."

One of them, a big man with a hard face, gave me a look that said, *now you tell me.*

I watched as they gingerly carried the box to Stutka's car, slid it across the back seat, and closed the door without a slam.

"Unless you examine those specimens under very careful conditions," I warned, "you put yourself at great risk."

"Oh, no risk, Dr. Armstrong. We have one of the finest minds in the field and access to the laboratory resources."

"Where?"

"Never mind," he smiled. It was the kind of smile a nasty child makes before kicking the dog. I suddenly got very nervous.

"Mr. Stutka," I said. "I don't know what you plan to do with those rocks, but I don't think you fully understand their power."

"It's you who don't understand," he said. "Power is what this is all about. It's all it's *ever* about."

Stutka turned to Romero and held out a hand. Romero handed him his automatic and Stutka turned and aimed at me.

"Sorry, Doc, but business is business."

I saw him squint and then there was a flash and explosion as he pulled the trigger.

A burst of fire exploded in my chest. The impact pushed me backwards and then I was lying in the dirt.

I was on my back. I think my eyes were slitted to just the barest opening; I could still see the cold, white light they were using, and their shadows came closer and loomed over me. My vision focused and the horrible faces of Romero and O'Brien were visible in the gloom. Romero said, "Good shot, boss." Then I closed my eyes.

So this is what it's like to die, I thought.

I heard the men pile back into their cars, I heard engines come to life, then I heard them drive away.

I don't know how long I lay there, but the next thing I knew was that my chest was in agony and there was a ringing in my ears.

I got up, gasping at the pain in my ribs. I grabbed the fender of my Lasalle and got to my feet.

So, I'm not dead, I thought.

It was nearly dawn. The sun was not up, but there was the subtle glow in the horizon that promised a new day. I knew that soon the birds would be singing. I sat on the running board and took off my gloves before pulling the protective boots away from my shoes. Each movement was excruciating. Then I got unsteadily to my feet and pulled down the protective trousers before slipping out of the tunic. I panted in pain, wondering if moving would shift the bullet lodged in my chest, and if that would do even greater damage.

I checked the tunic. There was a bullet hole right through the chest. The thick material and interlocking threads of protective material would have slowed down a bullet, but not stopped it completely. I should be very dead. Then I put my hand over my heart and saw where the bullet tunneled through my breast pocket.

Then I reached into my jacket and found my new copy of *Tarzan and the Lion Man*. I opened the book and found, flattened between its wet and swollen pages, the automatic's bullet.

Great. Now I have to get another copy.

I tossed the book into the back seat, pointed my Lasalle at the sunrise, and set out for home.

CHAPTER SEVEN

I did some hard thinking on the drive back.

Stutka said that he had one of the finest minds to help him with the stones. Did he mean Dick? I had to hold out hope that my friend was still alive. And what laboratory resources was he talking about…?

Then I remembered that Miss Welles said that Stutka's base of operations was in New York. If Stutka needed a first-class lab, the closest place he would find one was in New York. It was guesswork, but it was guesswork that made sense. If I was going to find Dick and the rocks, the first place I had to look was in the big city.

The sun was just coming up as I parked in front of my apartment. I left the containment suit in the backseat and quietly worked the lock of the front door. As I stepped into the vestibule, Mrs. Bradbury opened her door.

"Good morning, Dr. Armstrong."

"Good morning."

"Out all night again?" she grinned.

I gibbered something unintelligible.

"Was it that Miss Welles," she asked, grin ever-bigger, "or were you in 'jail' again?"

"Actually," I said, heading up the stairs, "I was shot."

She laughed. "You *are* a card!" and she went back inside.

My head was ringing and each breath took effort. I put up some coffee and stepped into the bathroom. I took off my jacket and tie, then my shirt and undershirt.

There was a nasty bruise on the left side of my chest. I moved my arm and rivulets of pain ran across my chest. I wondered if some of the ribs were broken.

In the kitchen I wrapped a handful of ice in a dish towel and held it against my chest. I drank most of the pot of coffee once it was ready, eating eight pieces of toast with grape jelly.

Finished, I tossed the ice aside and climbed into a cold shower. After a shave and running a brush through my teeth, I felt human once more.

Stutka had a several hours start over me, but that did not matter all that much since I had no idea how to find him. I fought back the impulse to call Miss Welles once again—I still wanted to get the stones examined by Princeton scientists before I handed them over to the War Department.

I took my suitcase from the bottom of my closet and loaded it with clothes. Then I got into my old navy-blue pinstripe and put on my lucky red tie. I took the latest issue of *Amazing Stories* and tossed it on top of my clothes, along with four packs of Lucky Strikes. I also grabbed my calculations from last night, along with the photos of the pages from Mason's notebook.

I was back in my Lasalle and on the road before the clock struck eight. It would take nearly two hours to drive to New York and my exhausted brain was struggling with next steps. How do you find a gangster in New York? That should be easy—but how do you find a *particular* gangster? I can't just walk up to a policeman and ask. And I doubt Stutka was in the phone book. There was no clearing house or directory for criminals that I knew of. Just how was I going to find him?

I had no choice but to just press on and hope something came to me.

I was happy to emerge from the oppressive darkness of the Holland Tunnel and into the open air of New York. Even though it was after nine, the streets were crowded with cars and people. I sought out the spire of the Empire State Building and headed north.

There are many people who love New York. As I drove uptown, I saw a vibrant city filled with happy, on-the-go people. New York is an unusually clean city (immaculate, compared to some of the places I've seen in my travels), and it has a vibrancy and energy that is already becoming mythic.

All around me, people hailed cabs, men whistled at beautiful women, and the overhead elevated train passed by, throwing off a shower of sparks. Corner newsstands sold pulp magazines and fruit, and every few blocks stood a paperboy with the morning edition.

But where most people are galvanized by the almost supernatural energy of the place, New York leaves me mostly exhausted. I was raised in a small-town, and I think it would've been impossible for me to get through school if I grew up here: the noise, the distractions and the manic pace negatively affected the wiring in my brain: like a radio I could not turn off.

I decided to stay in the New Yorker Hotel while I made my plans. I had stayed there last year during an astronomical conference sponsored by Griffith Observatory and liked it a lot. It stood in the shadow of the Empire State Building, a forty-three-story monument to Streamlined Modern architecture. The Empire State Building and its surroundings always make me think of Doc Savage[16], the scientist-hero in the pulp magazines who lived on the eighty-sixth floor of the world's tallest building.

I parked off Eighth Avenue and hoofed it over to the hotel. The lobby was just as I remembered it: a two-tier, Art Deco wonderland. I walked beneath chandeliers all hard right-angles and clean lines, and past long, frescoed murals in the Modernist style, as if they were painted by robots.

The carpet was plush and its design had an almost mathematical precision. There was a second-tier balcony from which revelers could look down into the lobby. Here it was, hours before lunchtime, and already the city's beautiful people were drinking cocktails.

The man at the reception desk was small, trim and finicky, with a

---

16   Doc Savage was the hero of 187 pulp novels written between 1933 and 1949. The majority of the novels were written by Lester Dent (1904-1959). A surgeon, inventor, world-explorer, adventurer and philanthropist, Doc lived on the 86th Floor of the Empire State Building. When not in harness, he retired to The Fortress of Solitude in the Arctic, where he worked on his many inventions. Known as The Man of Bronze because of his deep tan, Doc was the template for the later comic book hero, Superman.

pencil-thin mustache that did not help him look like Ronald Colman[17] in the slightest bit. He looked at me expectantly.

"I'd like a room."

He opened a large book. "Of course. Do you have a reservation?"

I reached into my pocket for my card. "No. I'm Dr. Armstrong from Princeton University. I'm in town unexpectedly on business."

His eyes went from my card to me. "We are very crowded at the moment," he said.

"I'll pay in advance."

"I was about to say, we're very crowded at the moment, but I could let you have a room on the thirty-third floor."

"That would be fine."

He pulled out the registration book and dipped a pen in the inkwell. As I signed the registrar he said, "We have another scientist staying here. On your floor."

"Really?" I said, writing my address. "Who is that?"

"A man named Nikola Tesla.[18] Ever hear of him?"

"Tesla is here! Of course, I heard of him."

"We try to keep most scientists, academics and ..." I'm sure he would've said *cranks* "... and writers on the same floor. They appreciate the company."

"Thanks. I appreciate it."

"See what I mean." He slapped the bell beside the registration book. "Boy!"

A young man of about sixteen in a red jacket with gold buttons and cream-colored trousers was at my side in a moment. He smiled and saluted us both.

"Take the gentleman to 3324."

The young man picked up my suitcase and we went to the elevator. The elevator doors were made of gleaming brass with designs of tight, concentric circles. The doors opened and a small, red-headed girl dressed like the bellhop, except she wore a skirt of the same color rather than pants, worked the mechanism.

"First time in New York?" the bellhop asked.

"No," I said. "I'm right nearby in Princeton."

"Come often?"

---

17   Ronald Colman (1891-1958) was a suave leading man famous from the silent era throughout the 1950s. His pencil-thin mustache was his trademark.

18   Nikola Tesla (1856-1943) was a Serbian-American inventor, electrical engineer, futurist and—screwball best known for his contributions to the modern alternating current (AC) electricity supply system.

"Not if I can help it."

"Ah," he said." You're going to the egghead floor."

I couldn't help it. That made me grin. "Yeah. That's me."

The elevator operator smiled us out the door and the boy led me to my room. It was a pleasant room, cream-colored, like his trousers, with a three-line maroon trim running along the top. Four conical lamps lined the walls, and when the bellhop opened the curtains, sunlight flooded the room. There was a desk, couch and a few armchairs, a radio at the bar, and a small bedroom and bathroom beyond.

"If you need anything," he said, putting my suitcase on the floor, "call down for Nick and I'll bring it right up."

I reached into my pocket and gave him a nickel. "I'll remember that." I walked with him to the door. "Oh, there is one thing. Have you ever heard of someone named Leon Stutka?"

He looked at me, face blank. "Nope. Is he staying at this hotel?"

I smiled. "Just a stab in the dark. Thanks."

I quickly unpacked in the bedroom and put *Amazing Stories* on my night table. That made me think of my damaged Burroughs book, and I decided to go to the nearest newsstand for another copy while I considered what to do next.

Despite the pain in my chest and sleeping for only a few hours on the side of a deserted road, I figured I was doing pretty well, all things considered. I stepped out into the morning sunshine and looked up at the Empire State Building, hoping that I might see a dirigible mooring at the top.

No such luck. I decided to walk towards Fifth Avenue and Herald Square. Right at the corner of Macy's, on Seventh and Thirty-fourth, was a newsstand. I went over and examined the magazine selection.

There were the usual pulps—*Thrilling Wonder Stories, Weird Tales, G8 and His Battle Aces, The Phantom Detective*—and there, too, were the only two I followed regularly, aside from *Amazing: Doc Savage* and *The Shadow*.[19]

Both looked pretty terrific. The Doc Savage yarn was something called *The Metal Master*, and on the cover, Doc was parachuting to the earth with a beautiful, auburn-haired woman in his arms. (It was probably his cousin, Pat Savage. She was always trouble.) The Shadow cover was especially

---

19   *Amazing Stories* is a Science Fiction pulp magazine started in 1926 by futurist Hugo Gernsback (1884-1967). The influence of Gernsback and Amazing cannot be overestimated. The Shadow was a pulp hero who first appeared in 1931 and lasted until 1949, the majority of the novels written by magician Walter B. Gibson (1897-1985). Just as Doc Savage was a great influence on Superman, much of Batman can be traced to The Shadow. *Thrilling, Weird Tales, G-8* and *Phantom Detective* were also influential pulp magazines.

terrific. It was for something called *The Voodoo Master*. He was bathed in a lurid red light, and the black-clad avenger was firing his twin automatics into the distance.

Doc and The Shadow would make pretty short work of Stutka, I thought.

I checked for new, hardcover books, but there was no trace of the Tarzan. I found a few Agatha Christie novels and a Philo Vance,[20] and even a pocket-edition of Sherlock Holmes. I hadn't read Sherlock Holmes since I was a boy.

And then it hit me.

At this moment, I didn't need Doc Savage or The Shadow. I needed Sherlock Holmes. What would Mr. Sherlock Holmes do to find Stutka?

Well… first off, he wouldn't get in this fix. But if he was, I knew exactly what he would do. He'd call the Baker Street Irregulars!

I put the book back and ran all the way back to the New Yorker. A yellow cab grazed the heels of my shoes as it sped by me on Eighth Avenue.

I raced through the lobby and went back to reception desk. The same trim, mustached man was there. He turned as I reached the desk.

"Can I help you?"

"Yes!" I said. "I'm looking for a young boy."

His face darkened.

"Dr. Armstrong, this is not *that* kind of hotel."

"Huuuh?"

Then, he leaned closer and lowered his voice. "But, if you're interested, I know of a gentlemen's establishment downtown."

I blinked. "No, you misunderstand. I'm looking for boys who spend most of their time on the street. Um, like corner newsboys."

He looked at me, uncomprehending. "Never mind," I said, walking away. I crossed through the lobby and breathed a sigh of relief when I saw Nick. I walked up and clapped him on the shoulder.

"Nick," I said. "I need a young man."

He looked at me. "Wrong number. But I can dig one up for you."

I blinked again. "No, no. I'm looking for a newsboy. I have an errand for him."

He squinted. "What kind of errand?"

"I need information, and I'm pretty sure a newsboy and his friends can get it for me."

---

20 Nearly forgotten today, Philo Vance was perhaps the most famous "gentleman detective" of the 1920s and 1930s. He was created by art critic and dilettante Willard Huntington Wright (1888-1939), writing under the name S.S. Van Dine. The 12 novels that make up the corpus can still be read with satisfaction.

"Got it. I'll be up in ten minutes."

I smiled as he ran off and lit out for the elevator.

I had barely gotten to my room and taken my jacket off when there was a knock at the door. I opened it and gasped. Nick was on the threshold with someone I could've sworn was the double of Leon Stutka.

He was a slim, young boy of twelve or so with short, blonde hair and hard eyes. He and Stutka could be father and son—or doubles, as they were the same height.

Of course, Stutka would have blanched at the boy's clothes. He was dressed in a rough, flannel shirt, corduroy knickers, high socks and scuffed shoes. Bright red suspenders completed his kit.

"Come in!" I made way.

"Doc, this is Albert Frost," Nick said. "He sells papers on the corner for the hotel."

I stretched out my hand. "Hello, Mr. Frost. I'm Dr. Armstrong."

He took the hand with deep mistrust. "I don't need a doctor, dammit."

"Just call me Pete," I said. "Would you like to make two dollars?"

He balled his fists and put them on his hips. "How?"

"It's legal," I said. "I figured a young businessman like you would have lots of contacts, and I need them to find a friend of mine."

He folded his arms. "If he's your friend, how come you don't know where he is?"

"What are you, a lawyer?" I shrugged. "We fell out of touch. You'll understand when you get older."

"Who is he?"

"A man named Leon Stutka. I've heard these days that he's, um, well... a gangster."

Albert sneered. "You a cop?"

"No."

"Swear?"

"Scout's honor."

"That's all right, then." Satisfied, he asked, "What else can you tell me about him?"

"He's blond, very well dressed, and he's a midget."

"No kiddn'?"

"Nope. About your height, I think, but he's full grown and you'll get much bigger. I need to know where he lives, where he spends most of his time, anything you can find out. Do you think you can do it?"

"Mister, I got friends on every street corner in this city. If he's in New

York, we can find him."

"Then it's a deal?"

"No."

"No?"

"No."

I looked at Nick then back at Albert. "Why not?"

"I can't do it for two bucks."

"How much?"

"Two bucks now. And four bucks when I bring you the dope. Take it or leave it."

"Six dollars!" I reached into my pocket.

"And two for Nick."

"What?"

Nick shrugged, as if to say, *kids these days*.

I peeled off two dollars for the kid and handed another two to Nick. "When do you think you will have something for me?"

Albert neatly folded the dollar bills and stuffed them deep into his sock. "Are you kiddn'? A midget gangster? I'll have a line on him before tonight."

"I'm paying for results."

"Keep your shirt on Dick Tracy,[21]" he said. When he said it, it sounded more like *schoit* then *shirt*. "I'll be back. Thanks for the tip, Nick."

Albert turned on his heel and was out of the door. Nick and I were now alone. To my dismay, he did not offer to return the two dollars.

"Doc, if you need anything, you know where to find me."

"If I don't go broke first."

And now, I had nothing to do but wait.

~~~

By one that afternoon, I was beginning to feel the effects of exhaustion and gunshot. I hadn't eaten anything but toast that morning, and I needed to get out and find something to eat.

I had nodded off in an armchair by the window. The afternoon sun was warm on the back of my head; probably another reason I nodded off. I shook myself awake and straightened my tie in the bathroom mirror. I ran my palms over my jacket to smooth the wrinkles and put it on.

---

21   Dick Tracy was the titular hero of the celebrated comic strip created by Chester Gould (1900-1985) in 1931. The adventures of the rough-hewn Tracy still appear in newspapers. Actors Warren Beatty and Madonna starred in a 1990 film version of the strip.

I locked the door and padded down the corridor when a door up ahead opened. It was just dumb luck that I saw them before they saw me.

William Benet stepped over the threshold and turned, talking with whomever was in the hotel room. His simple, elegant gray suit was highlighted by a white boutonnière and he carried his Homburg in his hand.

I dashed into an alcove and edged forward as much as possible to see what I could.

"Thank you again," Benet said, extending his hand to the figure within the room. "Remember, this remains vital to the security of your country. The country that took you in and supported you all these years."

Whatever was the reply from within, I did not hear it.

Benet listened and then blinked as the door was closed in his face. He bristled, smoothed his mustache with the back of his hand, and made for the elevator. I watched until the silver and chrome elevator doors opened and he barked an order at the operator.

Alone again, I stepped out of the alcove. I made my way down the corridor and stood outside the room Benet had visited. The Art Deco numbers read 3327.

I stood there, dumbly registering the numbers, when the door suddenly opened. Instantly I found myself looking up into the face of a tall, thin man with the eyes of a hypnotist.

"Yes?" the man asked. His voice was deep and heavily accented.

"Pardon me," I said. "I must have the wrong room."

The man paused, gazing openly. I returned his look. He was tall, very tall, and thin, very thin. His blue pinstriped suit was once of excellent quality, but now showed signs of wear. His jacket was open, and I saw that his trousers were supported by a belt wrapped around a skeletal waist. The hands were large and thick with veins.

His white hair was brushed back and his penetrating eyes looked down on me from beneath darkened brows. The orbs themselves, deep within his skull, lie hidden in shadow.

"Have we met before?" I asked. "You look very familiar."

"Perhaps you have seen my photograph in the newspaper, young man." His voice was perfect for radio, and his outrageous accent instantly gave his every word a melodramatic intonation. He reminded me so much of Bela Lugosi,[22] it was frightening. "My name is Nikola Tesla."

---

22   Bela Lugosi (1882-1956), born Bela Blasko in Hungary, was, of course, famous for his portrayal of Count Dracula on the American stage and in the 1931 film version of *Dracula*. Actors to this day imitate him, to one degree or another, when playing the character. Lugosi was celebrated for his flamboyant screen style, as well as his—unusual diction.

I didn't bother to contain my surprise. "How do you do?" I extended my hand. "I'm Dr. Peter Armstrong, a scientist at the Princeton Observatory."

He smiled—a rather sinister smile, if truth be told—and took my hand. "A colleague," he said, much like Dracula would say, *soup's on*. "It is always a pleasure." Holding onto my hand he nudged me into the room. He smelled of turmeric, damp wool and Wildroot Hair Cream-Oil. "Come. It is always a pleasure to speak to a—colleague."

I found myself on the other side of his door and heard it close behind me. He now released my hand and placed an arm over my shoulders as if we were boyhood friends. "I hear so much of the Princeton Observatory these days," he said, eating every word like cotton candy. "I would love to hear what progress you are making. Allow me to provide you with a drink."

He led me into the drawing room. A quick glance told me that Tesla had lived there for quite some time. The walls were covered with framed testimonials and proclamations, as well as various maps and a few photos of Tesla himself with other titans, like Edison, Wilson and Eiffel.[23]

The couch and armchair had seen heavy use in the past, and end tables were placed around the room, all covered in scientific journals and papers. There was a bar in the corner and Tesla went to it. I noticed his strange gait: he walked like a praying mantis.

"Do you like gin?" he asked. "It's my only weakness."

I didn't want a drink, as I was exhausted, underfed and very possibly concussed. But I thought to decline would somehow break the mood. "Do you have something less potent?"

Tesla stood at the bar, with his back to me. He poured a generous amount of Gordon's gin into a tumbler, then opened another bottle. "Sherry?" he asked with something like disdain.

"Yes, please."

He poured sherry into an aperitif glass and returned to where I sat, looming over me like a vulture. "This is very old wine," he said. "I hope you will like it."

I took a sip. It was slightly rancid, I think. "It's delicious," I said.

"Excellent, Dr. Armstrong. Excellent."

I wish there was some way I could reproduce Tesla's bizarre speech patterns, pauses and intonation. What he just said sounded to my ear like:

---

23   Gustav Eiffel (1832-923) was a French engineer, remembered today for designing the Eiffel Tower in Paris, France. Thomas Alva Edison (1847-1931) is the most famous inventor of the 20th Century, responsible for the light bulb, the phonograph and moving pictures. Tesla was once employed by Edison and they grew to be great rivals. The Wilson mentioned is possibly former US President Woodrow Wilson (1856-1924).

XXXX-allant, DOK-tor ARM-strong........... XXXX-allant. He strode to the couch and sat, knees high, his beaky face peering at me like a vulture. "I do not approve of stimulants, but this is not a stimulant but a veritable elixir of life." He took a long swallow and laughed in his throat.

I took another sip. "Well, good stuff sure is hard to find." I moved to put my glass on an end table, but it was so overrun with books that I dared not. Instead, I placed it on the floor at my feet.

"No, no," Tesla said, waving a hand like Chandu the Magician.[24] "If you do that, the monster might get it."

"Monster?"

There came a rustle from the room beyond. In seconds a tiny, chocolate-colored chihuahua scuttled into the room and made a bee-line for my glass.

I reached for my sherry but Tesla made a long arm and plucked the dog from the floor and placed it on his lap. "He is very fast, my friend."

"Sorry," I said. I moved aside some books and made room for my glass. "What's your dog's name?"

"Alva,[25]" he said, as if he had a boil on his tongue.

"Ah."

"So—you are an astronomer," he said, sipping gin.

"Yes."

"Tell me of the heavens."

That was a tall order. "What do you want to know?"

"For some time I have believed that human organisms are only part of astrochemistry, controlled by radial forces from the sun."

I like to think I'm fairly smart, but I had no idea what that meant exactly. Astrochemistry is the intersection of chemistry and astronomy, but I'm more a practitioner than a theorist. I said, "What do you mean?"

He leaned further over his knees. Alva was trapped on his lap and mewled. "I mean that great rays from the sun have created all life. I believe that there is some super-violet ray of life-giving properties. It is possible that cosmic rays are the source of life itself, as is believed by many of our most profound scientists."

"You think—radiation is the source of life?'

"Radiation. Cosmic rays. Or perhaps something else." He pointed a

---

24 *Chandu the Magician* was a popular radio series that ran, on-and-off, from 1932 through 1950. An American who learned the mystic arts in the Mysterious East, Chandu was the precursor to such characters as Dr. Strange and Mandrake the Magician. Oddly enough, Bela Lugosi played both Chandu and his nemesis, Roxor, in alternate film versions.
25 "Alva" was also the middle name of Tesla's former employer and rival, Thomas Alva Edison. The name could not have been a coincidence.

long finger at me, his skeleton frame throwing fantastic shadows on the walls. "You mother gave you birth, but you father was—the lightning—or—something more elemental. Mark my words. Life here, started …" and here he pointed heavenward, "out there. In the farthest reaches of sidereal space."

"Ah—Dr. Tesla—"

"Mr. Tesla." He leaned back in the chair with a grimace. "I have no advanced degree."

"Mr. Tesla, then. I cannot speak for Princeton, but if there is anything I can do to help you in your researches, you have only to ask."

He looked at me, little bolts of lightning flashing in those dark eyes.

"Young man, why are you here?"

I picked up my glass. "I'm in town, seeing the sights."

"A lie is a very poor foundation for a friendship."

I sipped the foul sherry once more. "Are you offering friendship?"

"Are we not part of the same brotherhood? The Brotherhood of Science."

"Science is a tool for finding the truth," I said. "Not a truth in and of itself."

He smiled. I could see no teeth; indeed, his mouth was just a blackened grin. "You—have possibilities."

"Thanks. I think."

"I will tell you of my work. And then—you will tell me why you are here."

"I just said—"

"Come, my young friend. Here, alone in these rooms, just the three of us…"

I realized he meant the dog.

"Just the three of us, let us know the truth."

Frankly, I was spooked. If Tesla pulled a cape from the cupboard and turned into a bat, I would not be surprised. Also, the longer I played games, the longer Dick Pierson was in danger.

"Fair enough," I said. "You first."

He was silent a moment longer, as he continued to evaluate me. Finally he put down his gin and got to his feet. He extended a bony hand. It was white and bloodless in the cold hotel light.

"Come, my friend."

I got to my feet. He walked through the room with the queer praying mantis gait, Alva following at his heels.

I quickly realized that Tesla had two suites here at the New Yorker, and the cojoining door was left open. I followed him into a darkened room and he closed the door behind us. I felt Alva pawing around my ankles in the dark.

The light flicked on and I saw that Tesla had converted the bedroom of his second suite into a mini electrical-laboratory. Coils stood silent sentinel atop a black-tiled table, snippets of electricity snaking from the bottom to the top in a steady rhythm. There were several black boxes, each festooned with switches, dials and gages. There were even the odd beaker and Bunsen burner.

I realized instantly that the breadth of Tesla's scientific interests dwarfed mine by any conservative measure. I held my breath and wondered what came next.

"You admire my apparatus, my friend?" he asked.

"It's quite a layout."

"All of this equipment, all of my electrical power, and still I have only scraped the surface of the many forces that surround us."

"The lifeforce itself?"

He grinned. He flicked a switch on the table and a machine whirred to life. It threw off a greenish light that underlit Tesla's skull-like face. When he grinned, the effect was otherworldly.

"If the Brotherhood of Science means anything, it must make an end to the machineries of war. Do you agree?"

"I don't know."

His face fell.

"What I mean is—well, I guess it's our job to make discoveries, and for humanity to use them as they see fit."

"Humanity!" he sniffed. He rose to his full height, hands aloft like a hypnotist. "In past ages, the law governing the survival of the fittest roughly weeded out the less desirable strains. Then man's new sense of pity began to interfere with the ruthless workings of nature. As a result, we continue to keep alive and to breed the unfit."

"Who decides who is unfit and who is not?"

He continued as if he did not hear me. "The only method compatible with our notions of civilization and the race is to prevent the breeding of the unfit by sterilization and the deliberate guidance of the mating instinct. Several European countries and a number of states here in America sterilize the criminal and the insane. No one who is not a desirable parent should be permitted to produce progeny. A century from now it will no more occur to a normal person to mate with a person eugenically unfit than to marry a habitual criminal."

I didn't know what to say to something to patently—crazy. It sounded more like something from our English or Political Science departments than the hard sciences. I bunted. "You were saying about war?"

"War destroys the strong, the dedicated, the brave. To destroy the means of war is to maintain a healthy people. And that is why I have dedicated my life to the—Teleforce."

"Teleforce?"

"Why, my friend, do we persist in the savage practice of killing each other off?" Here he tapped his chest. "I inherited from my father, an erudite man who labored hard for peace, an intractable hatred of war. Like other inventors, I believed at one time that war could he stopped by making it *more* destructive." He leaned forward, his eyes gleaming in the green light. "But I found that I was mistaken. I underestimated man's combative instinct, which will take more than a century to breed out. We cannot abolish war by outlawing it. We cannot end it by disarming the strong. War *can* be stopped, not by making the strong weak, but by making every nation, weak or strong, able to defend itself!"

"And the Teleforce will do that?"

"Every gift of science has been corrupted, perverted into mechanisms of destruction. Devices created for defense are, in turn, turned into weapons of offense. This nullified the value of the improvement for purposes of peace. But I was fortunate enough to evolve a new idea and to perfect means which can be used chiefly for defense." Another puff of the chest. "If it is adopted, it will revolutionize the relations between nations. It will make any country, large or small, impregnable against armies, airplanes, and other means for attack. My invention requires a large plant, but once it is established it will be possible to destroy anything, men or machines, approaching within a radius of two hundred miles. It will, so to speak, provide a wall of power offering an insuperable obstacle against any effective aggression."

It all sounded like he had said it many times already, like an actor reciting lines that come too naturally.

"Without the ability to attack, the fact of war becomes obsolete, my friend."

"I don't think you could do that entirely without making people obsolete."

I don't think he heard me. He continued on. "My discovery ends the menace of airplanes or submarines, but it ensures the supremacy of the battleship, because battleships may be provided with some of the required equipment. There might still be war at sea, but no warship could successfully attack the shore line, as the coast equipment will be superior to the armament of any battleship."

"So you're saying you could build a wall of power that surrounds people and places, making them impregnable?"

"That is the direction that my researches have taken. I could destroy anything within two hundred miles, and still provide this invisible, protective shield of power."

"So..." it sounded ridiculous when said out loud, but I felt I had to say it. "So—you created a *death ray*?"

Tesla elevated his eyebrows and threw out his bottom lip—like an actor who, whatever his emotions, he telegraphs them to the back row. "I? A death ray? No, my friend."

"But—"

He stomped his foot. "I have not created a so-called death ray. Rays do not enter into this equation because they cannot be produced in requisite quantities and diminish rapidly in intensity with distance." He waved an arm to encompass our surroundings. "All the energy of New York City—approximately two million horsepower—transformed into rays and projected twenty miles, could not kill a human being, because, according to a well-known law of physics, it would disperse to such an extent as to be ineffectual."

"But you said—"

"My apparatus projects particles which may be relatively large or of microscopic dimensions, enabling us to convey to a small area at a great distance trillions of times more energy than is possible with rays of any kind. Many thousands of horsepower can thus be transmitted by a stream thinner than a hair, so that nothing can resist. This wonderful feature will make it possible, among other things, to achieve undreamed-of results in television, for there will be almost no limit to the intensity of illumination, the size of the picture, or distance of projection."

I have been hearing about television for some time now, but the promise of movies inside my own home seemed like small compensation for the risk of long-distance destruction.

"How far have you gotten with this?" I asked.

"My theories are nearly ready for a test!" he said. "But ..." and here he lowered his voice, as if he was afraid Alva was taking notes. "But—I must safeguard my findings. I must ensure that they do not fall into the wrong hands."

Finally Tesla was saying something that made sense. I had harvested those stones and wanted to keep tabs on them before I let Benet get hold them. It was one of the many reasons I had to get them back before it was too late. It was an instinct I understood and respected.

"I approve of your reservations, Mr. Tesla."

"The secrets of my Teleforce are something that governments—any government—would kill to control. That is why I must be ever vigilant. Ever careful! Even the small working models I have made I keep under lock and key."

"Working models?"

Tesla stepped back from the table and took a key from his pants pocket. He unlocked a drawer at the bottom of his laboratory table and took from it a gun unlike anything I had ever seen before.

It was a metallic blue with a long barrel ending in three concentric rings. The grip was bulb-shaped and bright yellow with a lightning-shaped zigzag engraved on the sides. It was like something from Buck Rogers brought to life.

Nikola Tesla took his ray gun and pointed it at me.

"Yes, my friend," he said. "And now it has come time for you to tell me about yourself."

"Like what?"

"What really brings you here?" His black, cavernous smile grew wider. "And, more importantly, tell me of the stones uncovered by Dr. Mason Cooley."

CHAPTER EIGHT

I gulped hard.

"And if I don't, are you going to shoot me?"

Tesla laughed—or what could be called a laugh. It was more like Dracula slowly saying *heh-heh-heh.*

"Shoot you, my friend?" He regarded his Buck Rogers ray gun, then extended his arm, the barrel level with my head. "You have been reading too many pulp magazines."

Tesla pulled the trigger and there was a metallic *click.*

My heart skipped a beat, but didn't stop.

"It's tin, my friend," he said, putting it down. "You don't think that I had invented a *ray gun*, did you?"

Now that I was breathing again, I reached out. "Let me see that."

Tesla handed me the gun and I examined it. It *was* a Buck Rogers toy ray gun. I heaved a sigh of relief. "What are you doing with this thing?"

"I have a fondness for you—junk culture," Tesla said. "I cannot get enough of you Buck Rogers and Flash Gordon."

"Me neither."

"It takes my mind from more pressing concerns." Tesla bent over and scooped Alva into his hands. "Let us have another drink. Are you sure you will not have a gin? It is my only weakness."

I followed him back into the parlor and let him pour me a gin. I needed it. He handed me the glass and clinked his own against mine. "To the Brotherhood of Science, and the brave new world it hopes to create."

I wasn't sure that I wanted any part of a world envisioned by Nikola Tesla, but I took the drink. If anything, his gin seemed even more rancid than his sherry. I made a face, but fortunately his back was turned as he made his way back to the couch.

Alva jumped on the couch beside him. "And now, my friend, tell me of Mason Cooley."

I looked into my glass, wondering what was the best thing to say.

"You should know," he said before I could start, "that I know Dr. Cooley."

That got my attention. "You know Mason?"

Alva climbed onto Tesla's lap and the old man absently patted the dog's head. "It was my impression that Mason knows everybody."

"Knew everybody."

Tesla's face fell. "Knew? Has something happened to him?"

"He's dead." I swallowed more gin.

Tesla grew even more grave—which is like saying ice grew even more cold. "I think it is time we compared notes."

"You first."

"No."

"No?"

"No."

"Why no?"

"Because, my friend, people want things from *me*. People like your Mr. Benet."

"He's not mine."

"No matter. I know my answer already, but what I know may be of benefit to you. So—you first." He then gave me that *heh-heh-heh*.

I don't know why—especially after becoming so fluent in lying to everyone from Elson to Miss Welles—but I decided to tell Tesla everything. I started with the kidnapping and didn't stop until my trip to New York. All the while he listened, his great brows knitted over his glistening eyes. For all I knew, he was in a trance.

Finally he said, "So, Mason Cooley is dead."

"Yes."

He nodded. "And now, my young friend, I will talk to you. First off …" here he gazed into space. If he was an actor, I would've said he was overdoing it. "First off, I can tell you that Mason had gambling trouble."

"How do you know?"

"He borrowed money from me. Lots of it—more than I could spare."

"I didn't know."

"I also know that he was desperate. If these hellish rocks had any value at all, he would've sold them. Quickly. If not, the gangsters would have killed him. As simple as that."

"So you believe me about the rocks? I know it's outlandish, but it's not baloney."

Nikola Tesla rose and poured himself another gin. "Outlandish—perhaps. Baloney—perhaps not. There are many things under the sun." He drank and said, "Would you care for another?"

"No, thanks."

He poured and sat once more. "What is you theory regarding these—Lucifer Stones?"

I shrugged. "I have no idea. I would imagine it's some kind of weapon. Probably developed in Europe. The Nazis would be a good bet, as I believe they came from Germany."

Tesla's hypnotic gaze traveled into the distance—like he was communing with the spirits. Then he came to himself and said, "Perhaps. But you still have not determined what gives them their strange properties?"

"No. And I don't have time to figure it out. I have to find Pierson and get them back before I do any real analysis. Now let me ask you one. Why did they put the bag on Dick?"

"That's easy, my friend. Once Stutka traced the journals to Pierson's house, he thought he could find the stones on his own. He had the journal—but he did not know the vital pages were missing. Why keep Mason around—an old and sick man—when he could just *put the bag on* a younger, healthier expert?"

"But they have the stones now?" I took a deep breath. "Do you think they've killed Dick?"

"To die. To be really dead. That must be glorious."

"What?"

He looked up and his eyes burned into mine. "There are far worse things awaiting man than death."

"What the hell does that mean?"

"Never mind," he said. "Now, I will tell you of your Mr. Benet. He told me a story similar to yours, but without the fact that Dr. Cooley is dead."

"What did he want?"

"What they all want!" he said. He leapt to his feet with more energy than I expected. Alva dashed to the side of the couch and cowered.

"What they all want!" he continued. "The secret to my Teleforce. And, more important, if there was a way to merge the power of the stones you found with that of my—ah, defensive ray."

"Is there a way?"

"I do not know." His brows knitted. "The challenge has always been how to concentrate the power of any powerful beam so it does not dissipate. But, perhaps, there is a way."

"What did you tell him?"

"What I tell all of them—that my genius is not for sale."

Well, that's a relief, I thought.

"But that does not help you," he said. "What helps you is finding this man, this—dwarf. And then tracking down you friend."

"Yes. Will you help me?"

"Yes."

"How?"

"To properly analyze these stones, the dwarf Stutka must have a well-equipped laboratory."

"Yes."

"These, my friend, cannot be built quickly without leaving a trace. There is always a trace in the natural world." His eyes hardened. "And finding traces is—exactly—what I do. I will find the laboratory. *You*—you find the dwarf."

I don't know why, but something in his commanding manner and outlandish presentation gave me a sense of—security. It was like being on the Devil's good side. I put out my hand. "Thank you."

Tesla shook my hand and scooped up his dog. "Now go. You have work and so have I." He led me through the cluttered room and I stood while he unlocked the door. It was then that I noticed, there on a table beside his hotel key and a dirty cocktail glass, a book.

"You have *Tarzan and the Lion Man*," I said, picking it up.

"I have all of Burroughs' books," he said, turning the key. "They give me—inspiration."

"May I borrow this? I lost mine."

"Of course," he said, shooing me over the threshold.

He looked at me. "One more thing, my friend. Now that you changed the calculation that led you to the stones, you must reconfigure their origin."

I wasn't sure what he meant. I stuck the book under my arm and reached to pat Alva on the head. The chihuahua replied by snapping and snarling at me.

"Children of the night," Tesla said. "What music they make."

The door closed and I found myself alone in the corridor.

Now, on top of being exhausted, hungry and possibly concussed, I was slightly stewed. I decided to make for the hotel restaurant without further delay.

As I beelined to the elevator, I realized that while Nikola Tesla may be the most brilliant man alive today, I wouldn't trust him to walk my dog.

~~~

There is a restaurant in the lobby of The New Yorker that was a little too ritzy for my taste, but I was hungry and unwilling to roam around Manhattan when Nick and Albert might arrive with news at any minute. The eatery was almost an Art Deco temple of chrome and gleaming metal; it looked more like Dr. Frankenstein's laboratory than a restaurant. No wonder Tesla lived here.[26]

They made a crackerjack plate of ham and eggs, though, and I ate it while paging through *Tarzan and the Lion Man*. I hadn't gotten very far with it before, but it was Burroughs at his best. The book was about Tarzan and his lion friend coming upon a mad scientist in a jungle city full of talking gorillas. I was sopping up egg yolk with my toast when I realized that, at that moment, Tarzan had nothing on me.

There was a subplot about an expedition of movie people in the jungle making a Tarzan movie, along with an actor who could almost be an exact double for the Ape Man. Somehow, I found that part more hard-to-believe than scientifically altered talking gorillas.

---

26   There were actually several reasons for Tesla to feel at home in The New Yorker. The hotel was one of the most technologically advanced buildings in the world at the time, and it is very likely that Tesla often visited the hotel's giant power plant 70 feet below ground, which has been designated an engineering milestone by the IEEE.

"Yes. Will you help me?"

I paid for lunch (they gouged me for sixty cents) and I put my Tarzan under my arm and hit the lobby. No sign of Nick or Albert, though the desk clerk smiled at me in a fairly oily manner. I nodded and returned to my room.

I was nervy after recent events and opened the door to my room cautiously. It seemed to be empty. I checked the bathroom and bedroom and suddenly realized that bed looked very appealing at that moment. I untied my shoes, loosened my tie and lay on top of the bedspread.

I would only sleep a few moments, I promised myself.

The very next thing I knew, the room was dark and there was a hand over my mouth.

The hand was pressed tight against my face. I grabbed at the wrist before my eyes focused. As I wrenched myself free, I toppled off the bed and sprang to my feet.

Standing there, on the other side of the bed, was Tesla.

"You!"

"Good evening, my friend."

He was in the same dark suit and his vulture-like features seemed to glow in the twilight.

"What are you doing in my room?"

"I came to give you information."

"With your hand over my mouth?" I could still detect his scent on my lips.

"I could not have anyone know that we were meeting." He looked from side to side—his over-developed sense of drama strong as ever. "It would not do if you friend Benet learned of our alliance."

I blinked myself more awake. The venetian blinds were down but open, and the late afternoon sun was dimming. The clock on my night table told me it was nearly five thirty.

I stood there, looking at Nikola Tesla, the bed between us.

"You could offer me a drink, my friend."

"I don't have anything on hand."

"A pity." One skeletal hand reached into his inside breast pocket and pulled out a slip of paper. "I have tracked the laboratory. Calls to various contacts have told me that thousands of dollars' worth of scientific and electrical equipment has been shipped to this address over the last few days. It would take some time to construct it all. It improves the odds that you friend is still alive."

I came around the bed and took the paper. "It's on Duane Street. That's downtown, not far from Wall Street. Any cab could take you there."

"A home?"

"A brownstone. My friends could not identify the owner, but I am convinced that this is where you will find Pierson."

I gazed up into those hypnotic eyes. "I'm very grateful."

Before I could say another word there was a knock at the door. Tesla threw up his hands up like a startled marionette, his brows knit and bottom lip jutting forward.

"Do you expect anyone?"

"No," I said, walking to the parlor. "Wait here."

I closed the bedroom door and opened the front door. Standing there were Nick, still resplendent in his bellhop uniform, and Albert.

"Come in!" I threw the door wide.

The boys entered and took root in the living room. Albert went right to business.

"I found Stutka for you," he said. "And if you want my advice, you'd stay away from this 'old friend' of yours. I hear he's trouble."

I closed the door. "I know it. Where can I find him?"

Albert balled his hands into fists and put them on his hips. "Wait a minute. You said you'd pay six bucks."

"I did."

"Let's see da money."

I pulled cash from my wallet and peeled two two-dollar bills from it, and handed them to Albert.

"Wait a minute," he said. "We said six."

"And I gave you two before you left."

The hard little face under the tight blond hair got even harder for a moment, then broke out in a grin. "All right, mister. You can't blame a guy for trying."

"No indeed." I put my money away. "Where's Stutka?"

"I ain't got his home address, but he owns a nightclub on West Fifty-Sixth. It's called the Bit O' Honey, and he's there every night. Very swanky with lots of hot dames. But if you're in Dutch with this palooka, I'd keep away. They tell me he'd just as soon murder a fellow as look at him."

Albert's patios was not as melodramatic as Tesla's, but to my ear, what I just heard was *he'd just as soon moida a fella as look att'em*. I beginning to think I should keep these notes phonetically.

Tesla picked this time to open the bedroom door. He opened it, of course, with a sweeping gesture and glided into the room like phantom.

Albert actually let out a yelp and stood closer to Nick.

"Nerts," Nick said. "Dat's the egghead I was tellin' you about."

Tesla stood by the coffee table and glared at the two boys. Then he turned to me, gesturing with his long, skeletal fingers.

"You do not need to go to—The Bit O' Honey," he intoned, making it sound like a death sentence. "Go now. Get you friend and get out of town, while there is still time."

"Huh?" Nick asked.

"Long story," I said. I turned to Tesla. "That's easy to say. What do you suggest? I just knock on the door and say, *hello. I'm here to take the man you kidnapped. And while you're at it, just give me that pile of murder rocks.*"

"I have thought of that, as well," he said. He cast a baleful look at the boys, then reached into his hip pocket. In his hand was a small, black box, roughly the size of a packet of cigarettes. There was what looked like a tiny lightbulb at one end lengthwise, with a red button on top.

Tesla held it in his palm, and motioned over it with his other, eloquent hand. "This is a device I have been working on. Point with this end and it emits an electrical pulse strong enough to temporarily paralyze the central nervous system." He looked up at me, eyes burning under his brows. "It stops a man without killing him."[27]

Nick took a step forward. "Keen!" he said. "Can I have one?"

Tesla and I ignored him. "Are you sure it works?"

"I have tested it."

"How?"

"On the dog."

"You did that to Alva?"

Tesla brushed my concern aside. "Never mind. He is used to it." He then gave me that strange laugh—*heh-heh-heh*. He held it out to me. "Careful, my friend. It only stores four doses of electricity."

I took it.

"Careful!" Tesla barked. "You almost shot you self!"

I hefted it. It was cool in my hand and weighed next to nothing. "Thank you, Dr. Tesla."

"Mr. Tesla."

"Mr. Tesla," I corrected myself. "But I still have to get inside."

Tesla raised his brows, thinking. I pocketed the device and turned to the boys and when my eyes fell on Albert, it hit me.

---

[27] The similarities between Tesla's device and the contemporary TASER are remarkable. However, as will be seen, Tesla's device had a different mode of operation. No designs, papers or notes of the device were found among Tesla's papers, indicating his disappointment in its unreliability.

"Hey Albert. What size clothes do you wear?"

Albert's gaze went from Tesla to me and then took a step back. "Wrong number."

"No, no," I said. "I have a business proposition for you. You want to make a hundred dollars?"

"A hundred dollars?"

"Yeah. I'd have to buy you a suit, which you can keep, but I just need you for a few minutes to put on a suit and go somewhere downtown with me."

"I don't need no suit."

"You can wear it to church," I said. "Do you need a hundred dollars?"

"You are speakin' my language. What do you have in mind?"

"I need you to be with me when I knock on a door downtown. They're going to think you're someone else. And once I'm inside, get lost and forget all about it. Is it a deal?"

"No."

"No?"

"No, not for a hundred bucks we ain't got no deal."

"I don't have a lot more than that."

"I don't want no money."

"What do you want?"

He pointed at the device. "I want one of dem gizmos."

Tesla bolted upright—like *he* got a dose of electricity. He turned on Albert with that black and bottomless smile. "Young man. What would you do with it?"

"Are you kiddin? I got four brothers."

Tesla considered and slowly that smile crept back onto his face. "Of course—you must destroy it once you are done."

Albert crossed his heart and gave the Boy Scout salute.

Tesla nodded at me.

"Deal," I said.

"Wait a minute," Nick said.

"I cannot just hand these out," Tesla said, chin jutting forward. "They are not—*candy bars*."

"I don't want that," he said. He pointed to me. "I'll take the hundred."

"What for?"

"Keepin' my mouth shut."

I reached into my pocket and took five twenties. "You can do two things to earn that."

"Shoot," he was already putting the cash in his pocket.

"First, keep your mouth shut. And second, find a place where I can get Albert a suit at this hour, and a cab to get us there."

He was halfway to the door when he called over his shoulder, "I'm on it."

Like I said, at the rate I was going, Tarzan had nothing on me.

~~~

A few hours later I was in a cab with a twelve-year-old madder than a bag of snakes.

Nick had found a men's clothing store in Herald Square and Albert, protesting and scowling, was undressed, fitted for a double-breasted gray pinstripe suit, new shoes, spats and purple silk tie. He got a great deal of joy from the wide-brimmed black fedora, but vowed that he would ditch his *sissy clothes* the first chance he got. He spent the ride pulling on his collar, complaining that the pants were itchy and pulling his shirt cuffs lower and lower.

It was nearly eight-thirty when our cab rolled down Duane Street in lower Manhattan. I never understood the reason why, but I've read enough thrillers to know that the cab should always pull up one block short of the actual address. With that in mind, Albert and I climbed out of the cab on Warren Street and went westward. I was nervous—not only for myself, but for Albert. I made a point of repeating the ground rules.

"Now remember, Albert," I said. "All you have to do is ring the bell and stand there. As soon as the door opens, move aside and let me take over." I stopped and looked down at him. "Is that understood? Do. Not. Get. Involved."

"You think I'm stupid or something'?" he asked. "I ain't sticking my neck out for you. Hey, when do I get one of those gizmos?" Again, this sounded like *hay, when do I git onna doz gizmos?*

"When I come back."

"And what if you don't come back?"

"Thanks for the vote of confidence," I said. "Then you'll have to get one from Mr. Tesla."

"That stiff from Transylvania? Brother, include me out." He reached into his pocket, pulled out a package of Lucky Strikes and lit one.

"Hey, don't do that," I said.

"Why not?"

"You're just a kid. It'll stunt your growth."

"I'm not a kid. I'm twelve."

"Well, I didn't start smoking until I was fourteen. Put it out."

"Then you can just go on this little picnic alone," he said.

I thought for a minute. "Give me one," I said.

He flicked his pack upward and a Lucky stuck out. I grabbed the cigarette and then snatched the one in his hand and lit up with the hot end. He took his cigarette back and blew a lazy smoke ring.

"You *will* stunt your growth."

"Maybe I'll grow up to own a nightclub," he said.

I started us toward the address Tesla provided, more anxious than ever.

The address was a nondescript three-story home of grey stone. It was right across the street from a small park, and the streets of lower Manhattan were empty now that Wall Street had closed for the day. The house had a large bay window on the ground floor level, darkened by closed drapes. There were large stone pillars on either side of the front door, a door which was massive, oaken and had no peephole that I could detect. None of the windows on the upper floors were lit, and I could not tell if people were watching the street or not.

I crouched beside Albert. "I want you to go up, just like we said. Someone may pull the curtain back to look at you, but pay no attention. Ring twice if you have to. When the door opens, step aside."

He took a long pull on his cigarette and blew smoke. "And what if they don't answer?"

"I don't know. I'll think of something else, I guess. Let me go first, then count to ten and go to the door."

I walked as casually as I could manage past the house, then ducked behind one of the stone pillars.

Then Albert went to the door, took another pull on his cigarette, rang the bell and stood waiting, cool as ice. When he got no answer, he rang once more. I *think* I saw a flicker of his eyes—and believed he caught sight of someone checking on him from behind the bay window.

I heard the locks undone and reached into my pocket for Tesla's device.

A pause before opening. I held my breath.

Then, I heard the door open.

A voice said, "Hey, Boss. Why you ringin' the bell?"

I have no exact memory of it, but I stepped from behind the pillar, pushed Albert aside and brandished my Tesla device.

It was O'Brien. His scar flashed white and ugly in the corner streetlight. His eyes grew wide for the merest instant as I pointed the black box and its tiny bulb at him.

His hand was already reaching for his gun when I pressed the button. There was a loud crackling sound, and what looked like a streak of lightning shot from the box and hit O'Brien square in the chest.

O'Brien stiffened and fell like a redwood. He crashed backward into the house and I stepped over the threshold.[28]

I found myself in a dimly lit vestibule. The front door closed behind me—I paid little attention. I could see nothing in the gloom, and the fact that Tesla promised only four shots from his device and that Stutka's henchmen had loaded guns did little to increase my sense of security.

"Where now?"

I nearly jumped out of skin. I turned and found Albert standing behind me.

"Are you crazy?" I hissed in the darkness. "Get out of here before you get hurt."

"Shush!" he said.

We both heard a faint rustling upstairs.

"Go home!" I hissed again and opened the vestibule door.

The parlor was dark. I held the Tesla device before me with both hands and walked on the balls of my feet.

The furniture in the living room was covered with white sheets. I crept through the darkened room and next found myself in a dining room. A pale illumination from the streetlight outside fell upon the table. It had neither plates nor tablecloth; I had the feeling that Stutka did not use this residence with any regularity. The kitchen beyond was similarly empty.

"Hey!" a voice called out. "Who was at the door?"

I froze. The voice came from upstairs. I quickly padded to the stairs where the vestibule and living room intersected.

Whomever was upstairs opened a door, letting a long oblong of electric light spill down the stairway. And I gasped at what I saw.

Albert, still in his suit and fedora, stood at the bottom of the stairs, trapped in the light. His eyes turned to me, then traveled up the stairs.

He put a hand in his pants pocket and nudged his head to motion me over. Albert started up the stairs and I was right behind him, head down so my hat hid my face.

"Hey boss," the voice said. "What are you doing here?"

The man was now at the top of the stairs. Albert was two steps down from him and I four when I looked up.

Gold teeth glinted in the light.

---

28   Again, the exact specifications of the Tesla device are lost to history.

It was Romero. He was in a black shirt with a purple tie and gray striped pants held by suspenders. Under his left armpit was a holster, a silver-plated automatic inside it.

Romero's face dropped. Like O'Brien, he pegged me instantly. He reached for his gun.

I raised my Tesla device, but suddenly found Albert was between me and the target. I pushed the boy aside and heard him tumble down the stairs as I ran up the last four stairs in two jumps and grabbed at Romero.

Somehow in pushing past Albert I had lost the device. Romero already had his right hand on the butt of his gun. I grabbed his wrist and twisted him round.

Romero tried to point the gun at me, but I managed to keep the barrel averted. We tumbled out of the hallway and through the door of the room he had just left.

It was a bedroom. Romero staggered backwards, now grabbing his own gun hand with his left while I hung onto his right wrist for dear life.

Romero backed over the unmade bed, taking me with him. I was conscious of tumbling over the mattress and bedding, but somehow on the trip down to the floor Romero ended up on top of me.

He leered, his gold teeth wet and repulsive in the bedroom light. I was on my back and he straddled me, trying to wrest the gun from my grip.

My head was right beside the brass footboard. With a roar I jammed his wrists against it and he howled, dropping the gun. It slid away from me somewhere over my head.

Romero pulled back and clutched a handful of bedding. He dropped this over my head and scrambled off of my chest.

I rolled on my stomach and reached for his foot. I grabbed an ankle and he went down. I heard him clawing at the floor for the gun.

The blanket fell away from my face as I got to my knees. Romero, on his stomach on the floor in front of me, looked over on his shoulder, face panicked.

I just hopped on top of him, wrapping my arms around his head and neck in a lock. He scratched at my forearm and dug his nails into my hand. I might have been able to keep him in place until he passed out, but he snapped both thumbs out and jabbed upwards into my eyes.

The pain was excruciating. I let go and brought both hands to my eyes. And in doing so, I realized I had signed my own death warrant—Romero would now be free to grab the automatic and finish me off.

I took my hands away and my eyes opened to agonized slits. Romero was on his hands and knees, looking under the bed and night table for the gun. I thrust my forearms over my head and jumped, tackling him to the ground.

Now it was my turn to do a little damage. Romero lay on his right side and I sat on his hip, pinning him down. He clawed at my face with his left hand but I let loose with a haymaker that connected to his chin with a tremendous crash. He blinked, dazed, and I hit him again for good measure. He made a sad, mewling sound and then was out.

I sat on him, catching my breath. Once I was sure he wasn't moving, I got to my feet. I scanned the floor for his automatic, but did not see it. I would not waste my time on it.

I stepped into the hallway. There were three other doors—and if Stutka had any other goons on hand, they surely would have come at the sounds of struggle. I grabbed the handle of the closest door, but it was locked. The second was also locked. I anticipated the ugly chore of going through Romero's pockets for the keys when the third door opened at my grip.

It was a darkened room. I reached for the light switch and met with the second startling sight of the evening.

It was a cavernous room—the other two locked rooms had obviously had their walls taken down to make this one large space. Crates of laboratory equipment were piled in loose groupings, with several pieces of apparatus already unpacked. Piles of bricks in the far corner were already pressed into the creation of a contained space, along with a lead door. Black topped laboratory tables were makeshift workbenches, and retorts and electrical coils were everywhere.

But the most surprising thing in the room was the man in the center, tied to a large, wooden kitchen chair.

It was Pierson. He was in shirtsleeves and slacks, his tie askew. The kitchen chair had arms, and his arms were securely tied to them, and his feet were fastened to its legs. His mouth was gagged and there was a red-white-and-blue bandanna tied around his eyes. His head drooped and his thick, brown hair fell over his forehead.

I started with the blindfold. Dick blinked and shook his head as I started on the gag.

"Armstrong!" he said, voice dry and scratchy.

I didn't waste time on words. I pulled at the ropes on his arms and gave up on the knots. I turned to one of the lab tables and grabbed a retort. I broke it on the edge of the table and then started cutting his bonds.

"How did you find me?"

"Not now," I said, finishing one arm and starting on the other. "We need to get you out of here." I sawed through the ropes and now both arms were free. "Start rubbing your hands together to get the circulation going."

I dropped to a knee and began to cut the ropes at this left leg.

"I was beginning to think no one would ever find me." He dumbly rubbed his hands together. "How did you get here?"

"No time for that," I started work on his other leg. "Tell me everything that happened."

"Well …" he ran a hand through his thick bush of brown hair. "Well—I thought I heard people outside my house. I hid the pages from Mason's notebook in my telescope. Did you find them?"

"Yes." I had the last rope cut. I got to my feet.

"They broke into my house and hit me with something. I pipe, I think. I thought I heard or saw or imagined that Mason was with them."

"He was."

He looked up at me in surprise. "Did he explain what he was doing?"

"He's dead, Pierson."

"Good Lord." He got unsteadily to his feet. "Where are we?"

"New York."

"New York? What the devil am I doing here?"

"I'll tell you about it later. Listen, Dick. I need you to think. Did you see the stones? The ones I told you about?"

"No." He ran a hand through his hair once more. "I've been tied to that thing forever. They let me up to pee every now and then, but then tied me down again. I haven't had anything to eat in ages."

"What have they been doing?"

"Building a laboratory. Right here, all around me."

I thought quietly for a moment.

"All right," I said. "We have to call Elson. Then I want you to lie low while I go after Stutka."

"I'll go right home."

I coughed. "Well—that's the other bit of news I have for you. Your house burned down."

"What?"

"Your kidnappers burned it down after they took you away."

Pierson put a hand on my shoulder. "This is insane. Let's go to the police. You'll get yourself killed."

I looked into his face to answer and saw it slowly go blank. Then Pierson slowly put his hands over his head.

I turned around and there, at the door, was Romero. Not only was he awake, but he was awake and had the gun.

I put my hands up.

Romero's face was swollen and a string of blood trailed down his jaw. He smiled and the light glinted on his teeth: he looked like a gold-plated shark.

"Now isn't this sweet?" he asked.

"Let him go," I said, nodding towards Pierson. "He doesn't know anything about it. Besides, I can do the work for you just easy as he can."

"I could kill you both and get someone else."

"I don't think Stutka would like that."

"I could kill Stutka and keep the rocks for myself."

"Where *are* the rocks?" I asked.

The smile got broader. "There're in hell, so you'll see them soon."

Romero brought the gun up and aimed and that's when it happened.

There was a flash of lightning and the pungent smell of cordite. A bolt of lightning shot from the hallway and exploded against Romero's teeth. He didn't even have time to scream—the bolt of lightning pushed him back against the wall, and I squinted at the flash. When my eyes cleared Romero's mouth was a burnt-out hole and he was slowly sliding down the length of the wall.

Albert stepped from out of the hallway shadows. He held up Tesla's device, his face shining with pleasure. "*Keen!* Did you see what I did?"

"It's the dwarf!" Pierson yelped.

"Very good!" I said. "You knew that gold was the metal with the third highest rating of electrical conductivity."

"Once more," Albert said, looking at the Tesla device in awe. "In English."

"Never mind," I said. I came forward and held out my hand.

"But you said!" Albert cried.

"I said you'll get a new one, and I need that now. Hand it over."

"Oh, jeez," he said, putting it in my palm.

Then Albert turned his attention to Romero. He bent and wrenched the gun from the man's hand with a cry of delight.

"No-no-no-no!" I said and held out my hand again.

He slammed the gun into my hand with a grimace, cursing under his breath.

I handed the gun to Pierson. "Hold onto this. We need to search this place and then call Elson. Then, I want the two of you to go home."

"I have no home," Pierson said.

"Albert, I want you to take this man to a hotel. Don't tell me which one, just take him there. And once you're done, I want you to forget all about it."

"Check."

"Now, let's search this place," I said.

"Hey," Albert said, standing over Romero. "This mook is still alive."

"It's not supposed to kill you," I said. "Just incapacitate you."

"Well, look at his mouth. He's incap—whatever you said—all right."

I stood over Romero. He was in a mostly sitting-up position, lying against the wall. His eyes were partially open, but the iris was turned heavenward and I saw nothing but the whites. His breathing was heavy, his chest rising and falling with a frightening rattle. His hands hung loosely around his body. And his mouth—well, his mouth was a ruin. His lips had seared away from the lightning jolt, leaving nothing but a lipless, bloody and gaping smile of singed gold. A tiny whisp of smoke trailed up from the blacked ruins of his mouth.

"We better tie him up until we call an ambulance," I said.

With a scream Romeo lurched forward, hands at my throat. His fingers dug into the soft flesh under my jawline.

I stumbled backward but the deathlike grip was secure. There was a motion behind me and Pierson came between us. His arm swung in a wide arc and he brought the automatic down on Romero's temple. The man went down once more.

"Jeez," Albert said.

I grabbed a handful of rope that had secured Pierson and rolled Romero over onto his stomach. I wrenched both hands behind his back and began to tie him up.

"Take some rope," I said. "There's a guy lying in the hallway. Be very careful."

Pierson grabbed a fistful of rope and made for the stairs.

"Hey Mister," Albert said, following. "I'll hold the gun while you tie him up."

I next tied Romero's legs. A quick check on his pulse told me he was still alive, but he did need medical attention and he needed it fast. The clock was ticking.

Pierson and Albert were back. "What now?"

"Brother, we search for the rocks," I said. "But *carefully*."

"You don't need to tell me twice," Pierson said. "Let's divvy it up. I'll take downstairs and the basement. You take here and upstairs."

"What about me?" Albert asked.

"Stay with me," I said. *So I can keep an eye on you*, I thought.

I started with the newly converted laboratory. I could have spent hours going over the equipment and instrumentation, but I didn't have that luxury. Albert pawed over the glassware and chemicals while I searched for the stones.

They could only be safely held in a lead-lined container. There was nothing the right size in the nearly bricked-off alcove, and none of the crates held anything other than the equipment labeled on their sides. Ditto the drawers, cupboards and the three brand-new filing cabinets.

I then made a quick examination of Romero's bedroom. There was a dresser filled with cheap, and somewhat flashy, clothing. The closet held two suits and a pile of soiled laundry. The bathrooms were similarly empty.

I took the stairs up two at a time. Up here were three more bedrooms, two with a joining bathroom, and another *en suite*. The large bedroom boasted an over-size canopy bed. There were fresh sheets and the bed was made with an exactitude that would put the best hotel to shame. There were a host of girly pictures on the walls, and each night table boasted a scented candle. The clothes closet and dresser were filled with expensive, child-sized suits. Clearly Stutka's bedroom-away-from home.

"Will you get a load of this joint," Albert said. He had followed me upstairs and stood transfixed under one of the girly pictures.

"Don't look—it'll stunt your growth." I could find no papers or clues of any kind, and no trace of the stones and I led Albert down the stairs. I met Pierson on the landing as I came down. "Anything?"

"Nothing. Lots of furniture covered with sheets, a mostly unused kitchen. Cabinets, fridge, nearly everything empty. Came up empty in the basement, too."

"Did you find a telephone?"

"One on the wall in the kitchen."

The three of us went to the kitchen. Pierson hit the light and I saw the phone on the other side of the ice box. The operator patched me into Princeton and in moments I was taking with Thurgood Elson.

"Dean Elson, it's Peter Armstrong."

"I know who it is!" he snapped. "Where are you and what are you up to?"

"It's a long story, sir. I found Dr. Pierson. I'm sending him back home."

"Back home? Where are you now?"

"New York, sir. He was kidnapped and brought here by the same the same people who took the stones from me."

"*You had the stones?*"

"Yes, sir," I stammered. "I don't have time to explain. But I know who took them and I'm going to get them back. Be ready to have them examined."

"Listen here, Professor Armstrong! If you think you will continue to represent this University when—"

I hung up. I dialed again and called the police. I told them there were two injured men that needed an ambulance and hung up before they could ask further questions.

"Let's go," I said. We stepped over the unconscious O'Brien in the hallway and went into the cool night air. I turned to Dick and offered my hand. "Time for you to go," I said. "Go wherever Albert takes you and lay low until you hear from me."

"Where are you going?" His voice, always deep, now sounded like controlled thunder.

"To Stutka. Without you and without Mason, he can't do anything with them. I'll get him to see reason."

"Are you a jerk, or somethin'?" Albert said. "The only thing you'll see is a concrete slab."

"Shut up, Albert."

"The kid's right," Pierson said. "What assurance do you have that he'll let you go?"

"I gave up on assurances days ago," I said. I saw a cab a few feet away and motioned it forward. I opened the door when it pulled to the curb and ushered them both inside.

Pierson reached into the waistband of his trousers and handed me Romero's gun. "Take this, at least."

I took the gun and put it behind my belt. As I closed the door, Albert yelled, "Remember! You owe me!"

I watched the cab drive away. I heard police sirens in the distance and quickly looked for a cab of my own.

CHAPTER NINE

I never liked New York City.

I did, however, *love* Radio City Music Hall. I was in the city on Observatory business several times during its construction and last year went there four times to see *King Kong*. When the cab sped past 51st Street,

I had a quick glimpse of its clean art deco façade lined with red-and-green lights. I wondered if I would live long enough to ever go there again.

I got off at the corner of 56th and walked West. It was now nearly ten at night, but Gotham was still bustling around me. But the noise of the city was not nearly enough to drown out the jazzed-rhythms coming from the Bit O' Honey.

Stutka's nightclub took up the whole center of the Southside block between Sixth and Seventh Avenues. It was a mad, ziggurat-shaped three-story building of green-tinted glass. There was a string of four neon bees over the twin-front doors that lit up alternately red or yellow and ended in an illuminated honey bowl.

A doorman in red-and-grey livery stood at the end of a red carpet that extended to the curb. He held the door with a salute for a smart couple in evening clothes.

The strains of *Love, You Funny Thing* were audible to me from nearly a block away. The band went up-tempo as I approached the door, and I heard *Happy Feet* begin. It made me think about running away.

The doorman blocked the door as I approached. He folded his arms and said, "Formal wear, only."

I didn't even pause. "I'm here to see Stutka," I said.

His hard face fell a bit. He looked through the glass walls into the club and motioned to someone inside. He then turned to me and said, "Hat check to the left."

He opened the door and I stepped inside the Bit O' Honey. The red carpet extended to the foyer of the club. Bathrooms were to the right and a hat-and-coat check room to the left. I went over to the booth and presented the uniformed girl at the other side my Trilby.

As she took my hat, I felt a ham-sized hand fall on my shoulder. Her face never registered anything.

The hand turned me around and I found myself staring up into a mountain of a man. I had never seen anyone so tall—and if someone told me he was over seven feet; I would not doubt him. He wore an ill-fitting blue suit; his black hair was cut very close to his scalp and his lips were tight in what I thought was a permanent frown. He squinted down at me.

"Hello," I said.

"You want to see the boss?" he said.

"He'll want to see me," I said.

Without a word those two massive hands ran down the length of my body. I stepped back in surprise, but was pegged in by the hatcheck booth.

He found Romero's automatic first. He took that with a sneer and put it behind his own belt. He then took my wallet and, from my hip pocket, Tesla's device.

He pocketed the Tesla and checked my wallet before tossing it back to me. "Follow me," he said.

We stepped into the Bit O' Honey. I had never seen a nightspot so large and luxurious. We went three steps down into the club proper, the red-carpet giving way to a gleaming black parquet floor. In the distance was a large stage, festooned with red and green curtains, upon which the band was going full tilt. The neon lectern at the center-stage read Clyde McCoy.[29] A handsome man with a horn led the finale of *Happy Feet* and took a bow.

Surrounding the stage and dance floor was a green-carpeted section of tables. Like the façade itself, the tables were these large glass—almost crystalline—structures that seemed too small for a meal of any consequence. The chairs, too, were translucent and glassine.

The room was lit overhead by a massive lighting fixture of glass and metal. I had never seen anything like it before; it looked almost like the club itself as seen from outside, but upside down and bolted to the ceiling. And then it dawned on me that the entire conceit was as if the Bit O' Honey were one gigantic, art deco beehive of glass.

Leon Stutka sat at the corner table. The glass design did him no favors: I could tell that he was sitting on a special box that lifted him to table height. There was a woman in a silver lamé evening gown beside him; her hair was platinum colored and she sported a beauty mark at the corner of her full, red mouth. An enormous glass of champagne stood between the two of them.

The giant marched up to Stutka and jerked a thumb in my direction. The dwarf looked up, face impassive.

"Wallet says Peter Armstrong," the giant said. "Nothing on him but a pack of smokes," and here he put Tesla's device on the table, "and this." Here, he opened his jacket and flashed the automatic.

Stutka gestured to a chair without a word. I took it and sat.

"Want me to stay?" the giant asked.

He simply nodded his head no. When the giant left, Stutka turned to the woman. "Man talk. Scram"

The woman looked at the champagne wistfully and left with a polite nod to me.

Stutka reached into the folds of his well-tailored brown suit. He had a

---

29   Clyde McCoy (1903-1990) was an American jazz trumpeter and bandleader. His music is readily available online and highly recommended

yellow tie and matching boutonniere. For a mad moment I expected him to pull a gun on me; instead, he took out package of cigarettes.

"Smoke?" he asked.

"I have my own," I patted the Tesla device, drawing it closer to me.

Stutka lit a thin, brown cigarette and put the package on the table in front of him. He regarded me from behind the curling wisps of smoke.

"Why aren't you dead?"

"Tarzan saved me."

"Very funny." He didn't sound amused. "Why are you here?"

"We need to talk."

"So talk."

In the background, the band began to play *We're in the Money*. Spotlights hit both ends of the stage and twin lines of chorus girls spilled onto the dance floor. All were dressed in tight, one-piece dance suits with yellow and black stripes. The rear was padded for extra effect and they all wore sleek, black stockings. It took me a moment to realize they were dressed like stylized bees. Each held a gigantic nickel the size of a serving tray. The dance routine moved in steady harmony with the music.

"Pierson sends his regards," I opened.

"Really?" he tapped his cigarette at the ashtray.

"He's free now," I said. "I got him out of Duane Street and your two playmates are on their way to the hospital. He's on his way to an unknown location—I couldn't tell you where he is if I wanted to."

He looked up at me, face blasé. "What does that mean to me?"

I laughed. It was a nervous laugh, and maybe shorter than I wanted it to be. But I did manage it. "So, it's over. You don't have Cooley. You don't have Pierson. We know all about you. Why not give me the stones?"

He just stared.

"I can take them back to the Observatory for study and I could manage to forget all about you," I said. "You'd have nothing to worry about."

Now he laughed. "I may not have Cooley or Pierson, but I most certainly have you."

"You're going to kidnap me in front of all these people?"

"I don't have to kidnap you. You can just have an accident." He blew smoke. "It's been done before."

I pulled the Tesla device closer to me as innocently as possible. My gaze took in the Bit O' Honey. Patrons had returned to their tables as the floor show took over the dance floor. McCoy was in the middle of a horn solo as the dancers waved their plastic nickels.

Finally I asked, "What's your plan?"

Now he was angry. "Don't crack wise." He crushed his cigarette into the tray. "I don't have the rocks and you know it."

I felt like someone threw cold water over me. What was he talking about?

"You don't?"

He leaned closer to me. In the weird light of the nightclub, I could see the network of lines and age spots across his child-like face. "Your boss took them from me," he said. "I never even got them back to New York."

"*My* boss?"

"He highjacked the car transporting them in," he barked. "Two of my boys are dead. And now you come here, playing games. I know everything behind the whole masquerade, and that makes me dangerous. So—just what the hell do you think you're up to, *Professor* Armstrong?"

I was tempted to drain the glass of champagne and yearned for a real drink. My boss? Took the stones back?

And then I remembered what Benet had said. Stutka was not in this game alone; there was someone else. Mr. X. Leader of a criminal syndicate terrifying in its scope and ambition.

I opened my mouth to speak, but the words caught in my throat.

My boss?

I watched as *We're in the Money* wound down. McCoy bowed and announced a fifteen-minute intermission. Chorus girls moved among the tables, mingling with the crowd. But little of it registered, because I was thinking about—*my boss.*

Mason may have tried to sell the stones to Stutka for his gambling debts, but how did Mr. X know about them? It had to be someone who knew about Mason and his work.

And how were so many of my actions anticipated over the last two days? I only told one person where I was and what I was up to.

My boss.

I felt sick. Thurgood Elson was not a great scientist but he was a brilliant administrator. He always seemed to live beyond his means—and his interests ranged far outside of the Academy. Could Dean Elson, the man who I had known for so long but really knew so slightly—actually be Mr. X? Did he murder Mason and kidnap Pierson to gain control of the stones?

And, if he was, did he now have them?

"I know where he took them."

"Where?" I asked.

"Very funny," his eyes glinted. "I don't have them now, but I *will* get them back. And instead of Pierson, I'll have you."

"The hell you will," I said.

Before I could move away a chorine passed the table, her black-and-yellow outfit incandescent in the electric light. She glided past the seat the platinum blond vacated and slid into it.

Stutka was as surprised as I was.

The large, plastic nickel was affixed to her wrist by a piece of black, lacey elastic. With her free hand she pulled something from her bodice and held it under the nickel.

And then I looked into her face.

"Miss Welles!" I said.

The something she pulled from her bodice was a tiny, silver-plated, pearl-handled derringer. Even over the buzz of the nightclub I heard it *click* as she cocked it.

The outfit accentuated her glorious hourglass figure. Her auburn hair was pulled up, like the other dancers, and somehow her eyes were more liquid, luminous and magnificent than before. I had to blink to convince myself it was really her.

"Hello Leon," she said. She pressed the derringer against the little man's ribs. "Be a good boy and tell me where the rocks are and no one gets hurt. Understand?"

"Miss Welles—" I began.

"Quiet," she said. "The big people are talking." She caught herself for a moment and added to dwarf. "No offense."

"I was just telling your boyfriend here that your boss has them."

"She doesn't—" I started.

"Shut up," Miss Welles and Stutka said in unison.

"All right," she said. "We're all going for a little ride. We can make you talk."

I was about to turn around to plot our exit when the massive pair of hands fell on my shoulders. I looked up and the giant stared down at me. The fingers of his right hand slid behind my neck and grabbed hold right over my shoulders. He could snap my neck like a matchstick.

To prove it, he squeezed until I yelped, then relaxed his fingers.

Stutka reached for his cigarettes, ignoring both Miss Welles and the derringer. "Things just got interesting, no?"

I was tired of people talking around me and wanted out, now. "Mind if I smoke?" I said, pulling the Tesla device closer to me.

I heard it *click* as she cocked it.

I was not one hundred percent sure how the device worked, or how it picked a target. If I aimed over my head at the giant, what were the odds of the device hitting me, instead? And what of Stutka? Was Miss Welles too close for a safe shot?

I picked up the device and my eye caught the enormous art deco light over the dance floor. The dance floor was empty.

I flicked the device around and pressed the button.

A bolt of lightning shot from it. It streaked white-hot through the cigarette smoke and struck the metal struts of the ziggurat light. There was a brilliant shower of sparks followed by a terrific *BOOM!* The glass shattered and the entire fixture crashed to the floor.

Alarums and Pandemonium!

Women screamed and men hollered. I pushed down and forward, out of the giant's grip, smacking my nose on the table. The motion was too much for the little table and it turned over as I fell into it.

The table upending pushed away Miss Welles's arms, and I could not see if she still had the gun. Stutka spilled out of his booster chair and hit the floor.

There was *some* light, but the Bit O' Honey was now mostly dark. I scrambled to my feet and grabbed a hold of Miss Welles. She got up and pushed me aside. As I fell to the right, she stuck the derringer in the giant's middle and fired.

He grabbed his belly and went down.

If the light startled the crowd, the sound of gunfire terrified them. Tables everywhere were now knocked over as people scrambled for the door. Several dark-suited goons made their way towards the ruins of our table, but could not push through the crowd.

"C'mon," Miss Welles said, grabbing hold of my lapel. She pulled me away but I was stuck momentarily when Stutka grabbed hold of my foot. I tried to shake him off but the little man bared his teeth and buried them in my ankle.

I realized I still held the Tesla device in my hand. I had one shot left and was going to use it on him. I aimed and pressed the button.

Nothing happened.

I shook it, trying to make it work, as Stutka pulled on my trousers, using the leverage to get to his feet.

I smacked a palm on his forehead and pushed him into a nearby table.

I took Miss Welles by the hand and we dived into the crowd.

There were a few moments when I feared we would be separated, but she held onto me as tightly as I held onto her. I threw a glance at Stutka's men, but they were not getting through the crowd. However, once we were outside, all bets were off.

We were crushed, pinned in the center of a hysterical crowed. At one point I felt myself lifted off my feet as we surged through the door.

Miss Welles and I spilled onto the sidewalk. She nearly tripped over her heels as the tight knot of the crowd separated and ran willy-nilly into Gotham nightscape.

I spared a look through the glass façade. The goons were approaching.

I pulled Miss Welles by the hand and ran for the street. We dived between two cars and I almost sprang for the opposite side of Seventh Avenue when a sleek, yellow cab pulled up close enough to snag my jacket button. Miss Welles jumped into the front seat and I took the rear door.

"Drive!" she barked and the cab pulled into the crowd.

I checked the rear window and saw Stutka's goons. There were standing now in the street, having missed us by seconds, but did not dare pull their guns. I was about to say a silent prayer of thanks for the cab when I realized it was all planned.

"Thanks, Moe," she said, pulling pins from her hair. Her auburn tresses fell around her face. The bee costume, so ridiculous once outside the club, was now garish in the passing streetlights. "The New Yorker. No need to wait."

I leaned into the front seat. "How did you find me?"

"I didn't," she said. "I knew you would make your way to Stutka, so I just kept my eye on him."

"And what if you made a mistake?"

"Then we wouldn't be here."

She had me there. "Look," I said. "I found Pierson."

"Where is he?"

"I don't know," I said. "O'Brien and Romero were holding him in a place on Duane Street and I got him out."

She turned and looked at me with something like admiration. For a moment, I felt absurdly proud. Then she pointed at my hand. "What's that?"

I looked at Tesla's device and put it in my pocket. "It helped."

"What is it?"

"A friend gave it to me."

"Some friend," she said. "What do you mean you don't know where Pierson is?"

"I didn't want anyone to find him through me, but *listen*," I said. "I know who Mr. X. is!"

She and Moe exchanged a look. It was the first time I really registered anything about him. Moe was a small, thin man with over-sized nose and ears. A hand-rolled cigarette hung from the corner of his mouth. His hair was covered with a cap and he wore a plain, dark-blue shirt beneath a zippered jacket.

"Who?" Miss Welles asked.

"My boss, Thurgood Elson!"

"What makes you think that?"

I explained to her how I figured it out at the Bit O' Honey. "Stutka says he's got the stones. We've got to head back to Princeton right away."

She and Moe exchanged looks again, then she said, "Check, Doc. But first, we have to go to the hotel and pick up your stuff."

"That might not be safe," I argued. "Stutka could send his men there now."

"Don't worry," Moe said. "We got transportation all set."

I didn't know what they had planned, so I sat back on the seat. I had been delighted to see Miss Welles, but the anxiety that she inspires once more overwhelmed me. We sped down Seventh Avenue.

We made it to the New Yorker in under ten minutes. Moe slowed at the twin doors out front and Miss Welles and I hopped out. She turned at the passenger window and said to Moe, "Monitor the radio, signal K."

He nodded and the taxi sped into the darkness.

I had a host of questions, but before I could ask one, she grabbed my elbow and barked, "C'mon, Doc."

We hurried through the lobby. I did not recognize any of the night crew—the concierge was different, and I saw no trace of Nick. The man at registration frowned at the sight of Miss Welles hurrying me along, and I wondered if we would soon get a visit from the house detective.[30]

I tried to ask questions in the elevator, but Miss Welles nodded at the pert little operator, and it wasn't until we were in the corridor on our way to my room that I could say anything.

"Just what's going on?"

"No time," she said, pushing me along. "Got your key?"

I tapped my breast pocket—felt the Tesla device there—and then my trousers. Yes—I had. I unlocked the door and she pushed me aside, drawing her derringer.

She prodded the door open with her toe and then flicked on the light.

---

[30] During this period, it was not uncommon for hotels to employ private detectives to ensure no illegal or immoral activity took place in the rooms.

She stepped over the threshold, her bee-outfit somehow both adorable and ridiculous in the electric light.

"Clear," she said, turning around.

I stepped in and closed the door.

"You got a spare jacket?" she asked.

Fortunately for her, if ever there was ever a man who would have a spare jacket, it was I.

"Great. Get it for me, then pack your bag. Not too big. And if you have any papers, bring 'em with you."

"Where are we going?" I stepped into the bedroom and she followed.

"On a trip," she said.

I grabbed my Harris Tweed from the closet and handed it over. It had velvet lapels and patches on the elbows; it was one of my favorites. I pulled my small travel valise from under the bed as she put it on.

I piled the scant clothes in, along with the photos of Mason's journal pages and Tesla's copy of *Tarzan and Lion Man*. I snapped both clasps shut when there was a knock at the door.

I moved to the parlor.

"Don't open it," she hissed.

"It's probably just the house detective," I said. "You should've seen the look we got when we came in."

"Over here," she barked.

I hopped back into the bedroom. She turned off the light and went to the window. She slid it open silently and turned to me. "Fire escape."

The knocking at the door grew louder.

She threw a leg over the sill and stepped onto it. I handed her my valise and stepped out to join her. I eased the window down, but not before I heard the front door of my hotel room crash open.

Miss Welles started up, never looking behind her. I threw backward glances at the window as we raced upward. We had gone nearly two floors when my window opened and a man stuck his head out. When it turned upward, I saw the scar even in the dim light of evening—it was O'Brien.

"Company," I said.

Miss Welles pivoted and pointed her derringer. I dived out of the way and she fired.

I heard the metallic ping of the bullet hit the metalwork of the fire escape. O'Brien ducked and flattened against the metal stairs, offering as little target as possible.

I expected Miss Welles to fire again, but instead she opened the window nearest us and jumped inside. I followed.

The room we were in was empty—lucky for us. We stepped through the darkened bedroom and parlor and out into the corridor.

Miss Welles never faltered. She hurried to the stairwell and pushed open the door. She took the stairs down as fast of her heels would allow and, in seconds, we were one floor below.

"Let's keep going," I said.

She did not answer. She led me instead to the elevator bank. She watched the indicator overhead; the elevator was coming from below. In a moment the double doors opened and we stepped inside the elevator. If the operator had anything to say about Miss Welles' outrageous attire, she kept it to herself.

Miss Welles kept her hand over the gun at bodice as we went up one floor, then relaxed as we then shot to the forty-third floor.

We were out of the elevator in an instant and she waited until the doors closed and the overhead indicator trailed downward.

She nodded me along and hit the stairway once more. She led us up a narrow corridor leading to a room, just large enough to accommodate a door with a fire handle. She pushed it open and we were on the roof.

I gaped for a moment at the sight. The tar of the roof sparkled in the evening damp. There was a starry sky, and the brilliant panorama of New York spread out before me. The newly built Empire State Building loomed to my left, seemingly close enough to touch. There was a dramatic updraft and my hair blew over my forehead.

But that wasn't all there was to see.

There on the roof was a sleek, gunmetal gray autogyro.

I had read about them before, of course, in *Doc Savage* and *The Shadow*, but had never seen one in person. There was a long, cylindrical fuselage, supported in the front by two, high struts ending in large tires. (From the front, the autogyro looked like someone rising from a push-up.) The rear-end was low to the ground on two smaller struts-tires.

There was a propeller in front of the device, and a much larger one overhead—it looked to me about twenty feet wide. There were no wings; just two small rudders in the rear.

On top of the fuselage were two pits for the pilot and passenger. Miss Welles chucked my valise at me and walked towards it.

"You have an autogyro...?" I said, somewhat stupidly.

"I said transportation was arranged," she said.

I stood where I was, too surprised to move. She was only three steps ahead when the roof door behind me exploded outward.

The edge of the door clipped me between my shoulder blades and the back of my head. I staggered forward and hit the ground, dropping my valise.

I heard the door bang against the hutch. I rolled and standing over me was O'Brien.

If there was one palpable after-effect of the Tesla device, it was this: O'Brien was mad enough to kill. He looked down at me and roared like an animal. He brought up both hands and dived at me.

I rolled and he hit the ground beside me, but not heard enough to hurt him. His hands grabbled my shoulders as I tried to wrench free. All I managed to do was roll over again, O'Brien holding me like a vise. When he was on the ground on his back, I was lying on top of him, on my back, too. I scrambled to get off.

He growled and he landed a terrific blow against my ear. I fell as I climbed off of him, spilling onto my side.

He got to his feet.

I reached into my pocket for the Tesla device. It should still have juice for one more jolt.

O'Brien froze when he saw the thing in my hand. The scar that trailed down his eye to the edge of his mouth looked white and ugly in the nightlights of Manhattan.

I pressed the button.

Nothing.

I pressed again.

Still nothing.

O'Brien reached down with a horrible grin and took the device from my hands. He tossed it aside like a broken toy.

Miss Welles was on his back like a lioness. His hat flew from his head and she wrapped a forearm around his neck while she reached into the scarred-side of his mouth with her forefinger. She pulled at his cheek, screaming.

O'Brien reached up and over, trying to get a hold of the girl.

I got to my feet and punched him in the gut with everything I had. If he noticed, I couldn't tell. I then punched him again, and then a third time in the ribs.

O'Brien spun around and flung Miss Welles from his shoulders. She somersaulted as she hit the glistening ground.

O'Brien turned to me and I let him have one in the face, punching his mouth right under his scar. He grunted and I punched again.

He responded by pushing me away—hard. It was like being hit by a bus. I balled a fist to get closer when Miss Welles, once again on her feet, stopped the whole thing.

She just came out of nowhere and bopped in front of him, like a jack-in-the-box. She pressed the derringer in the center of his sternum and barked, "Move and you're dead."

I don't know whether O'Brien did not hear or understand, or if he was carried away by the moment. He slammed the flat of his palm against her forehead and Miss Welles staggered backward. Without another word she raised the derringer and fired.

The gunshot was louder than expected; the three of us stood stock still in surprise. Then O'Brien looked down at his chest. A red circle, like the crimson petals of a blossoming rose, expanded across his shirt front. He looked at me, then at her, then blinked. He dropped to his knees and then to his face.

"Jesus," I said.

"Hurry," she said.

She dashed to the autogyro and hopped into the rearmost seat. The front propeller started to *whir*, then the wide prop overhead came to life.

I threw my valise into the front cockpit and then climbed in myself.

The autogyro was controlled by a rudder Miss Welles handled behind me. She reached to the floor of the cockpit and put on a leather aviator's helmet and a pair of goggles. Over the roar of the propellers, she reached over, handing me a pair of goggles. I put them on as the propellers continued to run for a moment and the machine readied for flight. It was loud, but not impossibly loud—like standing next to a gigantic fan with a faulty bearing.

An autogyro, unlike a plane, needs very little runway—less than fifty feet. The machine slowly started it progression to the very edge of the roof of the New Yorker hotel. I grabbed the edges of the cockpit in terror.

We were feet from the precipice when O'Brien collided against the machine. I screamed and turned to find him holding onto the rim of my cockpit with bloody hands. With a roar he loosened his right and started punching at my face.

The machine, not built for that kind of treatment, shuddered with a tooth-crushing jolt. I blocked his fist with my forearm; it was the only thing I could think to do.

I'm not sure but I think O'Brien walked alongside the autogryo and simply stepped off the edge of the hotel roof. His body shifted downward a bit when he left solid ground, but he kept hold.

The autogyro lurched mid-air and hovered at a grotesque angle. Miss Welles struggled with the rudder to maintain control.

His weight and position on the machine nearly killed us. We started moving to a ninety-degree angle, and I saw the length of the gleaming Empire State Building loom closer and closer.

"Get him off!" she barked. "He'll kill us all."

I got to my knees on the seat, bracing a shoulder against the rim of the cockpit so I wouldn't fall out of the machine. The streets of New York were forty-stories below.

I punched at O'Brien, but he didn't even blink. With his left hand holding the rim of the cockpit, he threw another punch at my face with his right. I balled my fists and battered his ears and head. His hair went wild in the wind.

The autogyro continued to move sideways and upwards. We covered a block of Manhattan real estate as O'Brien and I grappled. An updraft buffeted the machine and we lurched mid-air.

O'Brien became less sure of his grip. He looked down at the city far beneath us, then turned to me with a look of rage and hate. He grabbed me by the tie. His weight nearly pulled me from the autogyro; as it was, he dragged my chin down to the very rim of the cockpit.

Had he held just a moment longer, he would have strangled me. But his bloodied hands, the intense wind and the silk of my tie saved me. He slipped slightly down the length of my tie, clawed for a better hold, lost it, and fell.

O'Brien spilled downward with a terrific scream. I watched as he fell down the length of the Empire State Building and into the streets below.

At his release, the autogyro gained altitude at a terrifying rate. The ninety-degree angle nearly up-ended us—in the other direction. Miss Welles bit her lip and grabbed the rudder with both hands. In seconds we were just over the dirigible mooring mast of the Empire State Building and heading south.

"Where are we going?" I yelled over the sound of the propellers.

"Don't worry," she yelled back. "It's under control."

I had little choice but to settle into the seat and wait for developments. The sight of O'Brien's drop had filled me with terror, and I held onto the interior of the cockpit till my knuckles whitened.

CHAPTER TEN

I don't know how long I stayed conscious.
 Shaken by O'Brien's death, I huddled deep in the cockpit, white-knuckling the interior of the fuselage. Miss Welles was silent behind me—at least, I could not hear anything over the *whir* of the propellers—and I closed my eyes and fought to remain calm.

I don't know how long I was out, but the sky was faintly streaked with dawn when I awoke. It must have been nearly eleven when we left the rooftop of the New Yorker; my watch now said that it was just coming up on six in the morning.

I clutched the rim of the cockpit and slowly raised my head into the slipstream.

It came as a shock to see below me the outlines of both the Capitol Building and the Washington Monument, still lit by nighttime spotlights. We were on the outskirts of town, and below us I saw the trucks, tractors and pullies of a travelling circus setting up a series of big tops. Miss Welles had spent the night piloting us to Washington, D.C. I turned to the cockpit behind me and she gave me an enthusiastic thumbs up.

We flew past the Capitol and I soon saw many of the older townhouses that made up the residential section of town. I had seldom strayed far from the Smithsonian during my previous trips to Washington, and I was surprised that the many federal buildings were surrounded by frame houses, and, beyond that, farmland and weedy swamps.

Miss Welles piloted the autogyro over a row of townhouses that would not look out of place in a photogravure.[31] The houses had a wide expanse of backyard, and Miss Welles pulled up her goggles, looked over the rim of her cockpit, and steadied the autogyro.

The descent felt very strange. We just gently—lowered, the propeller spinning overhead. It was almost as if a gigantic feather were falling to earth. We drifted away from the early morning sky, suddenly were level with the streetlamps, then the rooftops, and then, we gently touched earth.

---

31 Armstrong is indulging in a little personal nostalgia here. A photogravure is an old-fashioned print whereby a copper plate is grained (adding a pattern to the plate) and then coated with a light-sensitive gelatin tissue which had been exposed to a film positive, and then etched. Photogravure would have been a part of Armstrong's boyhood.

The machine stopped humming almost instantly. The propeller slowed overhead and Miss Welles was climbing out before I could ask a question.

The back door of the townhouse opened and a man in military uniform approached us. Miss Welles pulled away her goggles and leather aviator's helmet. The uniformed man—young, tall and well-made—blinked in surprise at her bee-themed chorus girl suit visible under my tweed jacket. It did not stop him from saluting her smartly. He then looked at me, confused, and saluted again for good measure.

"Don't worry about him," she said, shaking her hair free. Even in that ridiculous get-up, she was wonderfully beautiful. "Hustle us some breakfast."

He saluted again and she followed him toward the house. I stood, rooted where I was by shock, surprise and exhaustion.

She turned at the door and nodded. "C'mon, Doc. Breakfast."

I reached for my valise and followed her inside.

The door slammed shut behind me. By the sound, it was reinforced with steel. I jumped at the sound, but was too disoriented by my surroundings to register additional shock.

The interior of the townhouse had obviously been altered; connecting walls to perhaps two other homes had been torn down and a long, large open space remained. There were enormous tables lined with maps, alcoves populated by shortwave radios and their operators, a free-standing library, a theater-grade movie projector and screen, and, if I wasn't mistaken, the start of a small chemical laboratory. And that was just for starters.

A short man in a General's uniform approached. His hair and mustache were iron gray, his brows bushy and in need of trimming. He seemed heavy, but solid, and he walked like an angry tiger. He roared at Miss Welles before she could salute.

"Dammit, Penelope, how the hell are we supposed to keep this place secret when you land that goddamn thing in the backyard!"

"Good to see you, too," she said, handing the General her cap and goggles as if he were the hired help. "This is Dr. Armstrong. Have you got everything ready?"

Here the brows raised in surprise and he gave me a brief smile—I was reminded of a lion about to be fed a beef stake.

"Dr. Armstrong," he said, gripping my hand and squeezing. "Good of you to come."

I didn't have much choice, so I just nodded.

Miss Welles opened her jacket, giving the General an eyeful. "I need to change, and then I can brief you. Fifteen minutes?"

"Check," the General said. He turned to the young man who greeted us at the back door. "Corporal, show this man to his room and then go outside and cover that damned thing up with a tarp or something."

The Corporal saluted and gestured with his hand. "This way."

Miss Welles had already disappeared somewhere in the cavernous interior. I checked for her before going along.

"Nothing to worry about, Doctor," the General said. "We will come for you in a half hour or so. Better clean up."

The Corporal took my valise as an incentive and I followed him. As we walked through the open space, I gaped at the radio operators, various uniformed women listening to dictagraphs through headphones and typing a record of what they heard, men at small tables working with coded messages and one table surrounded by a battery of graybeards fidgeting over what looked like a model airplane.

The Corporal led me down a small, brick-lined corridor. "I hope you'll be comfortable," he said. "I didn't have a lot of advance notice."

"Join the club," I said.

At the end of the corridor was a small wooden door; one of the few things probably still original to the house. He opened the door and gestured me inside.

It was a nice-sized bedroom; the bed was made and turned down. There was a writing desk, paper and pens, and several bookcases. I went inside as the Corporal continued talking.

"Those books are what I could get from the Smithsonian on short notice," he said. He pointed to various celestial maps that we tacked to the wall. "And those are as up-to-date as I could get them."

He opened door off to the side and showed me the bathroom, then moved to the window and drew the shade. As it descended, I saw that the window led to the backyard of several cojoined houses.

"Make yourself at home until you're needed," he said, putting my valise on the bed. "And if there's anything you want, let me know."

"One thing immediately comes to mind," I said. "What the hell is this place and who the hell are you?"

He spared me a tight smile. "I'm the Corporal, sir."

"Corporal *what*?"

"Just call for the Corporal, sir, and I'll come running." The smile vanished. "Anything else?"

"The *what is this place*?"

"You will be fully briefed, sir," he saluted again. I didn't know if it was military protocol, or a nervous tic.

The door closed behind him with a grim finality. I looked around the room. The books—astronomy, celestial mechanics, a smattering of geology—were indeed up-to-date and profoundly learned. The maps on the wall were of the best quality. What were they doing here and what did they want from me?

I reached into my valise and took out my charcoal gray suit, white shirt and green-and-red striped tie. My hat was left at the Bit O' Honey, but I didn't think I'd be going outside soon. I took the photos of Mason's journal pages and stuck them under the pillow, and placed *Tarzan and the Lion Man* on the night table. At the rate I was going, I should just about finish it by the time I retired, or got killed, whichever came first.

The bathroom was equipped with a fresh razor and a cup for lather. With little else to do, I stripped and climbed into the shower.

I stood under the hot spray, thinking, *Mason, what have you gotten me into?* The insanity of the last few days paraded down my overtired imagination; it was a slightly shaky hand that handled the razor.

In the bedroom a breakfast tray had been placed on the desk. I hadn't eaten since lunch the day before and I fell to it. The three eggs, a healthy amount of bacon, toast and coffee were so enticing, I ate wearing nothing more than my towel.

Finished, I dressed. I had just knotted my tie when came the knock at the door.

"Come in."

It was the Corporal. "They're ready for you, sir."

"Am I ready for them?"

He smiled; a sunny look. "It's not as bad as all that."

I followed him back down the corridor and once more into the large, open workroom. We passed through that, into what must have been yet another hollowed-out townhouse, and went through a series of small rooms. He opened a door and deposited me in a small parlor. There were armchairs, a bookcase, bar, various end-tables of dark wood and a stone fireplace. The simple floral wallpaper would not look out of place in an English country house. On one of the end tables was a tray with cups, saucers and a metal pot. The smell of coffee filled the room.

"Just wait here one moment."

He left me alone in the room. There was an over-sized mirror over the fireplace, and I walked to it. I had read about two-way mirrors in books, and wondered if this was one. I walked over to it, cupped my hands around my eyes and tried to look "through" it. If there was anything on the other side, it was invisible to me.

Sun streamed in from the large bay window; I figured this room must face the street. But, despite the brightness of the sun, the view seemed little more than a bright, gray haze. I walked to the window and ran a hand over the glass. It was covered with an ultra-thin layer of some kind of Bakelite.[32]

"It's made from bituminous coal," said Miss Welles, coming through the door. She had changed into a navy-blue suit, a smart double-breasted jacket and matching skirt. Her dark stockings showed her legs to great effect and her auburn hair was stunning in the diffused light. "If you were standing outside, you would see what looked like a normal living room. It never changes—I keep telling them they have to work on that."

"Miss Welles," I said. "Where are we?"

"Thank God," she said, going to the tray. "Coffee. Want a cup of joe?"

"I've had some."

She poured a cup and added milk. "You're in Washington. I thought you had an advanced degree."

"Three," I said. "And that's not what I'm asking."

She sipped. "Sure you don't want some? It's good."

I waved a hand encompassing everything around us. "Just what is this place?"

Miss Welles stepped forward and cupped my cheek with her hand.

"I work here. Trust me," she said. "I'm looking after you."

She took my hand in hers. I stared down at it.

"Deal?" she asked.

"Deal" I said. *At least*, I thought, *for now.*

The General chose that moment to enter. He stepped into the room, nodded curtly at the both of us, and made a beeline for the coffee. "Want some, Dr. Armstrong?"

"I already asked," Miss Welles said.

"Sit down," he said, drinking his black. Once I sat, he fished a small, cardboard square from his jacket. He gazed at it a moment, then handed it to me. "Do you know this man?"

---

32   Bakelite, or polyoxybenzylmethylenglycolanhydride, was the first plastic made from synthetic components. It is a thermosetting phenol formaldehyde resin, formed from a condensation reaction of phenol with formaldehyde. It was developed by the Belgian-American chemist Leo Baekeland in Yonkers, New York, in 1907. Bakelite has a very distinctive quality, and it today prized for its "retro" vibe. Welles is incorrect, however, as bituminous coal has nothing to do with the process.

I looked at the photo. It was of a middle-aged man with a wild mane of white hair, a dark mustache and eyebrows, and large, sad eyes.

I handed it back. "Every scientist knows him," I said.[33]

The General sat, sipped coffee and looked at me again. "Have you ever been in contact with him?"

"No. He is at Princeton, of course, but we travel in different circles."

"What if I told you J. Edgar Hoover would like to send him packing?"

"Why?"

"He's a socialist."

"Oh," I said. I didn't say anymore because I never understood politics, and would have a hard time defining socialism on a high-school level exam. "What's he got to do with me?"

"This German professor was a friend of your friend, Mason Cooley."

"It seems like everybody was a friend of Mason's at one time or another."

"And recently," Miss Welles chimed in, "Dr. Cooley's friends have a habit of disappearing."

"Has this man disappeared?" I asked.

"Yes," the General said. "He vanished from his hotel room here in Washington late last night. Neither his family nor his assistant have heard from him."

"Stutka!" I said. Or was it even worse—*was it Elson*? Elson was not only in a position to meet the German professor regularly, but to even befriend him. It was a terrible thing to contemplate.

"Possibly," the General said.

"Did you get a line on him?" Miss Welles asked.

"He and several of his goons hopped a late-night train for DC," the General said.

"You picked him up?" I asked.

"No," the General nodded. "He shot two of our men at Union Station early this morning."

"He's gone!" I said.

The General nodded.

"The little rat," Miss Welles said. "When I get my hands on him, I'll twist his neck so hard he'll need a corkscrew to burp."

"Wait a minute," I said. "Why would Stutka—or anyone else—put the bag on the German?"

Miss Welles and the General exchanged glances. It is something that

---

[33] Clearly the German scientist is Albert Einstein (1879-1959) physicist, mathematician and philosopher of science. Armstrong never directly names him throughout the narrative for reasons that are now unknown to us.

I have seen her do several times now; she certainly wants me to trust her, but she is always reluctant to share anything with me.

"Let's just say that some of the German's research could be channeled into developing armaments."

The stones were dangerous enough. If they could be harnessed into some kind of weapon, then the entire world was in trouble. And if Stutka sold them to America's enemies, we would never be safe again.

"What would you like me to do, sir?" I asked.

"For now, figure out where those damned things come from," the General said. "If we can't trace where they're going, then we can trace the source. It's a start. We'll work on Stutka."

"I'll start now," I said. "You'll find that Princeton stands ready to help the War Department in any way possible."

Again, that shared look between the General and Miss Welles.

"Yes," he said. He gulped down his coffee. "Carry on. If anything occurs to you, just call out to the Corporal. He can find either me or Miss Welles at a moment's notice."

Without another word, he put down his cup and left.

Once again alone with Miss Welles, I wondered what we were going to do about Thurgood Elson. But before I could say a word, she ushered me to the door.

"Doc," she said, "get to work on this. We need answers and we need them now." She opened the door and the Corporal was standing at attention on the other side. For a moment, I felt he was more jailer than assistant. "Take him back to his room." She said to me, "If you need anything, yell."

"Wait a minute," I said. "What about—"

She closed the door on me.

"This way, sir," the Corporal said.

I smiled wanly and followed him back to my room. If anything, the activity in the large work area was even more intense. The graybeards had pulled apart the airplane model and were making notes on graph-lined paper. The radio operators fiddled with dials and made radio signals say uncle. It looked as if more people were huddled over codebooks.

We walked down the brick-lined corridor and the Corporal opened the door.

"Thanks," I said. "I had no idea that the War Department had such extensive operations."

"War Department?" he said, genuinely puzzled and amused. "We're not the War Department."

He saluted and closed the door.

Not the War Department?

Who were these people?

No wonder there was no sign of Benet. And, despite the uniforms and assurances of good will, could I even be sure that these people were Americans?

I plopped onto the bed and loosened my tie. Not the War Department? Should I even consider helping until I have a better understanding of who these people are?

Well—I thought. *I want to know as much as I can, no matter what.*

I threw my jacket onto the bed and took the photos from under my pillow. There was a sheaf of paper on the desk, a cup of very sharp pencils and a slide rule. There were no ashtrays, so I grabbed my bathroom glass and lit a Lucky, bringing the photographs over to work in earnest.

The process, I thought, should be easier this time. Since I had the correct figures for *finding* the stones, now it was merely a question of reversing the equations and seeing where they led.

But it was not easy. The correct numbers that led me to the stones in Grover's Mills made no sense when going the *other* way.

I re-did the calculations twice and, finding the answer ridiculous, then tossed out all of the original numbers and started work anew.

I was at it for several hours when there was a knock at the door. I looked up like a guilty schoolboy. I bundled the sheets together and turned them facedown.

"Yes?"

It was Miss Welles. "We have a little commissary and I was about to have some lunch. Want to come along?" Then her keen eye sized me up. "What's wrong with you? You look like you've seen a ghost."

I lit another Lucky and realized my hand trembled slightly. I also realized that there were ten dead cigarettes in my bathroom glass.

"Nothing," I said. "I'm just nervy after everything that's happened."

"Yeah, it does that," she said. "You should eat something."

I took a deep drag on my cigarette. "I'll catch up to you."

"Not in your wildest dreams."

"I mean for lunch," I said. "Where do I go?"

"Don't worry, the Corporal will guide you," she said. She opened the door and stopped at the threshold. "See you in a few minutes?"

"A few minutes," I said.

She left. I sat at the desk once more and checked my figures. Making allowances for Mason's habit of transposing numbers, wasting hours on dead-end numbers and figuring trajectories in every imaginable combination, I had to concede that my initial findings were correct.

Correct…? If correct, it was also incredible. Unbelievable.

I stacked the papers into a neat pile and folded them once. I grabbed my copy of *Tarzan and the Lion Man* and stuck them inside. And then I planned on how to get out of there.

I put on my jacket and crept to the door. I opened it slightly and saw, standing at attention in the corridor, the Corporal. He was facing the wide open-space work area. I eased the door shut.

I stuck my Burroughs in my jacket pocket and walked to the window. Like the front windows, this was covered by a nearly transparent Bakelite sheet. Other than that, however, it was an ordinary window. I grabbed the clasps and raised it quietly.

Outside was nothing but a large expanse of backyard. I had no idea how many townhouses were joined to make this complex, but from the rear the houses looked all the same. Across the way were another row of houses with *their* backyards.

Looking lengthwise up and down the backyards, I saw high stone brick walls.

Now, I figured it was possible that the houses opposite were also owned by my "hosts," so if I was going anywhere, it was over the wall.

I threw a leg over the sill and stepped onto the grass. I felt only half-dressed without a hat, but could do nothing about that now. I gently lowered the window.

Well—it was maybe five hundred feet to the nearest wall. The Corporal was certainly out back quickly enough once the autogyro landed—but I hoped to be less ostentatious than a flying machine landing in the backyard.

There were no obstructions out back associated with the individual houses. And the brick wall didn't seem that high—seven feet, at most. With a running start, I should be able to jump for the top, grab hold and hoist myself over.

I ran for it.

I think I had passed three of the townhouses before a backdoor opened. I heard "Hey Stop!" somewhere behind me, but kept running. I just prayed I didn't hear gun shots.

I panted—the wall coming ever closer as I ran. Behind me, the sound of footsteps, running, too.

Before I knew it, I reached the wall. I hit it hard in my panic, scooted up and grabbed the ledge and pulled myself over.

I didn't manage the descent well; instead of landing on my feet, I spilled onto the pavement. In seconds I took in my surroundings: a simple, residential side street.

Before I had time to blink another figure came over the wall. It was the Corporal. Unlike me he landed on his feet, arms bent and hands at the ready.

It was just dumb luck that saved me. I jumped to my feet; my forehead clipped him in the jaw (I heard his teeth *click* smartly) and he slipped back into the wall. He smacked his head against the bricks and slid down to his bottom, out for now.

My immediate instinct was to check that he was not hurt; then the survival instinct took control and I started running.

I had no idea where I was; I could be miles away from the Capitol and Smithsonian, or just down the block. I saw no subways or streetcars; there were no taxicabs. Just quiet, residential streets.

Better to keep them that way. I ran for three blocks till my wind gave out, then just walked briskly. In no time at all I made my way to into a small park. I hoofed it to a large oak, put my back to it and caught my breath.

I did not see anyone following me, but it seems people have been following me for days and I never saw any of *them*. But while I was free and on my own, I had better figure what to do next.

If there was just someone I could call! My first instinct was to call Elson, but I pushed that thought down with a bitter laugh. Then I thought of calling Pierson and checking my calculations with him, but I had no way of finding him! And if I called Benet—would he just turn me over to the General and Miss Welles? I could call my folks, but what would a middle-aged clothes salesman do in Illinois? Calling Mrs. Bradbury would be useless.

I moved on once I got my breathing under control. I went only three blocks further when I saw a bus approaching. I raced for the stop and reached the door just as it pulled up.

"Where're you going?" I asked the driver.

"Pal, if you want directions, buy a map," the driver said, face bland.

I put a nickel in the slot and took a seat. Wherever it was going would be fine with me. I looked out the window and watched the neighborhood retreat into the distance.

I was on the bus for nearly thirty minutes, and by then I was in the center of town. I saw Union Station in the distance and decided to walk from there.

"Here's fine, driver," I said.

"You think this is a cab?" he growled. He drove for another block until we were at the actual bus stop and he opened the door. "Sorry there ain't no red carpet," he said.

I took the stairs. "This is why they don't tip bus drivers," I said, as the doors closed in my face.

Despite the extra block out of my way, Union Station was still in my line of vision. I walked quickly towards it, thinking.

I could get a train to anywhere in the country. I could head to California and just forget the whole mess. Or I could go back to Princeton, confront Elson and get him to give himself up. Anything was possible.

These thoughts, along with my calculations based on Mason's numbers, filled my head as I crossed the street. I was still undecided about my eventual destination when I saw the poster wired to the corner streetlight.

It was gaudily colored and instantly brought a smile to my face. In the background was an elephant standing on his hind legs, rearing up before a clown holding a long whip. In the foreground was a cowboy hero, hat in hand as his arm flung backwards, astride a bucking horse. The thing was brilliantly colored, vibrant and irresistible—like a good pulp magazine cover.

And the cowboy—there was something vaguely familiar about him.

The poster read: DOWNIE BROTHERS CIRCUS! STARRING JACK HOXIE.

Of course! I saw lots of Hoxie movies when I was a kid; mostly silent. He was no Tom Mix, but Jack Hoxie was in some great westerns.[34] I even saw one of his talkies last year.

The topmost portion of the poster was blank, and written there in red, wax pencil was today's date, along with ONLY AT THE WHITSON FAIRGROUNDS.

The promise of forgetting this whole thing and going to the circus was almost overwhelming. I'd love to see Jack Hoxie in person, let alone the elephants, the clowns, the aerialists, and also the freak show with its fat ladies, tattooed men and midgets.

Midgets.

What was it Benet had said—Stutka started his career travelling with

---

34   Jack Hoxie (1885-1965) was a prominent rodeo performer who also achieved fame during the silent era as a movie cowboy. He spent much of the 1930s touring with the Downie Brothers. The westerns that Armstrong would have seen in his youth were, of course, silent movies. It seems Armstrong never lost his taste for the Western genre.

a circus. Why, it wouldn't be impossible to guess that he still had circus connections. And if he had to hide out in Washington—where better for a midget to be nondescript. A circus!

I pulled the poster off the pole and hailed a cab. In moments one pulled up and I hopped in the back.

I leaned over the front seat and handed him the poster. "Take me there."

He not only looked like my recent bus driver, he sounded like him, too. "Pal, that's a half hour out of the city. I won't get a fare going back. Take a hike."

"I'll pay you double."

He looked at me, suspicious. Then he took another glance at the poster. "The show don't start for a few hours yet."

"I don't mind waiting."

"And how are you going to get back?"

"I might be staying."

He shrugged and adjusted his cap. "Your funeral."

I sat back in the seat. "Maybe."

I had no idea where the Whitson Fairgrounds were, but it took us forever to get through Washington traffic, and then there was a long ride through some weedy countryside. After a time, the weeds gave away and we were in rolling farmland.

I actually smelled the circus before we saw it. The scent of sawdust, animals and gasoline instantly brought back boyhood memories. We followed our nose and soon I saw the huge yellow and red tents dominate the landscape.

I later found out that the Downie Brothers Circus is one of the largest travelling shows that does not rely on train travel. The Downie uses thirty-eight trucks, three tractors and three advance trucks to move from burg to burg, playing towns and cities, as well as the boonies and the sticks.

When the cab approached, the Downie people had already cleared a huge expanse of land to set up shop. There was one enormous tent—larger, certainly, than any mansion I had seen—buffeted on either side by a variety of smaller tents. There was an animal pen, where I saw caged lions and tigers taking the air, along with a substantive horse corral. The corral was peopled by some wranglers in full cowboy regalia, as well a few Indians—though, for all I knew, they may have been men in costumes.[35]

The cab rolled to a stop and I stepped out. I paid the driver double, and

---

35   Unlikely. The overwhelming majority of "Wild West" shows employed Native Americans; indeed, more Native Americans were employed by Wild West shows than any other industry in the US.

"I'll pay you double."

figured that was more than enough to skip the tip. He scowled at me but said nothing and drove off.

The evening's performance was still hours away. If I managed not to be too noticeable, I might be able to find Stutka, if he was even there. And even if he wasn't, I might be able to get a line on him from someone connected with the show. It was worth a shot.

I had done a lot of riding while in England, so I naturally went to the corral first. I must have been an incongruous figure, as both the cowboys and Indians looked up at my approach. The cowboys merely nodded beneath their wide-brimmed hats and spat; the Indians looked away, uninterested.

I put my hands on the wooden railing and let my eyes trail the expanse of the circus grounds. Teams of men were beating tent poles into the ground; smaller tents had sprung up to accommodate the clowns. On a bamboo mat a group of men and women were practicing acrobatic moves. In the distance, a lion roared.

Then I saw it: a large series of painted banners were going up for the freakshow. The Downie Brothers had their own geek, along with a man who drove nails into his skull, a mermaid, a dog-boy (whatever that was), a tattooed man (SKIN ILLUSTRATIONS the sign read), and various midgets. But, for now, it was simply a line of banners—the show tent beyond was not yet built.

Finally, one of the cowboys broke the silence. Looking me up and down, he asked, "You need help?"

Since I was the only man there in a suit, I figured I could be anything I wanted. I simply nodded and said, "Business."

He pulled on his Stetson and spat once more, considering. At length he said, "You looking for the boss?"

"I certainly wouldn't object."

It was one of the Indians who spoke next. "Pardon me, sir. But if you're looking for management, you can find them behind the ticket booth." Here he pointed into the distance. "Just on the other side of the Big Top."

I nodded thanks and moved on.

I walked slowly past the freak show—no midgets yet. I had nothing to lose, so I decided to see what I could learn from management.

The ticket booth was empty: a small wooden building, about three-times the size of a phone booth, with a wooden panel over the glass front. There was a trailer right behind it—a sleek, gunmetal gray thing that looked more like a luxury liner on wheels than a circus transport. The gray lines were unbroken expect for the name JACK HOXIE printed in gigantic red letters.

Wow, I thought. Jack Hoxie.

I circled the trailer, then took the three steps in the back to the door. It opened on one knock.

A giant of a man filled the doorway. I'm not small, but the cowboy towered over me. He wore the largest ten-gallon hat I had ever seen: it was chocolate brown and bigger than a New York City tenement. He wore a rust-colored shirt lined with mustard fringe down the sleeves and across the chest. His gun belt was studded with silver bullets, and his holster was hand-tooled leather, the name Jack Hoxie stenciled down the sides. His tight dungarees were tucked into the tops of his red-leather cowboy boots.

He was the best-looking ugly man I've ever met. His face was long and rectangular, his mouth too wide and lips too red; his brows almost met over the bridge of his nose. But it was an honest face, a welcoming one that shows friendship easily. He also looked haggard, and I would not be surprised if he already had one drink too many. He held out a gauntlet and I took his hand.

"Mr. Hoxie?" I said.

"You the reporter?" he asked.

"The reporter?"

"The reporter from the …." He absently waved a hand.

"Yeah, I'm from the …" and here I absently waved my hand. "May I come in?"

"Hell, that's what you're here for."

Hoxie stepped aside and I entered in trailer.

It was a marvelous place.

The walls were lined with photos of Hoxie and other luminaires: Hoxie with Buffalo Bill Cody, Hoxie with an elderly Wyatt Earp, Hoxie with William S. Hart, Hoxie with Tom Mix.[36] Wall space not covered in photographs held mementoes: a pair of silver-plated six guns hung in an X, there was an elaborate Dream Catcher, an old Charles Russell print and, suspended by two pegs, a vintage Winchester.

---

36   Among the most famous names of the Wild West, Buffalo Bill Cody (1846-1917), Wyatt Earp (1848-1929), William S. Hart (1864-1946) and Tom Mix (1880-1940) all loom large in history. Cody was an army scout and Indian fighter turned showman; it could be argued that the myth of the Wild West starts with him. Earp was the legendary lawmen who, with his brothers, fought the infamous Gunfight at the OK Corral. Both Hart and Mix were the first, and greatest, of the Silent Screen Western movie stars. It could be said Hoxie rubbed shoulders with Titans. Curiously, a signed photo of Mix was found among Armstrong's personal effects.

The trailer was furnished with two armchairs, a daybed that would make a courtesan blush, and a bar.

Hoxie walked to the bar, spurs jingling as he walked. "Set a spell, pard," he said, taking up a bottle. "Drink?"

"No," I sat. "Thank you."

Hoxie turned and gave me a look, then poured a drink and sat opposite me. He took a long swallow and said, "Well, where would you like to start? My Cherokee maw? My days with the Rough Riders? Or maybe a story about me and Wyatt Earp?" He waved absently towards the photo of him and Earp. "We knowed each other in Hollywood, back in the day."

"Let's start with the circus," I said. "Tell me about it."

"One of the biggest shows on the road," he said, taking another sip. "We got everything you could ask for—elephants, a lion tamer, aerialists, the works."

I nodded.

"But I'm going to let you in on a little secret," he leaned closer and took another sip. "Not for publication."

"Of course."

"I'm going to buy out the show and make it Hoxie's Circus. That's where the real money is. The circus is dying out," he said. "But the Wild West! The Wild West is forever." He drained the glass and got to his feet once more. He refilled his glass at the bar and asked if I was sure I wanted nothing. I was sure.

He sat and sipped. "You on the entertainment beat, or special events?"

"Just a general reporter," I said. "I wanted this assignment because I wanted to meet you."

He nodded as if that was a given.

"I grew up on your movies and just wanted to see the show." I paused. "I saw them setting up outside. Do you think the sideshow interferes with the Big Top show?"

"No one comes for just the sideshow."

"Yeah, but some of those acts have a following of their own," I said. "Tell me about the midgets."

Hoxie drained his glass and put it on the table, making a *smacking* sound with the roof of his mouth and tongue. "Pard, just who the hell are you?"

"A reporter."

"With?"

"With…" I made the airy gesture again.

"I ain't never knowed a reporter who turned down a drink."

I was quiet.

"You want an autograph?"

I cleared my throat. "Well, I'm here for something more important."

"What could be more important than my autograph?"

"Well, my name is Peter Armstrong and I'm a professor of astronomy at Princeton Observatory."

"Cosmology, observational or theoretical?"

"You know something about astronomy!"

"Just because I ride a horse don't make me ignorant. What do you want, Professor Armstrong?"

"I'm looking for a man."

"Wrong number."

"No, I mean a particular man. A dwarf named Leon Stutka."

I don't know how he did it while seated, but Hoxie slid a pearl-handled six shooter from its holster and cocked it. He pointed in my direction—with the same airy uncertainty he used trying to remember my "newspaper."

"Keep talkin'."

I gulped. "No need for that."

"Let me decide that."

"Well—this Stutka—"

"Is a low-down, mud-crawlin' sidewinder."

"I couldn't have said it better myself."

"He spent some time in the Gollmer Brothers outfit," he said. "I heard he killed a couple of people."

"Yes."

"And he's a pard of yours?"

"No!"

"You a lawdog?"

"No. He killed a friend of mine at Princeton. I traced him to Princeton and came here, looking for him. On a hunch."

Hoxie's eyes got flinty, then he eased the six shooter back into its holster. "What makes you think he's here?"

"He shot some government men at Union Station. I was there and saw the sign for your circus and got to thinking—where better to hide a midget than in a bevy of midgets?"

"You *are* an egghead," he said with something like admiration. "I don't think you'll find him here, but feel free to look. But don't kill him on the fairgrounds. Bad for business." He waved an arm. "The kids come, you know."

"I just want to find him," I said. "I don't plan on killing anybody."

"Most no one ever does," he said. "You packin' a smoke wagon?"

"I beg your pardon?"

"A gun, Dr. Big Brain. Do you got a gun?"

"No."

He got up and took one of the silver-plated six shooters from the wall. He cracked the barrel and casually loaded it with bullets from his belt. "Listen here, Doc. There ain't no such thing as a dead hero. There's only dead. And there ain't no cure for dead."

I thought of O'Brien, and his scream as he fell to his death.

"No."

Hoxie poured another drink and swallowed it all in a gulp. Now that both he and the gun were loaded, he came closer. "Take this," he pulled on my belt and stuck the gun behind it. "A remember, shoot low. They may be crawlin.'"

"Thanks," I buttoned my jacket.

"Now scat," he said. "I got a reporter from," he waved airily, "comin.'"

I took his hand and, for some reason, said, "God bless." It something I never say; I was rather surprised it came out of me.

"He does, Pard," Hoxie closed the door on me. "He does."

I stepped back into the circus grounds. I didn't want to haunt the sideshow tent and give Stutka a chance to see me—if he was coming—so I just ambled along. I saw the big cats and watched the lion tamer stuff the sleeves of his pendulous shirt with matting for protection. There was a long row of tables where clowns applied their makeup, and I even watched the boys wash down the elephants.

But I spent most of my time with the horses. The cowboys were taciturn but surprisingly comforting. I watched as they went through their paces, rehearsing trick riding, roping and wrestling a steer. They even shared their hamburger lunch with me—it was the freshest beef I had ever eaten.

Near the close of the afternoon the ticket booth opened and cars filled the adjacent field as customers flooded in. Some of the show tents started operation—there was a special pit where Hoxie's horse Dynamite—and the cotton candy and popcorn booths— were already humming. Huge arc lights were powered by a generator atop a flatbed truck. In the distance, I could hear the calliope.

Workmen had earlier created the sideshow platform, and later erected the tent around it. Petunia, the Fat Lady, was the first to arrive, followed by a young man with a full beard and a hairline that reached down to the top of his brow—obviously the dog-face boy. The Illustrated Man wore nothing but a loincloth and his tattoos undulated with each step. I saw two elderly midgets, obviously husband and wife, file in last.

This is hopeless, I thought.

Suddenly, a bag was thrust into my face and I could see nothing.

CHAPTER ELEVEN

"Popcorn?"

I pushed the bag out of my face and standing there was Miss Welles. She reached into the bag plopped a few kernels into her mouth. "It's good. Just salt, no butter."

She was still in that smart gray suit, but now accented it with a pert square hat balanced on her auburn hair. She blinked and her eyes were lovely.

"What are you doing here?"

"I'm here, I'm on business," she ate more popcorn. "Sure you don't want some?"

"How did you know I was here?"

"I didn't," she surveyed the circus. "But I can't say I'm sorry to see you. You'll have hell to pay with the Corporal, though. He still had a headache when I left."

"Say, just what's going on? I thought you worked for the War Department."

She made an airy gesture with her hand. "Roving commission."

I made an airy gesture with my hand. "Who do you think you are? Jack Hoxie?"

"Only in some ways," she said. "I'm prettier."

"Well, there's that."

"What makes you think Stutka is here?"

"You don't fool around."

"I don't have time."

"I figured a midget would be invisible in a field of midgets."

"Smart boy."

"You're the second person to say that today."

"The second?"

"Yeah," I said, "but you're the prettiest. What brought you here?"

"Informants," she said. "You'd be surprised by the things we know."

"It's good. Just salt, no butter."

Like hell I would, I thought.

A child wearing a plaid shirt and gray knickers walked close by. She held out the bag of popcorn and the kid grabbed it with a, "thanks, sister!"

"Cute kid," she said, as he walked away. "Didn't you get into Stutka's place with a kid dressed as an adult?"

"What about it?"

"What makes you think he's not now an adult dressed as a kid?"

"I hadn't thought of that."

"Don't worry," she said. "You're doing fine. It just gets easier."

"If I'm lucky, when this is over, I'll still be alive and with luck I'll never see you again."

She looked at me, grinning. "And I thought we were friends."

"My friends don't play me for a sap."

"That you know of."

"Oh, this is hopeless. Look, I've been here all afternoon and no sign of him. Do you have a car? Can you take me back to the city? Or am I under some kind of arrest?"

"I'm not ready to give up yet, and I may stay for the show." Her eyes continued to survey the circus grounds. "And I'd stick close to me, if I were you."

I slipped an arm through hers.

"What are you doing?"

"Taking you at your word." We walked along the fairway; there were games, fortune tellers and a menagerie. We toured past the Big Top, then made our way around one of the adjourning tents. Beyond the arc lights all was darkness. Then, I felt her body tense.

"What?"

She did not say anything, but nodded up ahead.

About forty feet away was a trailer, similar to Hoxie's, but nowhere near as grand. Stenciled on the side was the legend: THE FAMILY SMALL.

But the thing that really caught her attention was the man stepping out of the trailer. It was a tall man in a rumpled trench coat, a fedora pulled over his face. The bottom half of his face was covered with a surgical mask, like doctors wear in the hospital.

"So?"

"Think, genius. What did you do to Romero?"

I looked up at the man again. He hadn't seen us. He thrust his hands into his pockets and stepped into the darkness. "You think that's him?"

"You busted up his mouth pretty good."

"The Family Small," I read. "It could be midgets."

Now she pulled me along. "Let's take a short look."

The trailer had three small windows, round like portals, and all were lit. Still arm-in-arm, we went past the door in back. It had no window and there was nothing to see. We circled the trailer, saw nothing in the windows on the opposite side, and there was no driver in the cab up front.

Standing back where we started, I asked, "What now? Do we knock and visit?"

"I'll let you in," a voice came. And then something hard and cold pressed against the back of my neck.

Miss Welles twisted fast, but the voice said, "Keep calm, girlie, or I put a bullet in your boyfriend here."

"I'm not her boyfriend," I said.

Miss Welles released my arm and I slowly raised my hands level with my chest. Very slowly, I turned around.

It was Romero. The collar of his coat was pulled up, but I could still see the rust-stained surgical mask under his hat brim.

"I was hoping I'd run into you again." The words sounded mushy and indistinct.

"She's just a friend," I said. "And doesn't know anything about it."

He flicked the gun. "Both of you. Move."

I didn't move.

Romero cocked the automatic.

Miss Welles nodded and we walked to the trailer. At the base of the steps leading up to the back door, I almost stepped aside, with a gesture of *after you*. The grotesque nature of the gesture forced me to suppress a giggle.

"You'll think it's funny when you're picking lead out of your brain," the mushy voice said.

I opened the door and led the way in.

The occupants of the trailer turned in shock. The shock was not one-sided.

In the center of the room was Stutka. He had changed into a navy-blue suit and red tie; looking for all the world like a child dressed for church.

He was surrounded by six other dwarves—all men of middle age and each dressed in gaudy suits of good cut. One of them stepped forward but drew back at the sight of Miss Welles and then Romero.

It wasn't the occupants alone that were remarkable. The trailer was no larger than Hoxie's, but the miniature chairs, couches and child-sized bed made the interior loom much larger than it otherwise was.

"You," Stutka gasped.

"A man of short words," Miss Welles said.

That didn't strike me as a good opening gambit. I said, "I'm happy to see that you were not hurt at the club."

"I'm touched," he looked up at Romero. "Where'd you find them?"

"They were tryin' to see through the windows," the mushy voice said. He reached behind me and slid a hand down the front of my jacket. The six gun that Hoxie had given me was taken from my belt. "He had a gat. What do you want me to do with them?"

Stutka considered. He took a silver cigarette case from his interior pocket and lit a long, dark brown cigarette. Finally, he said, "Dr. Armstrong, take a seat."

I moved towards one of the child-sized chairs and settled into it. The arms pressed against my hips like long, wooden fingers.

"I think we can make a deal," the dwarf suggested.

"A deal? You've tried to kill me twice."

He waved that away—it seemed we were in the middle of an epidemic of hand-waving. "I am about to regain procession of the stones and will need a man with brains to handle them until I get them out of the country. You have brains."

"Where are you taking them?"

"What difference does that make to you?"

"If I'm making a deal with you, I'd like to know all the facets of it."

"The deal is simple," he said. "You help me, and I don't kill you."

That *was* simple.

"You know where they are?"

"Don't be stupid," he said. "Your boss has them."

Elson again—he must think we're working together.

"I've been squeezed out," I said. "I don't know where there are."

"I do," he said, blowing smoke. "Come along with me. You'll live longer. For now. And, I'll let her go."

"She just walks out of here?"

Stutka nodded towards Romero. "My associate will escort her out of the circus. Safely, I assure you."

"When do we leave?"

"Now. I was just gathering together my associates."

"All these people. They're gangsters, too?"

Before any of them could reply, Miss Welles said, "Only in a small way."

Stutka's face hardened. "I'm doing my best to let you out of this with your skin intact. Tell your girlfriend to keep her mouth shut."

I turned to Miss Welles and tightly said, "Please knock it off. *Dear.*"

She looked daggers at me.

"Deal?" Stutka said.

"Yes," I said.

Stutka turned to one of the dwarves. "Benny, start her up and let's move it. I want to be there before too late."

Benny took a tiny fedora from a peg on the wall, walked around us for safety, and left.

Stutka turned to me. He took another pull on his cigarette and then crushed it in the ashtray. "No need for a handshake."

"We should." I rose and the chair, pinching me around the rear, came up off the floor with me. I reached behind and pulled it off—then raised it high and brought it down on Romero.

The gunman dropped his automatic and staggered backward. I pushed past Miss Welles and grabbed him by the lapels and pushed him hard against the wall.

One of the midgets pulled a gun but Stutka barked, "Not here! You'll have the whole place on us!"

I reached up for Romero's throat and got hold. His powerful hands closed around my wrists and squeezed as I choked him.

I couldn't see what was behind me, but I heard the patter of little feet, then a yowlp as Miss Welles barreled into her tiny foemen.

The motor of the trailer hummed and suddenly everything lurched as the tires pulled from the soft earth. I lost my footing and Romero and I tottered from one side of the trailer to the other, still locked in our lethal embrace.

But now, my back was to the wall. Romero braced his forearms and slammed upwards, knocking my hands away from his throat. I was back on him in an instant, clawing at his face.

My fingers locked around the edge of his surgical mask and pulled. It yanked off his face like an unhealed scab. Romero howled and stepped back.

Where his mouth had been was now a blackened hole. His lips had burned away; charred lines encircled his mouth like errant electrical bolts. His tongue, shriveled and black, had burnt down to the size of a thumb. The gold teeth nestled in gums that looked raw and bloody.

Romero grabbed me in his rage and slammed the hard plane of his forehead into the bridge of my nose. I saw sheets of white lightning and almost went down.

It was Miss Welles who saved the moment. She was on his back, literally, having hopped on with her knees around his waist, and planted a finger in his ruined mouth and pulled.

The trailer moved over unpaved roads and the entire room jumped. Romero and Miss Welles stumbled back like a Siamese jack-in-the-box while I nearly fell into Stutka.

The little man planted a blow right at my belt buckle and the air went out of me. I smacked him on the side of the head and when he came back for more, I smacked him again. He fell into the remaining dwarves, two of whom climbed over him and went for me.

Romero reached over his head and clawed Miss Welles in the face.

I wouldn't have time for the midgets.

I pushed the two coming for me hard and they went down on top of Stutka. I stepped close to Romero. His eye grew wide as I approached, but he kept his hands on Miss Welles.

I reared back and punched him in the mouth. He cried out in pain and let go of the woman. She fell off his back and rolled on the floor.

I punched Romero again and he swung at me. It was just luck and the rolling of the trailer—I had stepped back and his fist went wild. I rammed a shoulder into him and we reeled backwards towards the trailer door.

Romero's back hit the door with a crash. My visual perspective changed as the trailer took an incline. Putting a palm on the door next to Romero's head to keep my balance, I punched him in the face once more with my other hand. Then I hit him again.

And the next thing I knew, I was floating in space.

As the trailer sped up an incline, the door opened and Romero and I spilled out. I landed on soft earth and rolled. I got to my knees but was blinded—brilliant white light seemed to be everywhere.

I blinked. When my vision returned, I saw Romero. He stood in the soft earth, unsteady on his feet. He reached into the folds of his trench coat and brandished the same six shooter that Hoxie gave me earlier.

"Die, you son of a bitch," he said.

"Don't do it, pard!" a voice came sharp and cold.

Romero blinked and turned. So did I.

It seemed we had fallen near the actor's entrance at the Big Top. Jack Hoxie stood beside Dynamite, holding a six shooter. Behind him, all on horseback, were twenty cowboys, all waiting for their entrance.

Dynamite was a magnificent horse—a black stallion standing seventeen hands with liquid-black eyes and bushy mane. His nostrils flared and he snorted, a sound like controlled thunder, at the prospect of blood. He bridled and Hoxie clutched more tightly at the reins.

Romero turned his attention back to me and aimed.

Then came a sound unlike any I had ever heard before. I looked—it was the sound of twenty-one six guns all cocking at once.

"Pard," Hoxie said, "you got two choices. Drop the gun, or be dead."

Romero looked from them to me and back again to them. He tossed the six gun into the soft earth.

I got to my feet.

"You okay, pard?" Hoxie asked.

"It's Stutka," I said. "He was here but he just got away in that van!"

I pointed into the distance.

"Good riddance."

"We've got to stop them. They've kidnapped a girl."

Hoxie considered. "Can you ride?"

"English saddle."

"Pard, you're trading up to Western. Here. Take Dynamite."

"A horse can't catch a trailer."

Hoxie pointed. "They took that road?"

"Yes!"

He pointed again. "Go over the pasture *there*. It's half the trip. You can cut them off at the pass."

I didn't need to be told twice. I ran over and climbed up the saddle. Dynamite shuddered and I patted his withers.

"Can you take care of him? He's wanted by the police."

Hoxie spat. "Yeah."

I grabbed the reins and Dynamite reared upward with a whinny. In an instant I was off. As the circus receded behind me, I heard Hoxie shout, "Call the police, but first call my publicist! And get the goddamn camera!"

Dynamite took the pasture like a rocket. The wind swept through my hair and I felt my heart beat in rhythm with his hoofbeats. Clumps of earth were thrown up behind us, and I crouched low in the saddle to keep down wind resistance.

In my frantic effort to get Miss Welles, I had no real idea of what I would do when I reached the trailer on the road. I did not think of getting another gun from Hoxie, and had no stratagem to get them to stop. Maybe I could block the road with something, I figured.

Dynamite kept top speed for ten minutes. It was then that I saw, off to my left, the road and its upcoming turn. I could see the headlights of the trailer in the gloom. At our current speeds, we would actually collide near the turning.

I spurred Dynamite on and we galloped through the countryside.

The pasture here cut lower, and in my speed I had a terrible moment where I feared Dynamite would break a leg. But the stallion took it in stride and somehow, and I'm not sure how, I took the gentle incline and found myself speeding beside the trailer.

I urged Dynamite closer to the car, hoping the animal would not be skittish. But decades of chasing stage coaches, careening wagons and legions of Hollywood badmen rendered the horse fearless. Dynamite knew exactly what I was up to and sped right beside the trailer.

There was a small ladder that ran up the rear-side of the trailer beside the door, leading to its roof. I had no real plan—I just reached out for it.

I had the cold steel in hand and tightened my grip. I felt myself sliding from the saddle and for one terrifying moment, feared I would fall beneath horse and trailer. Then, with a lurch from the trailer, I was suspended midair.

I slammed into the ladder with a bone-crushing smack. To my right, Dynamite galloped away from the road, and then back onto the pasture. In the gloom I could make out his silhouette as he retreated back to the Circus and to Hoxie.

The wind whipped my body, my jacket billowing around me. I held tight and waited for some response from within. With nothing coming, I started up the ladder.

The top of the trailer was smooth, with a slight upward curve. There were four knobby protrusions—probably for affixing some type of circus signage or tent extension. I eased myself on top of the trailer and slid towards them.

The surface of the trailer was slick and the slipstream from the drive kept me unsteady. There was a torturous minute as I groped for the knobs, and when I finally closed each hand around them, I sighed with relief.

I looked forward, wind whipping my face. We were driving through the sticks, and the lights of Washington glowed in the distance. I kept my head down and to the side, pressing the side of my face against the top of the trailer. I watched the blur of the passing landscape and tried to listen for anything inside the trailer. I heard neither voices nor screams, which gave me some measure of hope.

I was cold and my fingers grew numb. After a time, the fields of the countryside gave way to homes just outside the city proper and soon we were in Washington itself. From my crouched vantagepoint, I saw the spire of the Washington Monument against the dark blue sky.

I worried at first that the sight of a man atop a moving vehicle would attract undue attention, but I soon realized that the trailer was too high for anyone on the sidewalk or in an adjacent car to see me. I would be able to stay undetected if my luck held until we reached wherever we were going.

We soon left the heart of DC behind and were again amid houses on the outskirts of town. I chanced a look ahead and saw that we were approaching a winding road that led to an enormous gatehouse, done in the Greek Revival style. It had two towers on either side, a small building in the center with a peaked roof, and the building was buffeted on either side by a prodigious stone wall.

We slowly approached the facade; the front door was an entryway to the area beyond. There were posts on either side of the entrance, and the stone walls were adorned with bas relief anchors. There was a guard house, and two men in military uniform stood at attention on either side, rifles at the ready.

It took a moment to recognize in the darkness, but I quickly realized that I was at the Washington Navy Yard.[37]

The trailer slowed to a stop. I craned my neck to look down.

The soldier on the driver's side approached and I heard the midget in the cab say something—what, I could not make out.

Then came the noise. It came from both sides of the trailer, coordinated with exact timing. There was a low *bang*, like a loud exhalation of breath, that came from the portal windows on either side. It was the sound of two guns fired, at exactly the same time, but the sound muffled in some way unfamiliar to me.

Neither guard had a chance. Both men dropped dead to the ground, their rifles useless beside them.

The rear door of the trailer opened and five dwarves climbed out. They pulled the two dead men into the guard house and opened the gate. One stayed behind while the other piled back in.

We drove through the entrance and paused, allowing time for the remaining dwarf to close the gate and get back into the trailer.

Inside the Navy Yard looked like some kind of massive industrial

---

37   The Washington Navy Yard was built in 1799 and is the oldest shore establishment of the U.S. Navy. In the 1930s and 40s, it also served as a scientific research and weapons development site.

complex. There were dozens of low-brick buildings, many much of the same type, windows mostly dark at this time of night. There were loading bays and gated doors and the shadows of great machinery hiding behind smoky windows.

In the distance, it was possible to see the Anacostia River. There were several ships in the harbor, now mostly shadows at night, along with what looked like an old submarine.

We drove very slowly through the rows of buildings, only stopping at one of the low-brick structures right at the water's edge. The lights were out. The trailer flashed the headlights twice, stopped, then flashed them once more.

The doors of the building opened and four men in dark suits came outside. They pulled the doors wide and the trailer snaked inside the building. When the doors shut behind me, the lights overhead came to life.

I was in some kind of factory. There was a series of conveyor belts and piles of metal plates; long groupings of work tables and a network of overhead cables. The trailer once again opened and the dwarves piled out, Stutka and Miss Welles leaving last. He held an automatic on her.

One of the men who opened the door came forward.

"Take her to the office and keep an eye on her," Stutka ordered.

The man took Miss Welles by the elbow. She pulled away and walked unaided. He led her down the length of the room and through a wooden door.

The remaining man said, "What next?"

"We need to get the goods before they can be loaded onboard," Stutka barked. "But we can't take chances. Do you have the boxes?"

"Check," the man said.

"Let's see."

Stutka and the six other dwarves followed the man to another wing of the factory. They went through a door; the sound of it closing was final in the now-empty great room of the factory.

So Elson was somewhere nearby. Clearly his intention was to leave the country with the stones, either to transport them by water to a more secure site, or, like Stutka, to sell them to a foreign power.

I let go of the knobs on top of the trailer, my hands aching, and went down the ladder. My first thought was of Miss Welles, but the lives of many would depend on the final location of the stones. I needed to know first what Stutka had in mind.

I crept down the workroom towards the room Stutka entered. I kept close to the wall and the shadows, careful to not make a sound. I moved to the door, hoping for a look through the keyhole.

It was then that the door at the opposite end of the factory opened. The goon who had secured Miss Welles stepped out and closed it behind him.

I dived behind some metal plating and into the shadows.

The man walked through the factory and approached the door. I had a passing thought—insanity!—of subduing him and putting on his hat and taking his place, but dismissed it instantly. That was the kind of stuff that happened in pulp magazines, not real life.

The man passed me by and entered the room with Stutka and his colleagues. He did not, however, close the door. I heard them speaking, but not clearly enough to make out what they were saying.

I slid along the wall, back to where I was, and hid behind the now open door.

I heard wood splintering and nails pulled. Then there was a rustling sound.

I peered around the rim of the door.

Inside, Stutka's cadre of dwarves were pulling radioactivity-protective gear from boxes; suits much like those I wore when looking for the stones in New Jersey. One of the small men was already pulling the shiny, metallic gear over the trousers of his dark suit.

Well—they weren't going far in those heavy, protective suits. Elson and the stones had to be very close, indeed.

Whatever I needed to do, I knew I couldn't do it alone. I could risk looking for a phone and calling for help, but doubted the uniform police would be much use, and had no idea of how to reach Benet. If the cavalry was going to come, it would have to be Miss Welles.

I eased away from the door and nearly ran to the opposite end of the factory on my tip toes.

I made it to the door, which the gunman left unlocked. I gripped the handle, turned it as quietly as possible, and slipped inside.

The room was dark. I felt for the light switch and, in a flash, saw Miss Welles and her companion.

The room was normally that of the factory supervisor. There was a large desk covered with papers, and a leather chair. Several file cabinets were placed around the walls, and an enormous map of the United States graced one of the walls.

Miss Welles was sitting on a plain, wooden kitchen chair, hands and feet tied to the arms and legs of the chair. A red handkerchief with white dots covered her mouth. Her eyes widened at the sight of me.

Her companion was a white-haired man seated behind the desk, his head down atop the papers. He appeared to be either dead or asleep.

I ran to Miss Welles and took off her gag.

"What kept you?" she asked.

"A simple thank you would be nice," I said, pulling on her bonds.

"Thanks. Hurry, will you?"

I couldn't work the knots and went to the desk. Next to the unconscious man was a letter opener. I grabbed this and started to saw away at the ropes.

"Who is your friend?" I asked.

"We have to get him out of here," she said.

"We all have to get out of here," I said, getting her right hand free. She took the letter opener from me and started cutting her left hand free by herself. I walked over to the unconscious man.

I gently lifted his head. There, under a wild matt of frizzled white hair, was a kindly face with a dark mustache. He wore a gray tweed jacket, a black corduroy vest and gray flannel slacks. He seemed asleep or drugged.

"It's *him*," I said, seeing the German scientist in person for the first time. I lifted an eyelid and saw his eyeball rolled upward. "He's been drugged."

"Beats being dead," she said, now cutting her legs free.

I picked up the phone. "I'll call help."

She reached over and took the phone from me. She put the receiver to her ear and hit the button. "Operator? Hello, Operator?"

That's when the gunshots started.

She put down the phone. "Trouble."

I dropped to a knee at the sound of gunshots and pulled the old German scientist to the floor beside me. I quickly noticed that Miss Welles did not follow suit. Instead, she pulled the square hat from atop her head and turned it inside out.

There, under the red satin lining, was a thin, gray automatic.

"In case you were in a jam?" I asked.

She said nothing and moved for the door. "Keep down." Holding the gun aloft, she gently opened the door and peered outside.

She turned quickly and indicated the large bay window. "Do you think you can carry him?"

"He's dead weight," I said. "But yeah."

The gunshots came louder now. It was two shots in quick succession that rose the alarm, and after Miss Welles went to the door, I heard four more. Now, multiple shots were firing at once.

She came over to me and handed me the gun. It was surprisingly light. "Hold this."

Miss Welles went to the window. Like most factory windows, it was high and wide and made up of multiple panes. The lower panes were all latched for opening, but they had been painted over in the past and would not budge. Miss Welles went round the desk and picked up the wooden chair that previously held her. She went to the window and brandished it high above her head, about to break the glass.

Then came three shots—close by and close together—BANG, BANG, BANG! Miss Welles let go of the chair and dropped below the desk.

"You hit?" I cried out.

"Stay down!" she hissed.

The sound of scuffling was loud and something slammed against the other side of the door. I heard a high-pitched voice cry out and then there was another gunshot—again, right outside the door. Then, silence.

I crouched beside the unconscious man, listening to the sound of my own breathing.

Then, the doorknob slowly turned.

The door opened and in came Stutka, a long gash down the side of his face, his smart suit streaked with blood.

Stutka was followed by a hand holding a silver automatic. Then the rest of the gunman came into view.

I heaved a sigh of relief.

Standing in the doorway, a brace of government agents behind him, was William Benet of the War Department.

I got to my feet, letting the German slide gently to the floor. "Boy, am I glad to see you."

Benet smiled and held out a hand. "I'll take that," he said.

I crossed over, handing him the gun.

Just before he closed his fingers around it, Miss Welles popped up from behind the desk.

"DON'T!"

Benet's hands closed around the small gun. He passed it to one of the men behind him, and then pointed his automatic at me.

"And now, Dr. Armstrong," he said, "you will please put your hands behind your head."

CHAPTER TWELVE

"What?" Benet stuck his automatic under my chin. "Hands behind your head."

"I would do what he says," Miss Welles said.

Stutka looked at me, then Benet, then Miss Welles, and back again at Benet.

I raised my hands and interlaced my fingers behind my head.

The sound of a shot—loud with reverberation—erupted as he took the gun away and my entire body shook. Then, a few seconds later, came another shot. It had a terrible finality.

A man came to the door and whispered something to Benet. He nodded and said, "Then get ready for transport."

He now turned to Stutka. "Those were the last two of your confederates. Now you're really shorthanded."

"Hey," Stutka said. "What's going on?"

Something I would have liked to know myself.

"You won't get very far," Miss Welles started. "My people have kept careful watch."

Benet grinned—a curiously cold and nasty grin. "Penelope, dear Penelope. You treacherous bitch."

He walked closer and she glared at him with defiance,

He answered by slapping her hard across the face with the back of his hand. She did not cry out, but I did. I roared with anger and made a jump for him.

But Benet was ready for me. He glided around and, as I came closer, shoved the barrel of automatic into my mouth. The cold metal pushed between my teeth, jabbing the roof of my mouth.

Benet turned to one of his confederates. "Check on the German."

A man came in and took the pulse of the German scientist, then lifted an eyelid.

"Still out."

"Wake him enough to move," Benet said.

The man pulled a small packet from the hip pocket of his jacket and cracked it in half, holding it under the German's nose. The man mewled, coughed, and struggled to get conscious. Soon, he blinked, eyes registering his surroundings and trying to make sense of them.

Stutka never took his eyes from Benet.

Benet pulled the gun from my mouth—a welcome relief—and motioned toward the men in the doorway. Two more men came, each wrapping one of the German scientist's arms over a shoulder, and hauled him to his feet.

"Make him comfortable," he said. He turned to me. "He'll have company. Other people's brains, you know."

I didn't like the sound of that.

He said to the man who administered the smelling salts. "Check on Stutka's men. Make sure they're dead."

Stutka's face hardened even more.

"Then gather them up; we'll dispose of them at sea."

Benet now turned his attention to us. "Well, that's that." He said to Penelope, "I could kill you and Stutka now, if I wanted. But you might still prove useful." He turned to the dwarf. "But you—you've never been of any use to me."

He cocked his automatic and pressed it against the center of the little man's forehead. Stutka showed no fear; he did not even close his eyes. If anything, he looked more defiant than ever.

I winced, waiting for the shot.

But, before it came, another man appeared at the door. "Boss, they need you out front."

Benet looked up, then un-cocked his automatic. "You can wait for it," he told Stutka. "More fun that way." He turned to the man. "Keep them here. If they give you any trouble, remember I want the big man alive," he said, motioning to me.

And he left.

Stutka exhaled loudly.

Benet's stooge reached into his pocket and pulled a .38 police special.

"Just keep it calm, folks," he said.

Stutka paid no attention. "What the hell is going on? I thought you worked for him?"

"Wait a minute! Me first!" I turned to Miss Welles. "What the hell is going on? I thought you worked for him?"

"My people have been watching him for months," she said.

"*My people*?" I cried. "Who the hell are you?"

"Shut up, Brainiac!" Stutka barked. "Girlie, you ain't with the War Department?"

"No," she said. She looked at the gun-toting stooge. "But Benet's not doing this for the War Department. Is he?"

He pointed at me. "He's the only one I've got to keep alive. So watch your mouth."

It hit me then—the reason for all of her suggestive looks, her seeming disinterest in Elson, that secret satrap with the General—Elson never had anything to do with it. It was Benet. It was Benet all the time, and Miss Welles was after *him*. I graduated to Chump, First Class.

Miss Welles must have read my face. "He was going to sell the rocks to the Germans," she said, indicating Stutka. "But Benet was going to keep them for himself. With his resources and friends in the War Department, he could set himself up as a veritable emperor of the United States."

"Shut your mouth," the stooge said, voice full of warning.

"They were going to move them tonight to some more secure location," she said. She turned to Stutka. "But we know *you* have people in the War Department and wouldn't give up. So, to find Benet, we just had to find you."

I reeled.

That's when Stutka made his move. The stooge had his eyes leveled on Miss Welles and myself, so the dwarf was able to take him by surprise. Stutka reached up with both hands and grabbed the gunman's wrist and pulled down. When it came down, Stutka bit into the wrist.

The man howled and the gun slid across the floor.

I lowered my hands and ran to help Stutka.

The gunman pulled away from the dwarf and swatted at him like a housewife swats at a household pest. I stepped close and the man threw a punch at my head. I ducked, but his fist grazed the top of my forehead and I pitched to the side.

Before the gunman could press his attack, however, Miss Welles bounded across the room and savagely stuck two fingers into the man's eyes.

He cried out again and crouched, hands over his eyes. She hooked a long-nailed finger into one of his nostrils and pulled upward.

I was steady on my feet again. When the gunman shot upward, following both her finger and his nose, I hit him on the jaw with everything I had. The man staggered backward two steps and went down and out.

I turned to Miss Welles to see if she was hurt, but her attention was solely on Stutka. I followed her gaze.

Stutka had followed the gun and now held the .38. His flinty eyes squinted.

I raised my hands.

"Nix," he growled. "I want Benet."

"Me, too," Miss Welles said.

I opened the door. There was no one outside to have heard our melee. "It's clear," I said.

"There's a German U-Boat here," Stutka said. "Germany has re-started submarine construction."

"I thought that was against the treaty?[38]"

The face Stutka made could *almost* be a smile. "Not when you build them for research. The War Department got their hands on one of them, a Type 1 U-25. That's what Benet's using to move the stones."

"Where?" Penelope asked.

"Gulf of Mexico," the dwarf said. "Benet has a weapons development center south of the boarder." He motioned with the gun. "Let's go."

"What about him?" I pointed to the unconscious gunman.

Stutka walked over and kicked the unconscious man in the temple. Hard. "He isn't getting up."

We stepped into the factory. The silence was now eerie; the lights were on but, except for the trailer brought by the dwarves, the large space was empty. He led us to the trailer.

"We were going to take out Benet's men and take the submarine," he said.

"You know how operate a submarine?" I asked.

"Benny did."

Blood stains pooled in multiple places. The pools had smeared where it was clear that the under-sized bodies had been dragged away. If Stutka felt anything for his fallen confederates, he said nothing.

The trailer was still open. Stutka took us inside and opened a cupboard in the kitchen area. Instead of pots and pans were a network of handguns, all nestled in a wooden framework. He tossed the .38 aside and removed two large .45 automatics. He shoved one in his armpit holster and kept the other in his hand.

"Help yourselves."

Miss Welles didn't need to be asked twice. She stepped up and took a Colt six shooter that would have done Jack Hoxie proud. She opened her jacket and stuck it in a pocket beneath her breasts.

---

38 Though the Treaty of Versailles that ended the Great War made it illegal for Germany to build submersibles, the Germans had started a submarine design office in The Netherlands. They had already built 65 submarines, with 21 of them already at sea and set for war, at the outbreak of World War II.

My experience with guns was limited to the last few days, and I found myself wishing I still had Tesla's device. I looked them over and took an automatic—and hoped it would be the easiest to use.

The dwarf left first, creeping down the trailer stairs. I came next, followed by Miss Welles. She and I kept low, our heads almost level with Stutka's. We hurried to the large window and looked out.

No sign of Benet, but a group of men in protective suits carried a series of leaden boxes. Each box was carried by two men, one at each side, to prevent accidents. The line of ten boxes slowly and carefully filed past us.

"I'm open to suggestions," Miss Welles said.

"I got it," I aimed my gun at Stutka. "Put your hands up."

He turned on me, eyes wide. "Why you rat."

"No, no," I said and turned to Miss Welles. "You, too."

She grinned. "I get it." She put her hands up; Stutka stuck his automatic under his jacket and did the same. "Just be careful with that," Stutka said. "I wouldn't trust you college boys to walk my dog, let alone hold a gat."

I opened the door and they marched out into the evening gloom, my prisoners. I made a show of holding my gun on them and we paused, watching the stones make their way across the complex and towards the water's edge. I even nodded at one of the men carrying them.

"Don't overdo it," Miss Welles said under her breath.

I let the caravan of stone carriers get a good fifty feet ahead of us before I said, "Let's go."

We walked slowly, Stutka and Miss Welles with hands up, while I kept my eyes on the pavement. The last thing I needed was one of the men from the factory to recognize me. When we reached the water's edge, we stood on the far side of a large group of men in protective gear. They had paid us little attention. Without any set plan, I saw a grouping of oil drums nearby. I led both of my "captives" there and we ducked behind them.

Beyond, lying in wait in the water like a giant predator, was the U-Boat.

It was enormous. The thing had to be over two-hundred and twenty feet long and twenty feet wide. It was gunmetal gray, with a conning tower at its center and a big gun on its deck. The deck was fenced in by a metal gate, and various cables stretched the length of it. Its diesel engines were alive and humming with a quiet malignancy.

The operation of loading the crates was a complicated one. Two men with one box went one-at-a-time over the plank to the outer hull, then cautiously carried the boxes to the conning tower. They were met by two other men, also in protective gear, who used a series of support struts to elevate the boxes higher and then maneuver them over the hatchway. The boxes were then lowered slowly into the hull.

We watched as the operation was completed ten times. That was all of them, then, including the first stone I had seen kill a man in Mason's simple country house. After the last box went down, the two men who had carried the box followed, and soon all twenty men entered.

I surveyed the scene. No one was about.

"Do you think everyone is in?"

"How the hell should I know?" Miss Welles asked. It was the first time I had seen her at a loss. "What should we do?"

"You could always get your bee costume," I said.

"Very funny."

"What do you think?" I asked Stutka.

"We got guns," he said. "We could always make a run for it."

"And just carry the rocks out?" she asked.

"And what about the German scientist?" I asked.

"No chance that you could pilot that thing?" I asked Stutka.

"None."

"Want to call for help?" I asked Miss Welles.

"And miss the party?"

"And you?" I asked Stutka.

"I'm not going anywhere until I get Benet," he said.

"Then I got a plan."

"What?"

"We go in and—hope for the best."

"Brilliant," she said.

A sound at the conning tower drew our attention. A line of men filed out of the craft; I counted them one after another.

"Those are the rats that killed my boys," Stutka said.

"How many were there? Did you notice?" Miss Welles asked.

"Fourteen, fifteen," I counted as the last one left.

"It couldn't have been more than that," Stutka said.

The men went past us—fortunately, we remained undetected behind the oil drums. They did not return to one of the factory buildings, that I could see. After a moment, we heard engines start in the distance.

"They're leaving," Miss Welles said.

"How large is a submarine crew?" I asked.

Stutka shrugged.

"Depending on the model, between twenty and forty," Miss Welles said.

"We watched twenty go in with the stones," I said. "Let's say that they are the crew, along with a few more. Then there's Benet and the German."

"You have no idea how many people were onboard to begin with," Miss Welles said.

"Yeah, but the Doc is right," Stutka said. "It's definitely twenty-two, at least."

"We don't have a lot of time," Miss Welles said. "If we're going in, we have to move on before they move out."

Two more men left the U-boat. They walked past us and headed for the factory building.

"Game's up," I said. "They are probably on their way to bring us back."

"Game's not up till we give up," Miss Welles said. We waited only a few minutes. Soon, the men were hurrying back towards the submarine.

"Now!" Miss Welles said, as they moved past us.

She hadn't given us any warning, and that probably was for the best. Adrenaline kicked in and I jumped from behind the oil drums and swung my automatic. I cracked one of the men right at the ribbon of his fedora and he staggered back. I swung the gun again and clipped him on the jaw.

Stutka was like a monster. He tackled the other man at the knees and he hit the ground hard. Miss Welles then kicked the recumbent man on the jaw and he closed his eyes.

"Hurry," she said, pulling the unconscious form behind the oil drums. I did the same.

"Take his hat," she said.

I took the hat from the man I clipped and put it on my head. Way too small. I then took the hat from the other man. Way too large. But, it was perfect, as I was able to snap the brim over my eyes.

"Let's go," I said.

Miss Welles and Stutka moved from behind the oil drums and marched towards the U-boat, hands over their heads. I trailed close behind, my gun on them.

We stepped off the wharf and onto the outer hull. It was slick with sea water and oil. My first instinct was to help Miss Welles, but I checked myself, and, instead, kept my gun aimed at her.

We stepped around the jumping wire and up the conning tower. Stutka led the way, then Miss Welles, then myself. The hatchway was open and the sound of the engines grew louder.

I looked at Stutka. "Ready?"

He nodded.

I looked at Miss Welles. She nodded.

Stutka started down the ladder to the command room.

Miss Welles turned and climbed down behind him. I followed quickly behind.

As I climbed down, I thought that if Benet was at the bottom of the ladder, we had no chance.

Once inside, I turned. Miss Welles and Stutka stood before various control panels, hands up. I looked around.

The space was cramped, a virtual nightmare for claustrophobics. The room was little taller than myself, the walkway narrow, and the interior crowded with controls. There were gauges, what looked like hundreds of wheels of various colors and sizes, and overhead were a series of thick pipes. The electric light had a blurry quality, as if inside the submarine was lit with an eerie twilight. The air was thick with oil and the scent of unwashed men.

Several men stood or sat at various control posts. A brawny man with red hair and prodigious sideburns wore a captain's hat, but no other military uniform. No sign of Benet.

"Prisoners," I growled.

The Captain pointed toward the stern of the ship and I jerked my gun at Stutka and Miss Welles.

We padded through the narrow room and passed through a round door, its outline studded with bolts. We hurried through a narrow corridor of pistons and gears, and then spilled out into a larger corridor.

"Where now?" I asked.

A voice came over the loudspeaker. "Embarkation in ten minutes. Embarkation in ten minutes."

"Now we're on the clock," Miss Welles said. "And if we are here when they submerge, we never getting back up."

We pressed on into the next corridor. Here, tiny billets with bunk beds lined the walls. Beside one, a man bent, administering to a hidden figure in the bunk. We filed past, noting that the man in bed was the German scientist. He was conscious, but clearly weakened.

The German's eyes grew large at the sight of Penelope. As we filed past, I winked at the older man. He blinked, caught on, and then winked back.

Once behind the stooge helping the German, it was easy. I brought my gun down hard behind the man's ear. With a muffled *huummphff* he dropped to the floor. Stutka and I bundled him into a lower bunk, the gangster covering the body with a blanket.

The German said, "*Gütiger Himmel!*"

"Relax," Miss Welles dropped low beside him. "I'm with the secret service and we're here to rescue you."

"They have a weapon—" he started.

"We know," I said. "Do you know where it is?"

"Where's the man who brought you here?" Stutka asked.

"He said he was with the government," the German's voice was plaintive. "I said I would do anything to help."

"We know," I said. "Where is it?"

"Don't know. Drugged." He looked around. "I'm not even sure I know where I am."

"On a submarine in Washington, D.C." Miss Welles said.

"I have to get home," the German said, like an absent-minded husband realizing he's late for dinner.

"Sit tight," I said. "We'll come for you."

Miss Welles assured him once more with a pat on the shoulder and we left.

The body of the great metal beast shuddered; there was a lurch and I felt us moving. The U-boat was pulling from dock.

"Hell," I said.

We then stepped into a dimly-lit room that looked like it was lined with gigantic snakes. Bunches of cables, pipes and metal struts lined the walls. Various gauges and instruments were nestled between the coils; one man in dark pants and naval sweater checked the instruments.

I ushered Stutka and Miss Welles through at gunpoint, purposefully not engaging the man in any discussion.

It was in the next room that we hit pay dirt.

Clearly, the normal, cramped environs of the U-boat had been cleared away for a workroom and storage facility for the stones.

It was a large room, for a U-boat. The walls were covered in a greenish tile, and the floor was a bright white Bakelite. There were four chemical tables, surrounded by wire struts to keep bottles, specimens and other items for falling to the ground if the U-boat should pitch or roll.

Two men in laboratory coats were examining papers on a clipboard; a third gazed through a portal in a door that led to a small ante-chamber.

Miss Welles and Stutka entered first, then I followed. Without hesitation I took a clipboard from the wall and examined the documents.

The man gazing into the anteroom turned and gave me an enquiring look.

I looked up from the papers and nodded at Miss Welles and Stutka. "For the experiments."

The man nodded and returned to his gazing.

I approached him and looked through the portal.

It was an isolation room almost exactly like the one in Mason's New Jersey home: a long, narrow room lined with lead on the inside. The portal door was steel with a window at its center; lead lined the door interior and the glass was coated with a transparent lead film. The room was equipped with an overhead light, and a black-tiled platform in its center.

The platform was partially covered by a lead dome. The dome had retracted inside the table and there, just a few feet away from me, were the ten stones.

One of them was uneven, with multiple facets. It shone like crystal in some places, but also flatly, like metamorphic rock. It glowed with a brilliant, crimson intensity.

The remaining nine stones were still black, smooth and round, the size of baseballs, though even these now showed signs of cracking. Glowing traces of red illuminated the cracks, like light from the next room coming from under an ill-fitting door.

I thought of my recent calculations of their origins and swallowed the lump in my throat. I turned from the isolation room and nodded at Stutka and Miss Welles. I then turned back to the man at the door.

I thrust my gun under his jaw and pushed him against the wall. I heard Stutka and Miss Welles scuffling with the other two scientists.

"Make a sound and I'll kill you."

His eyes grew wide with terror.

"Experiments, eh?" I said. "I should throw you in there. Would you like that?"

He made a choking sound.

"Where are the containment cases. Now!"

His right hand fluttered at his side and I realized he was pointing to a low section of cabinets.

I turned. One man stood stock still as Miss Welles held a six shooter at his temple. Stutka kept the other at bay with an automatic in his groin.

"Tell him to put them in the cases," Miss Welles said.

"You heard the lady," I said, pressing the gun deeper.

Protective gear hung on a series of hooks. I backed away from the man and he took down the hood and long, tunic-like shirt.

Stutka grabbed the belt of his prisoner and pulled him toward the other man. "Get the boxes ready," he said.

I had no plan for getting the stones off the submarine, but would come to that problem once they were safely secured.

Miss Welles, as always, was ahead of me. She stepped away from her prisoner and now pointed the gun in his face. "Radio the command room. Tell him there is a potential breach. Move personnel to the front of the sub."

The man did not move.

She cocked her six shooter.

"I'd do it now," she said.

The man nodded and backed towards a table with a radiophone. He picked it up and clicked the line open.

Miss Welles moved the gun closer to his face. "Don't…"

The man gulped. "Captain," he said. "Possible breach leak in the containment room."

"What?"

"Move personnel to the fore," he said. "As a precaution."

"Understood. Apprise me immediately of developments."

"Aye," the scientist said, breaking the connection.

My man continued to get into his suit, while Stutka's pulled the containment boxes closer. Miss Welles moved around her prisoner and pulled the radiophone wire from the wall.

"Help them," she said.

The man looked at the containment suits, then the boxes, and opted for the boxes. Nearly all ten were opened and ready.

My man was completely suited-up except for the boots. These he pulled over his shoes, sitting on the led boxes as he did so. I pointed my gun at Stutka's prisoner. "Now you."

The man moved to the row of suits and took down a hood.

He would never put it on. A voice at the door cut him short.

"I'm just going to have to kill you."

It was Benet. He stood just outside the door, the red-headed giant of a captain standing behind him. The captain held a Tommy gun.

I thought of throwing a bullet his way; Miss Welles must have read my mind. She said, "Don't. He'll cut you in half."

"They were trying to steal the stones!" the half-dressed man cried.

"You will please put your guns on the floor," Benet said.

I crouched and placed the automatic on the ground; Miss Welles did likewise with her six shooter. Stutka placed his gun near hers, but did not pull the automatic he held under his jacket. I held onto a faint hope.

Benet said to the half-dressed man, "Kick the guns over here. Careful—don't get in the line of fire."

The man, sweating, did so with gentle kicks.

My captive, at this point, continued to put on his protective gear; his confederate did likewise.

"I had hoped," Benet said, "that I could keep both you and your German colleague. Now I'll just have to get along with the one."

"You could do worse," I said.

"It's a pity that he won't be here to see the demonstration. It might make him more pliable."

"Demonstration?" Stutka whispered.

"I have never seen these things in action for myself," Benet said. "Until now." He said to the Captain. "Radio the crew. Tell them they can return to duty."

The Captain held the machine gun steadily on us and inched to the radio. Stutka followed him with his eyes. "They wrecked it," he said.

Benet turned to Stutka's former captive. "Go to the fore and tell the crew to resume positions."

The man left without a word.

Benet turned to the man who I had captured. "Status?"

"The isolation chamber is secure," he said, voice shaky. He was now completely in his protective togs except for the hood. "But we didn't have sufficient time to test the pneumatic doors. I advise no unnecessary personnel enter the chamber, or do so without protective gear."

"Show me," Benet said, stepping around the Captain.

The lead technician stepped aside and gestured to the porthole in the isolation room. Benet peered at the rocks inside.

"The cracks in the stones harvested by Armstrong first appeared yesterday," he said. "We expect that the outer shell, if you will, will crumble, leaving the more variegated rock exposed."

"Heat?" Benet asked.

"None," the technician consulted a thermometer mounted near the door. "Room temperature never varies. In fact, aside from radioactivity which can only be detected with a Geiger counter, there is nothing to distinguish them from normal rocks." Here he stood to his full height. "Aside from their destructive properties, of course."

I looked from the two of them to Miss Welles, Stutka, the Captain and the remaining technician. All of them gazed deeply at the portal, except for Stutka. His eyes never stopped darting from place to place.

"And the isolation chamber?"

"This lever here," the technician said, "closes the protective dome. This lever, here, activates the pneumatic door. They are connected by a circuit; in theory, it's impossible to open the door when the dome is retracted into the specimen table. But—we built all of this quickly and without sufficient testing."

Benet reached for the dome control. He eased the lever downward with a slow, methodical hand. Inside, a black dome emerged from the specimen table and swept over the rocks. The weird red glow diminished, then vanished.

Benet turned to us. "Time for a closer look."

Miss Welles gasped.

"But sir—" the technician said.

"Now," Benet said.

"But sir—" the technician started once more.

Benet turned on the man. "We could have four test subjects."

The technician reached for the door lever. He pushed it downward.

First, there was a loud blast and the sound of air escaping—like a giant's jar of preserves opened after a long time closed. Then protective struts separated from the door, and the sound of pneumatic gear filled the makeshift laboratory. Then, slowly and silently, the door opened inward.

This was it, I thought. I would die in that tiny room.

Stutka, however, had a different idea. As we watched the slow opening of the door, he reached into his jacket and pulled his automatic. In a twinkling, he put a bullet through the Captain's head.

The red-headed giant was pushed against the wall on impact, blood and brains staining the green tile. He slid to the floor.

The third technician jumped at Stutka, but the murderous dwarf put a bullet through him as the man sailed mid-air. His momentum kept the body flying, and he was dead before he fell over Stutka.

The head technician screamed in terror.

Miss Welles ran towards the Captain to grab the Tommy gun. Benet pushed me hard and I lost my footing. As I hit the floor, Benet had his own gun in hand.

Miss Welles backed away from the dead Captain.

Growling a curse, Stutka pushed away from the dead technician, gun at the ready. Before he could steady himself and aim, Benet put a bullet in his chest. Blood spurted over his shirtfront and suit, and the little man lay still.

The room was thick with smoke; the head technician screamed once more.

I got to my feet.

Benet held his gun on me and Miss Welles. "Shut up," he growled at the technician.

The man, now that his screaming stopped, seemed to be crying. He said nothing.

Benet's eyes were wild and there was a foamy blob of spittle at the corner of his mouth.

"You!" he said to Miss Welles. "Inside!"

She gave me a look, then approached the isolation chamber.

"NO!" I screamed.

Benet turned to me; teeth showing. "You, too, Dr. Armstrong."

Miss Welles stepped inside first, then me. We both turned and faced the door.

The room was small, the air oppressive. I could not keep my eyes from the black dome on the center of the specimen table. In moments, I thought, I would know the answer of its mysteries—along with all the other mysteries of life.

Benet stood at the doorway, clearly enjoying the moment. Behind him, the lead technician was green with disgust.

Miss Welles and I moved closer to one another. I wrapped an arm around her shoulders and brought her close against me.

"Burn in hell," Benet said. He turned to the technician. "The lever."

"But sir—"

"I said throw the switch!"

"But sir—"

The technician lodged his last objection. Without a word Benet turned, shoved the barrel of his automatic into the man's stomach, and fired. The sound of the shot was muffled, but the results were not. I could hear blood and tissue splatter the wall behind.

Benet turned to us again, and I was stricken by the look of madness in his face. He grinned at us, then pulled the lever.

The pneumatic sound once more filled the room. Inexorably, the door started to close.

I felt sick. I threw my arms around Miss Welles and held her tightly. I felt her body press against mine—her body, and something else.

It pushed against my chest, tangled in the folds of my jacket pocket. I stepped back and reached inside.

There, in my hands, were my photos of Mason's notes, along with Tesla's copy of *Tarzan and the Lion Man*.

To this day,[39] I am still unsure whether I acted according to some instantly formulated plan. At any rate, I dropped Tarzan on the floor and kicked it towards the door.

The door caught it up with in its closing progression; then, the book wedged between the door and the jamb. It stopped

I could not see Benet through the portal, he obviously crouched to find the problem with the door.

Tarzan began to crunch and squeeze, then the spine and pages almost jackknifed.

Then, we saw a hand. It was Benet's—he was reaching under the door to push aside the obstructing book.

I pushed past Miss Welles and hit the floor, sliding to the door. I grabbed Benet's wrist just as he was pushing the book away. I held tight as the door continued its progression.

Benet screamed. His fingers clawed at me as the door pressed against his wrists, tighter and tighter, grinding the bones to paste.

I no longer had to hold on; the door kept him prisoner. I rose and looked out the portal window.

Benet was screaming, frantically grabbing the door mechanism with his free hand, but falling short of reaching it. He no longer held the gun, he clawed at the door, his screams filling my ears.

Miss Welles was beside me in an instant; the both of us started pulling on the door but it was impossible to budge.

Now Benet's wrist was bleeding freely. Blood pooled around our shoes.

It was then that I saw something that I will take to my grave. Stutka, blood dripping from his mouth, slowly got to his feet. He stumbled across the length of the room, between the bodies of the dead men, and loomed over Benet.

Benet writhed in agony at his feet. The dwarf reached up and released the door mechanism. There was another *woosh* of the pneumatic device and the door once more retreated inward.

Benet brought his mangled hand to his face, barely attached by a few strands of raw and bleeding flesh. Stutka climbed atop him, like a frenzied child.

I helped Miss Welles over the jamb, but she was more than equal to the occasion. She stepped over the two combatants and ran to the captain, wresting the Tommy gun from his dead hands.

---

39   This indicates that Armstrong did not record these events as a daily diary, but sometime soon after the events. However, forensic experts do date the paper, ink and etc. as 1930s vintage.

Stutka had his hands around Benet's throat. The bigger man lay there, eyes bulging, pain and shock leaving him defenseless against Stutka's onslaught.

I stooped and grabbed an automatic. I came over to the frenzied gangster and said, "Come!"

Stutka, straddling Benet, looked up at me, mouth filled with blood. "GO!"

I didn't need to be told twice. Miss Welles stepped into the adjacent corridor, I joined her at the hatchway.

I spared one more look at Benet and Stutka, and was glad I did. Stutka choked, "You bastard," and reached a hand for the lever controlling the specimen table dome.

We built all of this quickly and without sufficient testing, the technician said.

"Help me!" I cried.

I grabbed the laboratory door, Miss Welles taking hold of the wheel at its center that sealed it tight. It clanged shut and, with a heave, we twisted the wheel.

Then I looked through the portal.

Stutka never took his hands from Benet's throat. He raved as the red light washed over him. Then, the dwarf started to scream as his face melted over the body of his adversary. His flesh poured away in globs, teeth falling from his mouth and into that of his disabled foeman. In moments, there was nothing left of Stutka but a horrible black-and-red ichor covering Benet's prone form.

But now that the dwarf was no longer there to block the full effect of the stones, it was Benet's turn to scream. With his one good hand he tried to pull himself away, but the hand pooled into a mass of bubbling goo as it touched the floor. He screamed, his ears seeming to slide off the sides of his head, leaving a red trail that gushed over his shoulders. His eyes began to sink inside of his skull, his mouth crumble upon itself and his body liquefied within the confines of his suit.

"Run!" I said.

The door would provide us some protection, but I had no idea whether or not the effects of the rocks would penetrate it completely, or at all.

Miss Welles led the way, brandishing the machine gun. We raced through the sleeping quarters. I paused at the bedside of the German; she stopped, waiting for me.

"Go!" I yelled. "I'll catch up."

She hesitated. Then Miss Welles came up to me and brushed the top of my head. Her eyes locked on mine and she whispered, "You're really something."

Then she ran.

The German looked up at me, face filled with horror. "The screaming," he said.

"Everything's all right, Professor," I said, helping him to his feet. I took him by the arm. "Come with me. We haven't a moment to lose."

We stepped into the room of pistons and gears, the air close and unpleasant. We stopped dead at the sound of machinegun fire up ahead.

The German turned as if to return the way he came. I pulled him. "Come, come. Trust me."

Another burst of machinegun fire.

In the command room were several dead men. Miss Welles stood at the machinery, Tommy gun in hand. Dials, consoles and equipment were smoldering, bullet-shattered ruins.

"Come on," she said.

Miss Welles shimmied up the ladder to the conning tower, unlocking the hatch. A blast of cool air filled the cabin.

I led the German to the stairs. "Up you go, Professor," I said.

The man climbed confusedly up, I right behind him.

By the time we were both on the conning tower, Miss Welles had already stepped onto the gleaming outer hull. The night was dark and clear; stars twinkled in the distance.

"How far away are we from shore?" I asked.

She peered into the darkness. "Maybe two miles."

"What do we do?" I asked.

Then I heard the screams.

The U-boat door had *not* been enough to contain the power of the stones. The red, death-giving rays had started their progression throughout the ship.

"Hit the drink!" Miss Welles said.

She tossed her Tommy gun aside and jumped into the water. I led the German down from the tower and to the edge of the hull.

"*Aber ich kann nicht schwimmen!*" he said.

"What?"

"I can't swim!" he said.

"Even you can't know everything," I said, and pushed him into the water.

I dived in after him. He sputtered and fought me over the waves, but I was able to get my arm around his chest. "Relax!" I commanded.

We splashed closer to Miss Welles. "This way," she said.

We swam.

I can't tell how far we had gotten when the U-boat started to *hum*. The sound was weird, uncanny—a hum mingled with an unearthly trilling. It seemed as if the entire length of the ship vibrated, sending ripples of water in our direction.

And then, like a stone dropped in the water, the U-boat simply vanished. It dropped under the surface of the water, not with a slow sinking or a dramatic capsizing—it just dropped to the bottom.

There came a tremendous pulling of the water current, as if we would soon be dragged down along with it. The undertow was so great; I feared that the U-boat was tunneling down into the earth's core. Miss Welles took to the water like Buster Crabbe,[40] I made my strokes as best I could while accommodating the German. Even the Professor realized the danger and paddled water for all he was worth.

Then, the horizon changed. I was never certain and could not prove it, but it seemed as if the very tide changed; as if the waters hit low tide at a finger snap. I gulped water and kept swimming.

It was nearly thirty minutes before we reached a Naval Yard pier. Miss Welles made it up a rickety set of wooden stairs first, then she helped the German up while I supported him from the rear. Soon, we were straggled along the concrete pier, gasping for breath.

"I'll call the General," Miss Welles said finally.

"No," I said.

"No?"

"No. First, I need time with him." I jerked a thumb at the German.

"Important?"

"More than you know."

She considered. "Let's go."

She got to her feet and we both helped the German to rise. In moments she was helping him revive in the back of THE FAMILY SMALL trailer, while I steered us toward Princeton.

It took nearly four hours to reach Princeton Observatory.

We had stopped *en route* to gas up the trailer. When I popped my head in the back, Miss Welles was sitting up with the German, sharing a cup of

---

40   Buster Crabbe (1908-1983), born Clarence Linden Crabbe, was a two-time Olympic swimmer and, later, movie star best remembered for his portrayals of Flash Gordon, Buck Rogers and Tarzan. He is just the sort of personage who would reverberate in Armstrong's mental frame of reference.

coffee. The man had a blanket draped over his shoulders and he seemed delighted with her company.

We'll see how long that lasts, I thought, climbing back into the cab.

It was nearly dawn when we pulled up at the Observatory. Neither Pierson nor I had been on site to record any celestial observations, and, of course, poor Mason would never do the honors again.

We parked nearby and the three of us, cold, tired and still slightly damp, opened the heavy metal door of the Observatory and made our way to the great telescope. There were tables and chairs aplenty, and I went to a small kitchenette off the administrative office to make coffee.

I positioned the crevice in the ceiling of the observatory to catch the morning sun and the room was bathed in a great yellow light. And there, drinking coffee as the mechanism of the telescope ticked companionably among us, I told the German professor the whole story.

Finished, I took the photos from my pocket and grabbed a ream of graph paper. "And now, Doctor," I said, "if you would do these final calculations with me, I would be grateful."

The man brushed his thick mustache and licked the tip of a pencil. We both did the calculations in tandem; once, twice, and then a third time to be sure. He looked at me and nodded.

"What?" Miss Welles asked.

"These rocks," the German started, then fell silent.

I cleared my throat. "If our calculations are correct, they come ..." and here I paused, awed by the enormity of the findings. "They come from Mars."

"Mars!"

"*Ja, Kleiner,*" the German concurred.

"But I thought ..." she struggled for the right words. "But I thought you guys could see the surface. You've said that it's uninhabited!"

"We have seen the surface, my dear," the German said. "But—but for all we know, there could be an entire underground civilization there. One peopled by minds vastly superior to our own. A civilization that travels on subterranean waterways, living completely underground. It could be a world teeming with life, *ja.*"

"But that's not the real question," I said.

"Yeah, I know what you're going to say," Miss Welles cut in. "Were those rocks sent as part of an invasion force?"

"Or as gifts from a people immune to their properties?" I put in.

"Or," the German mused, "were they—eggs."

"Eggs?" Miss Welles and I cried out together.

"*Ja*, it's possible." The German drew a circle on the graph paper with is finger. "We never properly examined them. This *Herr Doktor Cooley* assumed they were mineral in origin, but who knows? Could those *stones* have been Martians, themselves?"

"But if they can travel through space, why haven't they contacted us before?"

The German shrugged. "Who knows how they measure time. A thousand years to us could be *that*," and here he snapped his fingers, "to them."

"It's also possible that they just cracked the propulsion problems inherent in interplanetary travel," I added.

"But it is possible, *nein*, probable, that we have not heard the last of them. But now that these stones have fallen, we must reject the notion that no life exists beyond the petty surface of our minute sphere. And our destruction of these stones may only be a reprieve. To them, and not to us, is the future ordained perhaps."

The room grew silent.

"What next?" I asked.

"First," Miss Welles said, "I call the General. There's a lot of clean up. He will want to comb the War Department, and uncover any traitors had who worked with Benet or Stutka. It'll be messy, but it can be done."

"And the stones?"

"We look for them," she said, simply. "And if we're lucky, we don't find them."[41]

I sighed. "It's over."

"Not yet," she said.

"Huuh?"

Miss Welles took a great breath, her breasts swelling under the folds of her jacket. She brushed some of her luscious auburn hair from her brow and pressed against me. She brought her mouth closer to mine.

"A kiss," she said.

I looked at her.

"I'd love to kiss you," I said, "but I just washed my hair."

---

[41] If the stones were ever found, there is no official record of it. The fact of (possibly malevolent) life on Mars is, of course, the root of the controversy surrounding this packet of Armstrong papers. As NASA accelerates its plan to explore the Red Planet through both robotic and human agencies, the authenticity of the document grows in importance. I had one senior NASA engineer threaten to "break [my] lying neck" when I announced publication. As for who or what we find on Mars, only time will tell.

ABOUT OUR CREATORS

WRITER—

BOB MADISON— writes all kinds of stuff, including magazine articles, blogposts, television documentaries, nonfiction books, cookbooks, novels,and even—trading cards. He grew up reading pulp reprints during the Nostalgia Craze of 1970s, and lived on vintage comic strips, adventure novels, Classic Hollywood and Old Time Radio. For most of his boyhood, his imaginative space was somewhere in 1933. Bob wrote the narration for 2021 documentary *Dark Shadows and Beyond: The Jonathan Frid Story* for MPI, produced and directed by Mary O'Leary. It was nominated for a Daytime Emmy Award. His first two novels, *Cash and Carrey*, a comedy, and *SPIKED!*, a young adult novel, were published by Vulpine Press. Bob writes the *Tales of Tom Mix* series of pulp westerns for DS Productions under the name Scott McCrea. Follow him on Twitter here at @ThatBobMadison, or, for Westerns, at @ScottMcCreaWest.

INTERIOR ILLUSTRATOR—

KEVIN PAUL SHAW BRODEN,— initially seeking a career in comic books, took art courses throughout his education— only to eventually discover that no matter what the media, he was a storyteller at heart. Kevin received a BA in Art (emphasizing Narrative Illustration) from California State University, Fullerton (Fullerton, CA); before that, he worked on the HORNET newspaper as a reporter/illustrator while earning his AA at Fullerton College.

One of Kevin's early jobs teamed him with some of the talent that launched Supreme for Image Comics. You can even find a special "thank you" to Kevin in SUPREME #1. He storyboarded the music video for BiGod20's "One," as well as videos for John Wesley Harding and Kristin Hersch as part of Summer Arts in Humboldt, CA. Also, he's been contracted to do illustrations for commercials and television series pitches. The textbooks GARDNER'S GUIDE TO WRITING AND PRODUCING ANIMATION and GARDNER'S GUIDE TO PITCHING AND SELLING ANIMATION feature all interior art done by Kevin. With his wife and creative partner, Shannon Muir, Kevin created the online comic FLYING GLORY AND THE HOUNDS OF GLORY, which has been in existence over 15 years. His artwork has also been seen as the interior illustration for Ralph L. Angelo, Jr's "Against Fire and Stone" tale in LEGENDS OF NEW PULP FICTION by Airship 27 Productions, the cover art for the anthology NEWSHOUNDS from Pro Se Press (which also features his story "Stop the Presses!"), and as cover art for self-published e-books he's authored and released which include the REVENGE OF THE MASKED GHOST series and the CLOCKWORK GENIE MYSTERIES.

Oh, and yes, he does have FOUR NAMES. It's a family thing, but it comes in quite handy... FOUR NAMES OF PROFESSIONAL CREATIVITY.

COVER ARTIST—

ADAM BENET SHAW –Accomplished painter, illustrator, and comics creator, Adam has garnered acclaim across a number of artistic media. After completing studies at the Cleveland Institute of Art in Ohio, the Edinburgh College of Art in Scotland and Watts Atelier in California, Shaw was selected as an emerging American artist to watch by European gallery owners and exhibited in London, England. He has been featured in "New American Painting", selected multiple times for the Arkansas Art Center's Delta Exhibit, and shown at the prestigious "Red Clay Survey" at the Huntsville Museum of Art. His work has also been shown in over 50 group and solo shows in the US and internationally. His figurative paintings are a prominent part of a 140-foot mural entitled "The History of Cotton" at the National Cotton Exchange Museum, St. Jude's Children's Research Hospital, the National Contact Bridge Museum, and a treasured part of private and corporate collections. He has created storyboards for several motion pictures, including Paramount Pictures' film "Black Snake Moan" directed by Craig Brewer, stage design for operas and corporate events, and character illustrations for the gaming industry. His published graphic novel work includes the series "Dead In Memphis", "Bloodstream" for Image Comics, "David: The Illustrated Novel" from Shepherd King Publishing and "Harpe: America's First Serial Killers" from Cave-in-Rock Publishing. He shares his love of art through teaching and workshops at his studio in the Broad Avenue Arts District in Memphis. Recently he has been painting book covers for pulp publishers Pro Se Productions and Airship 27 Productions.

During the golden days of American pulps hundreds of masked avengers were created to battle evildoers around the globe. The Black Bat, Moon Man, Domino Lady, and the Purple Scar to name only a few of these amazing pulp heroes. Now Airship 27 Productions introduces to pulp readers brand new pulp heroes cast in the mold of their 1930s counterparts. Get ready for high octane thrills and adventure with...

MYSTERY MEN (& WOMEN)

PULP FICTION FOR A NEW GENERATION!
Airship27Hangar.com

Made in the USA
Monee, IL
10 September 2025